Thank you for coming and being a part of this. You are phenomenal!!

2015

GAME OF *Love*

ARA GRIGORIAN

A Division of **Whampa, LLC**
P.O. Box 2160
Reston, VA 20195
Tel/Fax: 800-998-2509
http://curiosityquills.com

© 2015 **Ara Grigorian**
http://www.aragrigorian.com

Covert Art by Eugene Teplitsky

ISBN 978-1-62007-852-5 (ebook)
ISBN 978-1-62007-853-2 (paperback)
ISBN 978-1-62007-854-9 (hardcover)

TABLE OF CONTENTS

*When we were both nineteen, you asked, "What is your dream career?"
Without hesitation I said, "Writer." When we were both thirty-nine, you
asked me to stop dreaming. This book exists because of you. My first reader.
My best friend. My wife. Delia.*

*To my two boys, thunder and lightning—dream without limits, live fully, work
tirelessly, never give up.*

*To my grandfather—genocide survivor, war hero, actor, playwright, author,
poet, angel—you are why I have a passion for storytelling.
I hope I've made you proud.*

PROLOGUE

Australia: January

The Porsche's tires screeched as the skidding car plowed into a row of parked cars. Gemma Lennon's body slammed against the door as her head struck the passenger side window.

A few moments passed before she was able to focus on her surroundings again. The car stood motionless. The chase was over.

She glanced to her right and saw a smeared stain on the glass, then smelled the choking odor of burnt tires, and felt something warm flowing from her temple onto her ear. The music that had been blaring from the speakers moments earlier was now muffled, and the outside world's colors muted.

Then she saw the paparazzi, jumping off their motorcycles, clamoring around the car, snapping pictures. The world began to fade.

"Are you hurt?" a distant but familiar voice screamed.

She blinked as she turned to face the driver: Johnny, her boyfriend.

Something thick and warm trailed from her forehead and into her right eye. She wiped at the viscous liquid.

"But... tomorrow..." she said, before her world went dark.

PART I

LOVE

"Tennis begins with love."

~Author Unknown

CHAPTER ONE

*"We are made strong by the difficulties we face,
not by those we evade."*

~Author Unknown

Paris: Four Months Later

Gemma's security flanked her, their grip tight on her arms. Bedric, her coach, rushed ahead, slamming open the hotel's glass doors to the roar of the French paparazzi—a cacophony of questions, comments, and insults.

Gemma moderated her breathing, prepared for another three-second spurt of chaos.

Three...

"—What happened in your hotel room?"

They knew. Dozens of cameras from all directions chirped and flashed. She kept her eyes trained on her goal: the awaiting car.

Two...

"—Mademoiselle! Gemma! One smile."

The paparazzi bore in from her right. *Only a few more steps.* A knee rammed into her thigh. That one would leave a mark. A bruise that the papers would dissect and analyze gratuitously.

One...

"—Why were you hiding for four months? Were you going to quit tennis?"

Don't react. Say nothing. Bedric forced the car door open, giving Gemma the opening she needed to squeeze in. He followed.

Zero.

The door slammed behind them, and the sounds of commotion lowered to a gentle hush. Black tinted windows offered a veil of privacy. Bodies, camera lenses, and faces smashed against the glass. Only inches separated her from the paparazzi. There had been a time when she used to move to the center of the car, creating as much separation as possible. But now she knew better. Distance was a mere illusion of safety.

The locks engaged, and the car accelerated away.

She didn't like surprises—particularly on game day—but in this case, her security lead's demand to move her to another hotel had been spot-on. It was one thing for the paparazzi to gather outside. It was quite another when one found his way into her hotel suite... while she slept. The French paparazzi were setting a new standard.

"This is not good," Bedric said in stoic English.

She eyed her superstitious coach, who was always concerned with deviations from routine. But the concern etched on his face wasn't about superstition. He didn't want a repeat performance of the Australian Open months earlier.

"You have not rested," he continued, "and you have yet to get breakfast."

"We'll be fine. We *are* fine," she said, nearly believing it herself. "As for breakfast, we'll grab something at the new hotel."

The car swerved as the driver made a temporary effort to lose their tail. Memories of another car chase months earlier inched its way into her throat.

"There will be people. You don't need more distractions."

"More distractions?" She had woken to the sound of an intruder in her suite, and now she was rushing from one hotel to another on the morning of her quarterfinal match. How much worse could it get? "We'll be discreet. Run in, eat, and we'll be off."

The car's tires screeched as the driver took another quick turn. It was happening again. Another chase just before a critical match. Only this time, the driver wasn't drunk.

From her bag, Gemma removed a tennis ball and twirled it in her hand. *One point at a time.* She focused on the soft texture. Familiar.

Calming. Poking out from inside her bag, the newspaper article from the day before mocked her. Inch-tall letters above her picture: *The Great Hype—Five Years and Still Waiting.* She squeezed the tennis ball over and over again until her fingers went numb.

She dropped the ball back inside the bag, then closed her eyes, hoping to salvage some sleep. She crossed her arms and tried to control her shivering. No, she wasn't cold. She just wanted five minutes alone with the bastard who had violated her space. Gemma almost wished the coward hadn't bolted when she charged him, tennis racquet in hand.

The car pulled up in front of the Pullman Hotel. No paparazzi. Not yet.

As they slid out, she turned to her coach. "Can you grab my bag and find us a table? I'll be there as soon as I've freshened up."

"Maybe room service is better. More prudent," Bedric said.

She studied him. "Maybe more prudent, but I refuse to live like a prisoner. And stop worrying; I'm fine. I'll see you in a few minutes."

Hotel management waited. She didn't speak, just smiled and followed their lead and that of her team. Like a flock of birds, they moved together, shoes tap dancing on the marble tiles.

Her mobile rang. It was Tish. Gemma pulled away from the rest, wanting to hear her friend's voice.

"Are you already at the Pullman?" Tish asked.

"Yes, just arrived."

"Good. They tell me your room is ready. Are you okay, G?"

"I hope so," Gemma whispered.

"Don't let that pig get in your head."

Gemma remained silent. There was plenty she could say.

"I know what you're thinking. It feels like an encore performance of Australia. But it's not. You've been away for a while, that's all. They're just desperate to get anything on you. It'll settle down soon, you'll see."

"Maybe."

"Give it a proper chance. You've been amazing, dismantling your opponents throughout the tournament. And don't forget: this time we're in this together."

It was easy for others to tell her to go on. To try again and again. But

Tish didn't have to push through crowds of photographers, Bedric didn't have his every step scrutinized by the media. Giving Gemma advice was a hell of a lot easier than *being* Gemma. But after all this time, she had come back for a specific reason—redemption.

"Together then," Gemma said, hoping she sounded more convincing than she felt. "I must admit, you're nearly adequate at this motivational speech bit."

"Adequate? Nearly? I was brilliant. I had goose bumps on my arms as I spoke. Winston-bloody-Churchill would've been proud."

"Fine, you were brilliant. Are you on your way?"

"No, I'll meet you at the stadium. Be safe, okay? Too many jackals around here."

Gemma hung up, already feeling better. Adding her best friend to her team had been a stroke of genius. She turned her attention to her security team, deep in discussion with the hotel staff. Unfortunately, the staff's blanching faces did not convey confidence.

Years earlier, when she first broke into the game, Gemma had found it absurd when others complained about the cost of fame and the loss of privacy. Now she could look back at how foolish she had been. She used to hope people would one day know her name. Now she wished they would give her space to breathe.

Gemma evaluated her new suite. Spacious, modern. For the next week, this would be home. *If I make it all the way to the finals, that is.* She leaned against the wall, exhausted.

Despite her past successes, plenty already doubted her. She didn't need to add her own voice to the chorus. As the article had pointed out, until she won a Grand Slam, she would not live up to her potential—or the hype.

No point living in the past. She was here now, at the French Open, with a chance to finally prove them all wrong.

Her mobile's blare startled her. This time it was Wesley, her manager.

"I just heard from Bedric. How the hell are you?"

"Fine, I suppose. Just trying to—"

"I told Bedric you'd be fine. He worries too much. Listen, we need to squeeze in an interview. Ideally before your match this afternoon."

"Interview? This afternoon? You're not serious."

"Very serious. Check this out. Entertainment Weekly... cover piece."

"Entertainment Weekly? What do they want?"

"Don't go absent-minded on me. *'Triton Warriors'* premieres next week, and your role has generated a lot of buzz. A scene leaked on YouTube and the fans have gone ape. They want to see more. Your return from hiding couldn't have been timed better. Isn't this awesome?"

She had nearly forgotten about that one. They had filmed her scenes six months ago, back when she was still a dolt. Back when she had allowed Johnny Flauto to talk her into a cameo appearance for his next blockbuster film. Back when she had taken her eye off her true love—tennis.

"No, it's not awesome, Wesley," she said. "I want to be clear about this. We have one goal now. Win a Grand Slam. I don't care about that movie and what the press are saying. We need to remain focused—and that starts with you."

"Then let me be clear also. Your success has always been my focus."

Even when she wanted to take a strong stance she couldn't do it properly. She may have been the talent, but in truth he was the reason behind her fame and fortune. He had meticulously masterminded her climb to success. To ask Wesley to shift gears was like asking him to alter his DNA.

"No interviews, Wesley. Not today."

She got off the call, and as she stepped outside she asked for one little miracle. Only one. An uneventful breakfast.

Andre Reyes glanced at his watch. His boss was late. Andre would have preferred room service, but Roger had insisted on a "game plan" discussion over breakfast before meeting with the client's team.

Perched on the twenty-third floor of the Pullman Hotel, the window-encircled restaurant was filling quickly as waves of jet-lagged guests lumbered in. Business travelers and tourists alike appeared depleted. A feeling he understood all too well.

Business trips were considerably less painful when Roger didn't join him. Now Andre would have to explain how he planned to dazzle the client when his plan was to wing it, like always. That would have been the truth. Roger's firm, however, wasn't built on truth but on premium, mapped-out consulting services. Roger wanted well-thought-out guarantees, and those were hard to provide with these types of engagements.

On his cell phone, Andre scrolled through additional information his assistant had delivered on the client. If his instinct was right, the challenge of this engagement wouldn't be the technical matters, but the corporate egomaniac who was intent on placing blame on everything but his own leadership deficiencies.

Andre used to have a lot more patience with bad leaders. They were clients after all. But over the last year, his patience had been dangling on a fine thread. Maybe because he was so close to the end of his contract. Or maybe because he never liked those who blamed everyone else for their own mistakes.

The headache that had been threatening bloomed now. The day just kept getting better.

Andre scanned the restaurant for the waitress. No luck. He could smell the coffee. Now he needed to taste it, to quench the headache that, like a burgeoning monster, continued to transform from a nuisance to a debilitating migraine.

The hostess escorted a tall man in Andre's direction. He must have been near seven feet, long arms and even longer legs. The man's leathery skin made it hard for Andre to guess his age. He walked with an off-center gate. An injury? Or because of the oversized bag he carried slung over his shoulder? The man was seated at a nearby table.

Stop staring. This habit would one day land him in trouble. Unfortunately, it was his nature to observe, study, and wonder. It was this curiosity about everything that had piqued the attention of his kindergarten teacher and had started a chain reaction of tests and evaluations, eventually tethering him to a career path before he'd even hit puberty.

He rubbed his temple. Where was that coffee?

Andre glanced up, hoping to find the waitress. Instead, he heard a woman shout across the restaurant, "Bedric, move the bag!"

The tall man perked up. *Bedric, I assume,* Andre thought. When Bedric glanced down, so did Andre. The oversized bag lay blocking the path between tables, and a waitress was heading their way fast, tray held high, obstructing her view.

Bedric reached for the bag, but before Andre could utter a sound, or even move, the waitress tripped, and the stainless carafes of coffee flew off the tray like stray bullets—nailing Andre dead-on.

One container exploded against his chest, the other slammed into his shoulder. A third skidded off the table then sloshed the piping hot contents onto his lap.

After the instantaneous paralysis, boiling pain howled along his skin. Andre leapt from his seat. He wanted to scream, curse, yank off the steaming suit. His heartbeat danced erratically while his jaw pulsed, and twitching neck muscles hardened to stone.

The next few moments were surreal, full of muffled screams…

—*Mon Dieu!*

… Commotion…

—*What happened? Is he okay?*

… And apologies.

"I am so sorry, *Monsieur.*" He turned. The waitress. Tears clung to her lashes, her cheeks flushed. Worry darkened her eyes.

He blinked. "Not… your fault," he managed.

"What have you done?" the *maître d'* yelled. His puffy red cheeks bobbed as he marched toward them. Spittle gathered at the corners of his mouth. "Stupid girl, leave, now! *Sortez d'ici!*"

"It's not her fault," Andre said as he regained his breath. "She tripped—"

"*Monsieur* Reyes," the man said, "this is unacceptable. This is an embarrassment—"

"Stop." Andre took a deep breath and straightened, towering over the Frenchman by a good foot. "If you cause problems for her, I'll cause problems for this hotel. It was not her fault. Do we understand each other?"

Andre's gaze shifted slightly behind the *maître d'*. Next to Bedric, a tall, striking young woman stood motionless with her mouth agape. Was this the Voice who had yelled for Bedric earlier?

The *maître d'*'s brows furrowed, then loosened. "I understand," he said, then leaned in for privacy. "Doctor Reyes, the hotel medic will be sent to your room at once. And of course, we will take care of your suit. Please accept our sincerest apologies."

Andre put out his hand. "Apology accepted." The *maître d'* shook it. An old-world contract. The type his late uncle would've appreciated.

The sounds of the crowded restaurant returned to life. Silverware clinked against china, and voices in dozens of languages rose to a sustained crescendo.

As the *maître d'* scurried away, the waitress turned to Andre. "Thank you, *Monsieur*," she said.

The plea in her almond brown eyes reminded him of a deer—lost, scared, at risk. He handed her a business card. "Let me know if they give you any trouble."

She held the card in both hands and studied it. She wiped a tear that finally fell, and tucked the card into her pocket before she continued to clean.

Andre studied his Armani suit, suddenly feeling flustered—maybe even angry. Why hadn't Bedric and the Voice spoken up? His suit was ruined, his chest and lap throbbed in pain, and the waitress was blamed for someone else's carelessness. No maybes about it, he was pissed. And the damp stink of coffee on cloth did not help.

He started to march out, finding Bedric and the Voice in his path. He considered giving them a piece of his mind, but at the last instant navigated around them, avoiding eye contact. *It doesn't matter. It's over.* Right now, he had to tend to his wounds and take another shower before his meeting.

A light tap on his shoulder caught his attention. He turned, coming face-to-face with the Voice. Their eyes locked, and in that split second, everything slowed. Sounds muted.

Breathe. Remember to breathe.

He stared, with only a passing realization that his mouth might be open. But he was not in control. Like sunlight against precious jewels, her azure eyes seemed to collect light and add an unreal level of luminosity.

"Be sure to quickly drench the burn with cool water, not cold," she said, her British accent transforming even the most obscure words into poetry.

"Don't rush the process." She stepped closer. "Allow the cool water to soothe the burn."

He inhaled her faint scent of jasmine and took in details: Jet black hair pulled tight into a ponytail, eyes, round as a cat's, smooth, tanned skin.

Her face, somehow familiar.

She was no longer talking. "Are you done evaluating me?"

Heat flushed his face. *What's the matter with you? You're gawking like a preschooler.* "Right, sorry," he mumbled. "Cool water, not cold. Got it."

Her once gentle eyes narrowed before a perfectly formed eyebrow lifted. "Do call the hotel medic." Her voice cold, distant.

"Thanks." He offered a small smile. She didn't return it. Great. He was supposed to be mad at her. Not the other way around.

Bedric approached her. "Gemma, maybe we should leave?" The man had a heavy Eastern-European accent.

Were these two together? Bedric couldn't be her father—no resemblance. Her husband? No rings, thankfully. Her boyfriend? Ouch!

Without turning to Bedric she said, "We're staying." She studied Andre for another moment, then spun away, muttering, "Unreal."

Andre stood planted, watching. He wanted to leave, but couldn't. As she strode past, heads turned and gazes shifted in her direction. She was tall, maybe six feet. A few inches shorter than him at any rate. In fact, her body seemed a bit disproportional. She was mostly legs and wide shoulders—like a swimmer. She was probably in her twenties, like him. She wore mid-calf, body-hugging Capri pants, perfectly detailing her long, killer legs. As she slid around the tables, her ponytail danced, each sway exposing the back of her elegant neck.

He pulled away from the trance and rushed out, surprised at his behavior. When it came to beautiful women, he was typically reserved and indifferent. The beautiful floated through life expecting others to grovel. Andre bowed to no one. Not even to someone who looked like her.

But those eyes...

He took a deep breath and exhaled the bad karma.

As he reached the elevator, the door opened. His boss stepped out, then recoiled.

"What happened to you?" Roger asked.

"Not now. I'll see you in the lobby."

Inside the elevator, Andre rested against the wall and pulled his wet clothes away from his tender skin. He raked his hands through his hair and focused on the not-too-distant future. Soon he wouldn't have to put up with this crap. Airplane to hotel to client to airplane. All he had to do was stick to his plan. In six months he'd be done with all of this.

So much for being discreet. Gemma could feel the probing eyes of the other patrons as she sipped her tea. Eating breakfast at the restaurant had turned out to be a mistake, but she was tired of being caged in a suite. On the other hand, she was tired of faces that stared and analyzed, always studying her body language, her eyes, her expression, her anything for any indication of stress, hoping to be witness to her next public meltdown.

Stay calm. No emotion, show nothing.

She never knew who might be filming her, snapping pictures, or listening in on conversations. Every move she made was news. From the type of socks she wore to the number of times she applied lip-gloss on an average day. No one cared about the real Gemma. They only cared about the image that had been carefully crafted over the last five years.

"What is going on?" Bedric asked.

"Let's see, you scorched an American, ruined his five thousand dollar suit, and nearly had a Frenchwoman sacked. Other than that, nothing." She displayed her well-rehearsed, confident smile.

"You know what I mean."

"I have a match in a few hours. I'd prefer you remain focused."

"I was about to say the same to you." A smile nearly crossed his lips.

Well played, she thought.

"I don't have to remind you, do I?" he said. She just stared at him. "I have seen that look in your eyes before. With Flauto. We agreed this was a new chapter."

"This *is* a new chapter. And what you saw in my eyes was anger."

"Hmm," he murmured then sipped his coffee and turned his attention to his mobile.

Gemma forked a piece of melon and savored the sweet nectar as she took in the panoramic view of Paris from the restaurant windows. Focusing on today's match was key, but one thought kept interrupting—the American. Bedric was right.

For a moment she'd thought maybe he was different—a modern-day knight. His display of empathy for the waitress was nearly chivalrous. But she had been wrong.

Gemma was certain that when he'd recognized her, he started to plot—just like Georg years earlier and, of course, Johnny. Her idyllic image of the American instantly crumbled when he practically undressed her with his eyes. She'd known too many like him. Polished blokes who dressed and spoke well, but in the end all wanting the same thing: to bed her, then sell a story, a picture, or any remembrance that would widen their wallets or stroke their ego.

When it came to Gemma Lennon, everyone was out to make a profit—she had no savior. Would she ever?

"It is a question of trust," Bedric said.

She gazed at him. His eyes still trained on his phone. "What was that?" she asked.

"People like you must learn to trust very few," he said. "Most are untrustworthy. They have agendas."

Money, she thought. Would he sue her? She could see the headlines now—*Tennis Star Burnt Me.* Of course, he could have embarrassed her in front of the whole room by pointing out it was her bag that tripped the waitress. But he hadn't. Also, he did get burnt.

She shut her eyes, momentarily allowing the choking weight of her life to win. It would be so much easier to walk away and try to live a normal, simple life. And she almost had quit after the Australian Open debacle. Almost.

But she'd come back to convert her critics into believers. And somehow, she'd find it within herself to believe also.

CHAPTER TWO

"Hollywood is a place where they'll pay you a thousand
dollars for a kiss and fifty cents for your soul."

~Marilyn Monroe

The war of tennis was won and lost on the court, but the mental game began long before the first serve was launched. The way she had been embarrassed at the Australian Open semifinal after the accident was evidence of that.

From the hotel lobby, Gemma observed members of the so-called press hovering outside. Like vultures, the paparazzi seemed one step ahead, always knowing where to go. It had taken them less than one hour to find her.

She didn't think she'd stay at the Pullman next year. It was nice, but it was no Hotel Sofitel. The ocean of marble tiles were pretty, the leather sofas were artsy, and the lobby's brass stairwell was striking. But she was not impressed with the hotel's ability to control the chaos that followed her. The hotel porters were already losing the battle at the doors.

"We're ready," her security lead said.

She slid on her sunglasses, slipped on the noise-canceling headphones, and rose. She pressed play and turned the volume up—as high as possible—hoping maybe *System of a Down* would drown out the voices.

Her security, one man on the right and another on the left, held her by the arms. Bedric took the lead. They marched toward the lobby doors. On the other side of the glass, the hordes ignited into motion and surged forward, while the hotel staff tried to push back unsuccessfully. Gemma's gaze lowered to her feet and stayed there.

When the doors opened, the noise hit fever-pitch. She shut her eyes and held her breath. Through the music, she could still hear them call her name. *Gemma. Gemma. Gemma.* Security rammed their way through, their bodies pressing hers, her feet barely touching the ground.

Three. Two. One. Zero.

She was in the car.

The door slammed behind her and the locks engaged. She slowly opened her eyes and breathed again. The paparazzi smelled, a putrid stink of the unbathed who had given up hygiene for the opportunity to get the one picture that would earn them a payday or a month's rent.

She slid the headphones to the back of her neck, then turned to Bedric, who was perusing the scouting reports on her next opponent.

"Doesn't all this bother you?" she asked.

"They're here for you, not me," he said, eyes trained on the papers.

"Did it bother you when you played?"

"No one cared about me when I played."

"Am I bothering you?"

"You have been bothering me for nearly six years now. But I am a patient man."

"And a lovely man as well."

He snorted.

Gemma grinned. Bedric was dry as a cork, but lovely nonetheless. She couldn't have asked for a better coach and match strategist.

Through the madness of the crowd, she caught a glimpse of a little girl—maybe eight or nine—trying to see through the forest of people, saying something, tears in her eyes. She read the girl's lips. "Gemma."

Gemma scrambled toward the driver's privacy window just as the car pulled away. "Don't leave," she told the driver. The car came to an abrupt stop. "Do you see that young girl in the crowd?" she asked the security guard in the passenger seat while she dug into her bag. "She's wearing a red top."

"Yes, but Miss Lennon, we really should leave."

"As soon as you give her these." She handed him match tickets, then grabbed a tennis ball from her bag and wrote a note. "And this. Please."

The security guard leapt out of the car, and Gemma returned to her seat, watching intently. The guard made his way to the girl and handed her the ball and tickets. The girl's eyes widened. A warm smile spread on her lips just as she spun toward Gemma's car, waving vigorously.

This is the prize. Moments like these kept her sane.

"What did you write on the ball?" Bedric asked.

"You are the magic."

Because life was so vicious, and often unfair, Gemma wanted girls to believe in themselves—if they did that, no matter the obstacles, they could make it.

After all, hadn't she? She could have lost everything at sixteen when she had fallen for the wrong guy. And again, just a few months ago, when the person she thought she could love had nearly killed her a day before her seminal match in Australia.

Yet after all that, she was still standing, fighting because a Grand Slam had been her dream—and her late father's. The reason why she had worked day and night and sacrificed so much since she was five. When her father was on life support, did he hear her when she promised she would win one? Did he believe her? She trained around the clock after he passed, driven to win in Australia. She should have listened to her instinct to distance herself from Johnny during those critical days. Instead, she had caved to her weak heart.

The guard jumped back in and the car lurched forward. Like an organic outgrowth, the paparazzi followed. Some ran, some jumped on bikes and mopeds, others jogged alongside. A scene she recalled all too well.

Minutes from the venue, she leaned her head back and started meditating. *One point at a time. I can defeat anyone if I take it one point at a time.* With that chant in her head, she drifted.

"Wake up, we are here," Bedric said, nudging Gemma.

She came to just as the door opened.

"Bonjour," Wesley said in an inexcusable accent. Her manager, an American transplanted to London, seemed to have acquired a new tan.

His exaggerated smile pushed his long nose out further.

"An in-person visit by His Greatness?"

"Shush, you," he said, and kissed her cheek. "How are you feeling?"

"Ready."

"Everyone's talking about how well you've been playing. They all want to talk to you, to understand what's different this time around." His smile was rehearsed, yet reassuring. "No one's even mentioning Australia."

Fine Caribbean sand on an open wound would have been significantly more pleasant.

"Gemma," Bedric said, his ears and the tip of his nose crimson, "focus on this match. And only this match."

"Right, of course." Wesley glanced at his watch. "Good, we have plenty of time. Come with me." He took her by her arm and hustled her through the gathering faces and cameras.

"Wesley, I already told you no interviews. Not today."

"This is not an interview. There's someone who wants to meet you."

"Wesley, really. Can't this wait?"

"Believe me, you want to meet him."

Gemma's movement was pure machinery, driven by forced momentum.

"Why aren't you carrying the Ferragamo purse?" he whispered.

"Bloody hell, Wesley, we don't use purses on the court."

"The sponsors want your fans to see you using their products. I'll have Tish remind you."

"Yes, you do that."

A heavy-set man brightened as they approached.

"Gemma, I'd like you to meet Mr. John Seevers. He's the—"

But she no longer listened. Another sponsor or similar. A Vice President of this, that, or the other. Another person who wanted something. She knew the name of this game. She smiled, shook hands, exchanged pleasantries, and signed a couple of tennis balls for him. *Another day, another minute of my life stolen.*

The locker room facilities at Roland Garros were reminiscent of an exclusive spa. Considerably different from the days when she'd changed in a car or public restroom. The lighting was warm, the wood-inlaid locker doors built by craftsmen, and the aroma of oils and designer shampoos accented the air. Now, in the latter rounds of the tournament, the locker room was mostly empty, desolate, providing Gemma with the quiet she needed.

She turned her attention to the senior trainer, meticulously preparing Gemma's feet—or what was left of them. She padded the callouses, wrapped her jammed toe, then applied tape until her feet felt as indestructible as rhino skin. No blinged-out pink nails here. *What would Glamour or Cosmo think?*

As soon as the trainer finished, she cleaned up her supplies and walked away without a word. Gemma appreciated professionals who understood when to stay and when to leave.

Gemma slipped on her lucky socks then opened her bag. She removed all five racquets and squeezed their handles. *We're in this together,* she told each one. She carefully returned them to the bag then drank the first of three water bottles fortified with electrolytes. She ate one banana and kept the second one for later during the match.

She noticed Paulina, her opponent, stretching and talking to her reflection in the mirror. The loneliest sport in the world. No one to pass to, no one to speak to during the match. Athletes learned very quickly that they started alone and by the end, even if they won, they stood alone.

A few minutes later, the French Open match official entered. "We are ready," he said.

Gemma rose, hoisting her bags over her shoulder and exchanged a greeting with Paulina. They were friendly off-court, but war would soon be waged on the court, and the psychological match had begun. No awards were given for congeniality in tennis. From this point, win or go home.

Gemma knew everything about Paulina. She had studied hundreds of hours of footage. She knew what to expect from her serves, her returns, and her volleys. Gemma would exploit Paulina's single-handed backhand and sub-par second serve. No longer would she leave anything to chance or luck—or talent. Today she would be in control of her destiny.

They followed the official through the long corridor toward center court. The faces of past champions adorned the walls on either side. Would she be on these walls one day?

Gemma slowed, giving Paulina the lead by a few paces.

When Paulina's name was announced, she walked onto the court to a cheering crowd. Then Gemma's name was announced, and the cheers transformed into thunderous roars. Paulina flinched. Gemma could practically read the woman's mind. In that moment, both the home field and mental advantage transferred to Gemma. The first, albeit unrecorded, point of the day was hers.

Gemma stepped out, and the noise doubled, then tripled. The loose red clay on the field rattled. She had her share of critics, but she also inspired legions of fans. Fans who had remained loyal through all her failures. Fans who were her last remaining source of fuel.

She turned slightly to take in the complete view of center court, absorbing the waves of support. All successful athletes were coached to shut out the crowd. But she couldn't, wouldn't. What she couldn't get from her failed relationships she would get from the game. She searched their faces and smiles, longing for their energy. Unlike anywhere else, inside the stadium she felt loved.

Gemma's jaw muscles tightened, her throat went dry, her ears rang, and her eyes stung. Streaming through her veins was what she thought of as combustible adrenaline.

Game time.

"Time," the umpire called. Gemma had won the coin toss earlier and elected to serve, always preferring to draw first blood.

"Gemma, marry me!" a fan from the upper decks yelled.

"I'm quite busy right now," she yelled back.

The crowd exploded in laughter. Within moments, a persistent chatter draped center court. Not enough for the umpire to call for silence, but enough to be palpable. She scanned the anxious crowd. The French enjoyed long, competitive matches. Gemma preferred quick, decisive ones. Particularly on warm days like this.

She took a deep breath.

Done.

All sounds vanished. From now until the end of the point, she would hear nothing but her heartbeat and the sound of ball on string or clay.

She asked for and received three balls. With all three in her hand, she studied them as she rotated the spheres in her palm, trying to identify one that didn't belong. She dropped one, tucked another under her skirt, and squeezed the third.

At the baseline, she bounced the ball five times then glanced at Paulina. She stood exactly where Gemma expected her to stand—deep corner. A predictable move.

Focus. Toss. Hammer.

Gemma zeroed in on her feet, the grip, and the ball, nestled in the open throat of the racquet. Muscle memory took over, a movement refined in the course of thousands of hours of repetition. Her body executed the dance: where her knees bent, her arms rose, and the ball flew high above, exactly where she needed it. Her eyes bore in on the spinning ball as she leapt and the hammer slid behind her back, like an axe ready for the kill. And in one instant, the ball stopped—the world on pause—inviting Gemma to make contact.

She grunted, the hammer erupted, and the ball exploded down the line.

Ace.

The crowd roared.

Paulina had guessed poorly.

No, Gemma would not lose this match.

CHAPTER THREE

"Be the change you wish to see in the world."

~Mahatma Gandhi

Andre stepped off the elevator into the lobby. A large crowd had gathered outside the Pullman. He approached Roger. "What's going on out there?"

"Someone famous, I think. And the paparazzi found out."

A heavily-tinted car sped away, and the mob followed like a redirected swarm in pursuit of its prey.

"Did you get burned?" Roger asked. "The *maître d'* gave me the morbid details."

The hotel medic had been helpful—right after Andre had signed the release form. Also, he had taken Gemma's advice, *Cool, not cold.* He remembered Gemma's divine eyes in vivid detail. Sometimes photographic memory had its distinct upside.

Had she apologized? He reran the conversation in his mind. No, she hadn't. Sometimes photographic memory was annoying. Granted, he did behave like a perv, but considering the circumstances, she should've given him a pass.

"I have some blistering and tenderness, but—"

"Blistering?" Roger asked. "You should see a doctor. Maybe afterwards."

"Sure. Doctor. Next on my list."

Roger's attempted display of sympathy brought a smile to Andre's lips. This was no regular engagement. Otherwise Roger Trutt, founding partner of Meyers & Trutt, would not have come. The client's board had approved a large sum of money for this project. No Andre, no money—simple equation.

Andre was the reason Meyers & Trutt secured multi-million dollar deals. Although his credentials were indisputable, he realized he was an enigma. His youth alarmed most, and the natural question was whether a twenty-four-year-old could be trusted with business deals of this magnitude. Which was where Roger came in. He was the one with gray in his hair.

Also, since all of Andre's clients had tried to recruit him, Roger likely wanted to keep tabs on M&T's most valued asset. But with six months remaining in his contract, Andre wouldn't do anything to jeopardize the bonus payoff—his golden parachute. After seven years of hard labor, he was owed that windfall.

"There's Franck." Roger lifted his chin and produced his winning smile. "Our client awaits."

They stepped into Cinematique's spacious, modern conference room. The swarming began, and attendees converged around Andre. Hands were thrust, names with impossible accents were thrown, and positions were declared in quick succession. A different scene than the reception he used to get as an eighteen-year-old consultant with M&T. He had been asked to work behind the scenes, never had a seat at the table, and when he spoke, the others stared at him like he was a sideshow freak. Now everyone wanted a piece of him because they knew who he was and what he could do. But could he gain their trust? He needed to show them he was here to help.

"Dr. Reyes," Franck said once everyone sat, "we are ready when you are."

"Thank you," Andre said, standing and positioning himself behind his chair, looking out at his audience. He often thought of himself as a performer or a chess-master, all his actions calculated and deliberate. "Franck, I'm confused by the attendees. I had been specific. Only those who have an intrinsic understanding of the systems should be here. Instead, I also see executives."

Badeaux, the Chief Operating Officer spoke up. "Because I want to understand why this team continues to struggle with streaming 3D content," he said in a condescending drawl. "We are the largest broadcaster in Europe, yet our smaller competitors have solved their issues. They," he pointed to the engineering team, "are still lost. You will help me understand what has gone wrong."

"I'm here to solve the problem. Not talk about it. What led us here is of no concern to me. It's irrelevant."

"It is not irrelevant to me," Badeaux said, his voice sharp. "I want answers."

Roger shifted in his seat, ready to speak, but Andre stopped him. He would not let this corporate bully have his way. He peered in Badeaux's eyes. "How's this for an answer: twenty-seven questionable acquisitions in less than eighteen months. None integrated into the company, because of political decisions. Three-hundred-twenty-one technical experts laid off in that same period of time to justify the cost of acquisitions."

Badeaux's mouth had gone slack. The room was silent, but the technical team's eyes were glowing in shock, in awe.

Check.

He had read all the press releases in advance—Badeaux's ego plastered across all those acquisitions. As expected, now he was trying to find the scapegoat. "This company's core is a mishmash of technologies—a perfect mess. If you're still interested in solving the problem, instead of blaming people, I'd recommend you let me run this meeting my way."

"But our interest is paramount," Badeaux said, most of his bravado gone. "Our expectations must be addressed."

"Agreed." Andre held up a black marker. "Can you four articulate your expectations on the board behind me? We commit to address them. In your absence."

Badeaux's face went blank. After a nine-second stare down, the executive team rose, wrote nothing of significance on the board, then stormed out. Andre studied the team that remained. The dynamic in the room had shifted. They were all grinning and loose.

Checkmate.

The team didn't waste time. System-by-system, hundreds of functional schematics were analyzed, and after some time the logical flow of the video stream emerged. The spaghetti of connections evolved from a mess into a structured mesh. Five hours later, the overall ecosystem was represented visually—from start to finish.

"I think we got them all, Dr. Reyes," Franck said.

Andre rose, studying the system architecture in quiet contemplation. He blinked rapidly as he freed his mind's eye to run through countless scenarios, similar to what Einstein called 'thought experiments.' He searched for potential bottlenecks by processing one test case after another, visualizing a beam of light running through the web of connections. Once one path gave him a result, he tried another, then another—an iterative process until he had tested all permutations.

By the time he was done, more than three dozen bottlenecks had been marked for the engineers to investigate.

"Let's stop here for today," Andre told the team at just past eight p.m. "We'll pick this up in the morning."

Everyone approached Andre and shook his hand before leaving He took note of the awed look on their faces and acknowledged their gratitude, but was also grateful to them. They had trusted him. With trust, anything was possible.

Franck approached Andre. "Amazing. This has been amazing."

"Don't celebrate yet," Andre said.

"You don't understand." Franck ran his hand through his hair, his smile wide. "We have tried for over a year to solve this problem. We were treating the symptom, not addressing the core issues."

"I know." Andre grinned.

"*Touché.* I will get the car."

Roger, barely awake, stood and grabbed his coat. "I'm getting too old for this," he said.

"I know what you mean," Andre said.

"Hmph."

Andre attempted to sustain the smile, but he was spent. His mind felt tired, abused. And his chest, shoulder, and lap had been screaming with pain from the burns since noon.

"You got this one, right? Any doubts?" Roger asked. "Our deal is contingent on a guaranteed solution."

Andre studied Roger. "On moral grounds, I refuse to answer."

"Great. I'll tell the office to process the invoice."

"Shameless. You are shameless."

"By the way," Roger said, lowering his voice, "I've asked Franck to join us for drinks at the hotel bar. We will discuss future opportunities. They could become a major account for you."

"I don't know, Roger. I need to take care of the burn. Not sure—"

"Do it quickly. Change. Whatever. But you need to be there."

Andre remained silent. The high he felt when he helped clients solve the seemingly impossible was indescribable, but he needed to help himself now. He was burning out quickly. His years-long chase after financial independence had left him damaged.

"Clear?" Roger asked.

"Of course." He could do this. He had to—for now.

Gemma took a deep breath then phoned Tish's room. "Are you busy?"

"Watching some horrid French game show. So yes, mind-numbingly busy," Tish said.

"Good. Let's get a drink at the bar."

"Bar, as in, where real people congregate? That type of bar?"

"That's right. For maybe an hour."

"And your security?"

"They're manning the front lobby. You'll have to double as my bodyguard."

"Fantastic. I'm coming out now before you change your mind." Tish hung up.

Gemma needed to escape her room and breathe. No security, no Bedric, no Wesley. Breakfast had been a disaster, but she had a better feeling about this decision. Mid-week evening at the hotel's quaint bar with her best friend was definitely a good idea.

CHAPTER FOUR

"It is strange to be known so universally and yet be so lonely."

~Albert Einstein

D on't draw attention to yourself," Gemma told Tish.

"Me? I'm a fuckin' saint."

"Dear Lord."

The lift chimed, and when the door opened, she saw him. *The American.* He was leaning against the lift's back wall, studying his mobile. He wore a crew neck sweater, tight around his sculpted shoulders and chest, sleeves rolled up to expose muscular forearms. He had not seen her yet. She hesitated, considering her next move while Tish inched forward.

The American glanced up. A momentary pause, before his eyes lit up with recognition. But he said nothing, just smiled. When the door began to close, he leaned forward and stopped it, letting it slide back open. "Going down?" he asked, tone even.

"Yes," Tish said, and sauntered in. "That's one impatient door. Thank you."

"Any time."

Gemma stepped in then spun toward the closing door. The lift dropped, while her heartbeat accelerated. She zeroed in on the panel, watching the floor numbers flicker past one-by-one. Was he staring at her? She studied her reflection on the semi-shiny surface of the door, happy with her choice of clothes. She shifted her gaze to see if he was checking her out. His head was down, focused on his mobile, not her.

The lift chimed. Lobby.

The door had barely opened when Gemma slid out and marched toward the bar.

Tish hurried to catch up. "What's the rush?" she asked.

Gemma was not ready to speak quite yet. Instead, she listened to the footsteps behind her. The light tapping of leather soles against marble tiles. She glanced over her shoulder. He was following.

Tucked in a far booth at the bar, Gemma read through Twitter, Facebook, and e-mail messages, pretending to be catching up on things, but her thoughts were disjointed.

She now knew who she'd play in the semifinals. A rematch against Sonia Wilkins, no less. Her American albatross. The experts were already wondering if Sonia would dismantle Gemma again, just like she had in Australia months earlier. It had to be against Sonia if she wanted closure.

That had been her last tournament—the one that nearly ruined her career. But she was back thanks to Xavi—her Malibu home house-sitter, her personal guru, the man who had become her confidant. With his help, she had returned, determined to win a major by crushing all distractions in her path there.

At least that had been the plan. Right now, she had a distraction at hand. The American. Even Tish had noticed Gemma's wandering eyes. Thankfully, he hadn't been following her, but joined two older men. She glanced in his direction, unable to deny an interest, a curiosity.

What was this American's story? Was he the typical scoundrel she met in places like these? Possibly. After the way he had ogled her during breakfast, there could be little doubt he'd seen something he liked.

She glanced again. His humility and youth confused her though. The way he dressed and the way he carried himself shouted power—the type of man she'd fancied in the past, but had sworn off after Johnny. But the way he had taken a stand for the waitress was unexpected, beautiful in a way. To this day, no one had ever taken a stand for her.

"You keep staring at him. You want me to call him over?" Tish asked, never lifting her face from her mobile.

"What? You're mad," Gemma said, feeling a flush creep up her ears.

Tish lifted her eyes. "He's no Johnny Flauto, but handsome in his own 'Merican way."

"Shut it, will you?" Gemma said. She could do without hearing Johnny's name everywhere she turned. "If you weren't my best friend—"

"And only friend."

Gemma glared. "Fine, if you weren't my best and only friend, I'd sack you for insubordination."

"Promises, promises." Tish's green-gold eyes sparkled as she turned her attention to the American while she fiddled with the beads on her long braids. "Do you sometimes wonder if a relationship with a normal person would be different?"

"Normal? What's that supposed to mean?"

"You know, as opposed to celebrities and such."

Gemma shrugged. She didn't know, nor did she care. All relationships were trouble. Even innocent dates turned into a mess, leaving her ravaged. Her broken heart seemed to be a perverse form of entertainment.

An only child, gifted with the skills to compete in the loneliest sport… Maybe she was designed this way for a purpose. What she knew for sure was that in all her attempts to break her solitude, she had made one poor decision after another, falling for those who would eventually hurt her. Her latest with Johnny had been her poorest choice to date. She had to learn to choose better.

Gemma turned her gaze toward the American's table against her better judgment.

"So," Tish said, "what's the story with your friend?"

"Not my friend," Gemma said.

"If you say so."

Gemma sighed. "Remember how I asked you to contact the restaurant's manager and ensure the waitress wasn't reprimanded? Well, he's the bloke who was scorched this morning when the waitress tripped."

"Oh, no shit." A beat. "Wait. I'm missing something. Then why did you give him the cold shoulder in the lift? I thought we wanted to avoid a potential lawsuit. That was a perfect opportunity."

"It wasn't *that* perfect."

"Do you have marbles in your head? You could have made peace with him right then and there. Flash your smile, put on the charm, and we're in the clear." Tish shook her head. "A perfect opportunity blown. In Ethiopia we have a saying: Give advice; if they don't listen, let adversity teach them."

Gemma studied Tish, processing her words. A few moments passed as thoughts clashed. Months back, when she was ready to quit tennis, Xavi had reminded her that life was about choices and action.

Choices and action.

CHAPTER FIVE

"I don't like that man. I must get to know him better."

~Abraham Lincoln

Gemma waved down the waiter.

"Oui, Mademoiselle Lennon?"

"Can you please ask the young man at that table to join us?"

Both the waiter and Tish followed her finger. Then they turned back. Tish's eyes widened.

"Do you mean *Monsieur* Reyes? The gentleman in the gray sweater?"

"Yes, him," she said. At least now she had a last name.

"Right away, *Mademoiselle.*"

"Interesting move. Do you have a game plan, or are you improvising?" Tish asked.

A game plan? Of course not. But it had to be done. Closure was best. "We'll find out soon enough, I guess. Give me the play-by-play." She dropped her eyes to her mobile, feigning disinterest.

"Right. The waiter's saying something. They're looking in our direction now, but he's not moving. I'm smiling—hello."

A few seconds passed.

"Well? Now what?" Gemma sounded more anxious than she intended.

"We're good," Tish said, whispering now. "He's up with drink in hand, following the waiter. He's here in three, two—"

"Hi again," he said.

Gemma looked up. "Hello, Mr. Reyes, will you join us?" Gemma's voice did not waver, but inside she was a wreck. *Settle down.* Others were supposed to be nervous, not her.

"Sure, thanks," he said, then turned to Tish. "I'm Andre."

Tish introduced herself with a slight grin, as he sat across Gemma.

"I hope you don't mind being pulled away from your friends," Gemma said.

"Not a problem."

Men usually gushed and went out of their way to impress, but not him. He created the impression he didn't care. *Don't be an egomaniac. He's not interested.* But if he wasn't interested, then why had he stared during breakfast?

"How's the burn?" Gemma asked.

"Improving. Thanks for asking."

He locked on her eyes, and her heart rate quickened. She broke eye contact and shifted her glass. *What's wrong with you?* "About the incident this morning," Gemma said, "I'm not sure where to begin." She glanced up at him.

Something changed in his demeanor. "Don't worry about it. It was an accident. I'm fine and the waitress didn't get in trouble. It's all forgotten."

The waitress. *Forget the damn waitress, you're in the clear. He won't sue.* But she couldn't let go. The waitress was pretty and he had handed her a card. What kind of man was he? Why had he really protected her?

"Do you know her?" she asked.

"Who? The waitress?" A crease appeared on his forehead.

"Yes—the pretty one."

He blinked then his eyes narrowed. "I don't know her at all." He placed his arms on the table. "What are you asking?"

Crap. Now she'd done it. "I'm just curious, that's all. You don't see that anymore—jumping to a stranger's rescue the way you did." She paused. *You sound shallow.*

His gray eyes turned dark, nearly black. He tucked a strand of his longish black hair behind his ear, never breaking eye contact. "It's simple. If not me, then who?"

Silence.

Say something.

"I've seen too many who work hard, try their best, and yet bad things happen," Andre said. "I can't sleep well when the innocent get screwed."

The room faded. No one else was in the world, only the two of them. Gemma's self-assured smile faded while the flames danced in his eyes. "I would have cleared it up," she finally said.

"I didn't see you or Bedric jumping in."

How could she explain that she didn't want to draw attention to herself? "It's complicated."

"Not to me."

"But you are not me. And like I said, I would have cleared it up. In fact, we did. Afterwards."

He raked his hands through his hair. "Looks like you've answered my question."

She shot him a quizzical look.

"If not me, then who," he continued in a warm voice. "I guess it would have been you. I'm glad I'm not alone." He produced a handsome, yet honest smile.

Gemma cleared her throat. "I do apologize for being such a git. Not only for causing the accident, but also for questioning your motivation."

"No worries. I don't hold grudges."

His words rang true. Apologizing hadn't been so hard after all. "Good. Let me buy you a drink. As a peace offering."

"Didn't realize we were at war. But since we're coming clean, I need to apologize as well."

"Oh? What for?" What would he say? *Because I was starstruck? Because I wanted to see if I can get a chance with Gemma?*

He rubbed his face and grimaced. "For staring at you. It's a bad habit, but I'm not a pervert. Promise. You can ask my aunt."

Tish giggled, and Gemma smiled. "You were staring? At me? Why would a well-mannered American like you do that?"

"I don't want this to come across as a line—because it's not. But it was your eyes. Even now, sitting here in the dark, I find it hard to grasp the impossible brilliance of your eyes. It's insane how beautiful they are."

Gemma could feel Tish's stare. But she didn't dare look, nor break eye contact with Andre. Heat flared on her forehead. "I'll accept that—line or no line."

"Good, because I was about to propose a trade: I'd forgive the second-degree burn if you forgive the innocent gawking. Now I can hold on to my bargaining chip for the future."

"Oh? You have future plans for us?"

"Pardon me." They spun toward the middle-aged English woman.

"Hate to interrupt, but can I please have your autograph for my daughter?" she asked. "She adores you. It would make her year."

"Absolutely. What's her name?" Gemma asked.

After the lady walked away, Gemma glanced at Andre, who appeared confused.

"Are you famous?" he asked.

Tish threw her head back and laughed, pounding the table.

Gemma searched his eyes. Was he serious? Did he really not recognize her?

Andre scanned from one to the other. "Should I know you?" His eyes widened. "That came out all wrong. Didn't mean it that way."

Gemma wondered if he was pulling her leg, but his boyish honesty made it impossible for her not to believe him. "It's no big deal. Some people know me," she said. How ironic that her anonymity made her feel special.

"Boy, this would've been a real bad first date," he said.

A small snort escaped Gemma, and she immediately covered her mouth. She didn't snort. She hadn't snorted since she was eight. Her eyes froze on his. The moments ticked away.

Tish cleared her throat. "G, hate to break this up, but you have an early start tomorrow."

Gemma glanced at the time. "Blimey! It is late. I must turn in for the night," she said, forcing out the words.

"Yeah, me too. Hopefully I'll see you around," Andre said as he slid out of the booth. "Maybe at breakfast." He grinned then walked away.

Gemma studied the way he moved and how his pants fit him just right.

"A bit dishy," Tish said, her eyes trained on Andre's arse.

"Bloody hell, Tish," Gemma hissed.

They scooted out, leaving from the furthest exit and avoiding Andre's table. The women moved briskly toward the lifts.

"What was that all about?" Tish asked in a harsh whisper.

"Nothing. Nothing at all."

"Looked like nothing to me as well. Typical fan, but isn't a fan. In fact, he has no clue who you are, but you pulled a Spanish Inquisition on him because he helped some waitress. Then you sound daft, because he actually did what a decent person should do. Nope, nothing at all. I can see that, clear as day."

Gemma tried to keep her composure. "So, what did you think of him?"

"Handsome—did you see those biceps?—young, but talks like a man, and actually has no clue who you are, but was mesmerized by your eyes. Though frankly, my eyes are prettier, but that's neither here nor there. Clearly a sorry excuse of a man. Shall I get his number?"

"Can you just pretend to be professional? Why I hired my best friend to be my assistant I'll never know."

They broke into laughter as they stepped into the lift. Tish placed an arm around Gemma's shoulders.

"Seems like a decent bloke," Gemma said. "I guess I was wrong about him."

"Hold the presses. You have both apologized and declared you were wrong, all in the span of ten minutes. This must be a sign of the apocalypse."

Gemma closed her eyes and daydreamed of his bright silver eyes and honest smile. But like all others, once he realized who she was, those same eyes would probably see opportunity.

"They all start that way, don't they?" Tish said.

"Sorry?"

"Decent, charming. Then the profit motive kicks in. So hard to trust anyone."

Gemma was silent.

"Speaking of lost trust..." Tish eyed Gemma. "I received an odd note from Johnny's assistant saying he would not make it to your next match. The Brilliant One sends his apologies."

Gemma pulled away from Tish's hold. "Why would that daft cow think I was expecting him?"

"You tell me."

"Who were you talking to earlier?" Roger asked Andre once Franck left.

Andre knew better than to tell this man the truth. "Someone I met earlier today."

"I see," Roger said. Silence joined their table for a few moments. "I am concerned with some of our newer recruits."

Andre glanced at him. "Why's that?"

"They seem to struggle with keeping their priorities straight."

A headache tore at Andre's right temple.

"I preach to all our young consultants that there will come a time for all that other romance stuff. Now is when they have the opportunity to set the world on fire with their intellect." He finished his glass of wine and rose. "I wish they were more like you. I mean, look at what you've accomplished so far," Roger added. "You know how to keep your eye on the prize, son." The winning smile emerged. "And in your case, with your retention bonus on the horizon, that prize will be a game changer."

"Speaking of which," Andre said, "I'm getting married right after. Will you attend?"

"Don't even joke about that."

They both laughed, but Andre knew the truth behind Roger's joke. If Roger suspected that Andre planned to bail once he got his bonus, the next six months would redefine misery.

CHAPTER SIX

"Franck, this is awesome," Andre said. "I've never been to a tennis match." They strolled through the pathways of Roland Garros observing the ad hoc street performers, scanning the various stores, and shops.

"Our pleasure," Franck said. "I expect you will cheer for your countrywoman."

"That's the plan. I hear she's scary-good in person."

"Yes, but so is her opponent. She is the best server in the game."

"Nice. Should be a great battle."

He could have spent hours people watching. The smiles, the laughter, the incessant buzz, and intermingled languages from countless countries. As unsettling as they were, even the mimes were almost enjoyable. Almost. The energy was undeniable. A mass of people from across the globe brought together for one common love—tennis.

This was well worth delaying his flight by a day. He couldn't recall doing anything remotely like this in... well... forever.

Tomorrow morning he'd return home. For now, he'd revel in this match. And tonight he'd return to the hotel bar with hopes Gemma would show up. He had checked every night, but since their first encounter, no sign of either Gemma or her friend.

They joined Roger in the stadium. The athletes had not taken the court for warm ups yet. The seats couldn't have been better. Dead center, facing the judge, four rows off the court. He needed more of this. And he would do more. Soon.

Electricity ran through the crowd when the announcer introduced Sonia as she took the court. He finally felt his age, screaming, hooting, and hollering.

Mixed with the loud cheering and painful echo, the unintelligible blare of the announcer said, *"Representing Great Britain—"* but Andre was not able to catch anything else. Cheers escalated to a roar, resonating throughout his body.

"Wow, she's got loud fans," Andre screamed in Franck's ear. "Lennon, was it?"

"Lennon. Gemma Lennon."

Confusion stunned him.

Wilkins vs. Lennon.

Great Britain.

Lennon is Gemma Lennon.

Gemma is the tennis player?

At that instant, Gemma marched out. She wore an all black outfit, her toned body glistened, her ponytail danced. She was radiant. His heartbeat slowed, his lungs labored, and his brain stopped. He stood transfixed.

She waved to the crowd, who cheered in an explosion of love even while the judge urged the fans to be quiet. Moments later, they settled.

"Andre," Franck said, tugging at his arm. "Andre."

Andre pivoted in a semi-conscious move.

"Sit down."

He scanned around to find he was the only one standing. *Crap!* Andre dropped to his seat. Although Gemma was quite a distance away, he was nearly certain she was looking straight at him. His hand shot up, but he stopped it, not wanting to look silly. Instead, he raked his hair behind his ear. She didn't react. Maybe she hadn't seen him after all.

Gemma's eyes settled on the one person standing. Andre? Here at her match? Coincidence? Unlikely. She did not believe in coincidences. Maybe since their last encounter he had put two and two together. Was he trying to befriend her, get close to her? Had she been right after all, that he would be like all the others?

Her muscles twitched and her mouth went dry. Nerves? Self-consciousness? Why? He was just another person. That's all. Nothing more, nothing less. She had a street fight to get through. *Stay focused.*

She took the court to warm up. The smart move would be to phase out Andre and the crowd. But she could feel eyes trained on her, watching her every move. She scanned the crowd, prepared to see judgment in their faces. Instead hundreds, maybe thousands of people waved British flags. They were here for her, in support of her. Her heartbeat quickened. *Stay focused.*

After a few minutes, when she was ready to practice her serves, she risked a quick glance toward Andre. He looked young—full of life—sitting at the edge of his seat, watching intently. He was possibly a masterful scoundrel who had lied to her and she had bought it. Or maybe he was a good guy. Or maybe... *Stop it.*

Why was it that when he was around she suddenly felt like a schoolgirl?

She stretched her neck, and bounced up and down to loosen up. At the baseline, she took a deep breath, relaxed, bounced the ball, then tossed it...

He's just someone I met.

... She leapt...

Nothing more—nothing less.

... And ripped a 118-miles-per-hour serve.

The crowd exploded.

Andre could not claim to be an expert at the game. At best, he had seen highlights on TV. But watching Gemma play, he couldn't help but think she was the most amazing athlete who had ever lived.

Clearly this wasn't based on objective criteria. Just an instinct. Also, the score did not support his assertion. The match continued to be tightly contested. What made her the best was something he couldn't put his finger on.

Whether she was serving, or returning Sonia's hits, Gemma seemed to explode with power and focused energy. The clay beneath her feet detonated with her movements. Yet the same clay converted to ice when she needed to glide. He wanted to film her and slow down the footage to study what happened to the environment surrounding her. No, what she caused wasn't otherworldly. Quite the contrary. This was natural, innate greatness in action.

Gemma charged the net, slid gracefully, and volleyed the ball past Sonia's outstretched racquet. She was a handful of feet away from Andre now. She glanced at him and nearly smiled before she returned to the baseline.

"Do you know each other?" Roger asked.

Andre had to be careful. "Don't I wish," he chuckled.

Roger studied him. "I suppose most would," he finally said.

Andre didn't want Roger to meddle, nor give him reason to speculate. He didn't like the tone in Roger's voice, the shift in his eyes, the bunching of skin on his brow. All signs of stress.

Andre returned his attention to Gemma, the goddess on clay.

All Gemma had to do was keep her composure, and not react too quickly. She was grateful for the water bottle in her hand. She needed something to squeeze during the press conference.

"Gemma, this was the longest match of your professional career. You seemed fatigued. Was it a conditioning issue due to your extended time off?"

She hated post-game interviews.

"Anyone who competes in a three hour match against one of the best is bound to feel fatigued. Sonia is a phenomenal athlete."

"After you lost the first set, how did you turn it around by winning the second?"

"One point at a time, like always. Each set could have gone either way. The first set was close all along. So were the second and third. The ball sometimes bounces that way."

"How did it feel when you couldn't reach the last decisive ball? What went through your mind?"

The bottle whined in her fist. Did this guy actually expect an answer? How would he feel? She wanted to collapse when she hadn't reached the yellow furry ball that eradicated her chance at a Grand Slam. She wanted to fall and cry. She wanted to disappear.

The press awaited her answer. She drank water, counting to ten. *Don't snap.*

"How did it feel? Was that the question?" She crossed then uncrossed her legs. "As you astutely put it, it felt very decisive."

The press corps laughed.

"Gemma, the fans have voted online, and it's official. They say this is the best match of the year. What are your thoughts?"

"Those must be Sonia's fans." More laughter. "Tennis fans like to see good battles and athletes who leave it all out there. That's what we gave them today."

"Overall, a much better performance in this semifinal—"

"With unfortunately the same results," she said and stood. "Thank you, all."

Tish walked her to the locker room, but Gemma's thoughts drifted back to the end of the game.

When she lost, she wanted to hide, but the crowd had different plans. *"Gemma! Gemma! Gemma!"* they chanted.

She found the will to wave to her fans and her team. Wesley's eyes were swollen, while Bedric kept a strong face, and Tish tried to maintain her composure. Ravaged with dejection, she searched through unfamiliar faces to find Andre. He was screaming and cheering as loud as anyone else, waving a tiny British flag.

Her lungs felt raw and her joints like frail parchment paper. She had lost to Sonia—again. She should have been crushed. Instead she focused on the friendly face of the American man with the genuine smile.

A face she wanted to see again. A man she wanted to know better.

With Tish's help, Gemma finished packing her luggage. She could feel her friend's stare. "I'm fine," Gemma said, then playfully pushed Tish. "Don't analyze me like I'm some endangered butterfly."

"I know. You always come back stronger. Do you want me to join you?" Tish asked.

"Thanks for the offer. But I want to rest, do nothing for three days before I head back to London. I need some *me* time." The last thing she wanted was to deal with the press, paparazzi, and more Johnny Flauto fallout in London. Also, she wanted to see Xavi again. To ease her mind.

"You let me know when you want *me* time to be *we* time, and I'll be on the next bird out of Heathrow."

They hugged.

"Take this," Tish said, handing her a Sudoku puzzle book. "It'll keep the voices in your head occupied on the flight. Half the book when I see you later in the week, or you owe me fifty quid."

Gemma tucked the book in her carryon. "Remember, not a word to Wesley or Bedric until after I'm gone. They won't understand and will assume the worst."

"Understood."

Gemma was silent for a moment. "Tish, don't ask why, just do me a favor."

"Anything."

"Go and see if Andre, the American, is at the bar. Then text me."

"And I can't ask you why?"

"No, you can't."

"Can I guess?"

"No, you can't." Uncontrollably, Gemma beamed. There was that feeling again. Youth.

That night, lounging at the hotel bar, Andre watched highlights of the day's match on the flat screen. Gemma had not come downstairs. For all he knew, she had already left.

"She is staying here at the Pullman," the bartender said.

"The British player?"

"*Oui*, Gemma. She is so good."

"What makes her good?"

"How do you say, angry and active on the court?"

"Aggressive?"

"*Oui*, like Capriati. She runs to the net all the time. Like the men, taking chances, but smooth like a ballerina. Also, powerful serves. She makes the match fun to watch."

"Interesting."

"And, of course," the French bartender said with a dramatic flair, "she is the most beautiful woman in the world."

Andre laughed, fully agreeing with the man's sentiments, when a familiar sensation gave him pause. He swiveled slowly, scanning his surroundings. Nothing seemed out of place, but he couldn't shake that all-too-familiar, yet uncomfortable, feeling. Was he being watched?

Gemma read Tish's message. *"Not at bar. Sorry G."*

She considered going downstairs just to be sure. Gemma had wanted to do that for the last couple of days, but had talked herself out of it, each time remembering what falling for the wrong guy had gained her.

She strode to her bag, found her scraggly stuffed dog of twenty-one years, then went to her bedroom and fell on the bed.

Probably best he wasn't there. She couldn't afford to get in that trap again.

She closed her eyes, recalling the unforced errors and lost chances on the court. Even so, she had done well this time. Xavi had been right. So long as she remained focused and shut out the noise, she could have a shot at winning it all. Thankfully, she'd get another chance in three weeks at Wimbledon. But each passing day held the possibility of an injury, a new star, a new nervous breakdown. Talent guaranteed nothing. She could lose in the first round.

Her mobile rang. "Oh, bugger!" Gemma had forgotten to call back. "I'm sorry, Mum. I was packing and forgot—"

"You don't have to explain. I just wanted to say I'm proud of you." Her voice was solid, honest.

The emotion that overcame her was instantaneous. Gemma covered her eyes, pushing back the tears. "I was so, so close," she whispered.

"You played with heart. That's all that matters. That's what Dad always said."

Her chest cramped. "I wanted to win for him."

"Win for yourself, not him. He's in heaven, proud of you, cheering you on."

"Proud? Somehow, I doubt that."

"Despite what you think, he loved you deeply and unconditionally."

"Was he proud when I decided to find my birth parents? Did he love me when I told him he's not my real father?"

"You were an emotional teenager. He understood. I understood."

"I let him down in life and haven't been able to make him proud in death."

"My, you make your life sound like a Shakespearean tragedy. But it's all melodrama, I assure you." She wasn't mad, upset or concerned. She sounded amused. "He loved you. He just didn't know how to express it. Don't turn this journey of yours into his. It's yours. And you did bloody well today. Lift off from here."

When had she turned into a philosopher? She was right, of course. Which was why Gemma was going back to visit Xavi to heed his old-school advice. He knew how to center her. "I'm going to visit Xavi and Mari for a few days."

"Good. He'll set your head straight. Send them my best and remind Mari I still want her recipe for *Tortilla Española*. I know I've butchered her other dishes, but I have a good feeling about this one."

"I love you, Mum."

"Even though I don't know how to dress properly or apply makeup?"

"Particularly because of those things."

CHAPTER SEVEN

"A sex symbol becomes a thing. I hate being a thing."

~Marilyn Monroe

When Andre and Roger stepped out of the taxi at Charles de Gaulle Airport, he spotted a large, loud, and disruptive crowd. The mob flowed toward the Air France entrance. He caught a glimpse of the nucleus. Cameras flashed, highlighting a tall woman with long black hair, pushing through with two security guards and what appeared to be airport staff.

Gemma.

"Goddamn paparazzi," Roger mumbled under his breath.

Just then, from the way they moved and shuffled, focused solely on their target, Andre noted a pattern. They were susceptible.

"Do you like bowling?" Andre asked Roger.

"Bowling?"

Andre nudged his luggage, letting it roll down the entrance ramp's decline. "Three, two, and—"

The luggage collided with the edge of the paparazzi. One stumbled then grabbed the jacket of another. The chain reaction was immediate. Half fell to the floor. For an instant, the security personnel and Gemma looked confused.

"Strike!" Roger bellowed. Gemma whirled in their direction. Her eyes locked on Andre's, and even though her crew moved quickly, the tether didn't break until the sliding doors shut behind her.

"What the hell? Wasn't she the tennis star we saw yesterday?" Roger asked.

"Yeah, maybe. Let's go. Good deed of the day done. It's time for our full cavity search. Airport security and rectal examinations are becoming synonymous."

Andre eyed the headlines at the newsstand. Both English and French rags proclaimed the same message. *"Gemma is crushed after loss… Considering quitting tennis… Leaving country."*

Andre and Roger had just found their way to the departure gate when a voice announced, *"Can Monsieur Andre Reyes check in with an Air France agent? Monsieur Andre Reyes to any Air France booth."*

Andre spun around. "Did they just call me?"

"Yup. Probably screwed up something."

That's the last thing he needed. He just wanted to go home and enjoy his first vacation in years. An agent directed him to the Air France lounge, where he was then escorted to a semi-private table. A friendly face smiled up at him.

"Join me if you have time before your flight," Gemma said, her eyes soft.

"Love to," he said as he sat. The air seemed fresh, full of jasmine.

"Thank you for what you did," she said.

He shrugged. "If not me—"

"Then who?" she completed.

Andre peered into her eyes. He didn't see her typical posturing. She looked drawn, honest. She looked phenomenal. "Do you get that all the time?"

"Every waking moment," she said in a whisper. "I'm a target. Fair game. You see, fame inadvertently gives permission to have a camera shoved in my face wherever I go. I allow them to hang on my car, chase me down, and write anything they want about me. They know I will not retaliate. And if someone claims I did something wrong, true or not, I will always settle. Bastards like them can make a healthy living off me for as long as I matter."

She paused, her eyes glistening, and glanced over her shoulder. Andre gazed in the same direction. Eyeballs were trained on them. She produced a rehearsed smile. One designed for public settings.

"Furthermore," she whispered, "what I just told you will probably end up in *People* magazine. I can't trust anyone. So why am I telling you?" Her smile faltered. "Call it temporary insanity."

He was getting a sense for her world. Her small, suffocating world. "I've been meaning to ask you something," he said, leaning in for more privacy. "And if I don't, I'll kick myself. It's an important question."

She sipped water through a straw, never breaking eye contact.

"Gemma, are you stalking me?"

She coughed, nearly spilling the water.

"Everywhere I go, you're there." He crossed his arms and leaned back. "This is getting very uncomfortable."

"And I was so certain I'd covered my steps."

"I'm very perceptive. Nothing gets past me."

"I've noticed. Like, say, famous personalities?"

"Particularly those."

"Yet you found your way to your stalker's pathetic match."

"What made it pathetic? I thought it was phenomenal."

"That's because the American won."

"Are you sure? I was too busy watching two gladiators fighting it out. I wasn't following the score. The score seems to trivialize the result, don't you think?"

Her eyes widened. "Trivialize? In my world, the score is the only thing that matters."

He considered what drove professional athletes—the love or the outcome of the game. "You were amazing. Poetic in the way you played."

"Thank you, but I still lost."

"Technical matter. Do you always let facts get in your way?"

"And how did you end up there? You were so convincing when you told me you didn't know who I was."

He read suspicion in her eyes. "It's true. Sorry, didn't mean to bruise your hard-earned celebrity. I had no clue who you were."

"So it's a coincidence? Breakfast, the bar, the match, and the airport."

"Perhaps these things have nothing to do with you."

She gave a sly smile. "Are you saying I think the world is all about me?"

"Well…"

"How dare you? Are you calling me self-centered? Do you know who I am?"

He rose his hands in surrender. "Not exactly self-centered, Your Highness. All I'm suggesting is you shouldn't assume everyone's out to get you." He let it sink in for a few seconds. "Also, I thought we established you're the one stalking me."

"Sorry, I forgot."

"As for the game, my client invited me to the match."

"What type of work do you do?"

"I solve problems. The kind people think can't be solved."

"As in mysteries? What types of problems are unsolvable?"

"I suppose they are mysterious at first. I help with technical problems, obscure math, scientific issues, and other messy stuff. Once my clients give up, they call me for help."

"But you're so young. Are you one of those brainiacs?"

His smile froze. "I wouldn't go that far."

"How exciting. Do you like what you do?"

"Sure, I guess. But the constant travel gets old—nearly debilitating." The heaviness of his life weighed on him. Silence crept in. "At least on this trip I got to meet you."

Gemma's brow rose, and her lips parted slightly. A real, honest face emerged.

"So tell me, Gemma, do you like what you do?"

"*Boarding for Air France flight 77 to Los Angeles will commence in five minutes,*" the intercom announced.

"Crap, that's my flight." He paused, torn. He wanted to stay with her, but he had to go home, see his friends, and enjoy his first vacation in seven years. "Maybe we'll bump into each other again?"

"As your stalker, I'll be sure to find you," she said, then latched onto his eyes. "It was lovely talking to you. And again, thank you for coming to my rescue."

"Anytime."

He rose, ready to leave, when he decided to lean in close to say something. She stiffened. Electricity hummed off her body. He slowly regained his composure. "Not everyone wants to use you."

And when her eyes lit up, inches away from his face, he wondered if he could delay his flight home for just an hour. Or a week.

"There you are," Roger said. "What happened? Did they screw up something?"

"No, all's well," Andre said as he collected his bag and headed toward priority boarding. He could feel Roger's probing eyes against his back. There was no way he would tell Roger about Gemma. As good as M&T had been to him financially, they were no friend to the personal lives of their principal consultants.

"By the way," Roger leaned to whisper, "something's come up with Homeland Security. This is in advance of Project Sunrise."

Andre shuddered. Project Sunrise was the classified initiative led by the Pentagon. A project that would remove him from the grid for at least three months. These were the worst of the worst. In his career he had been part of a few such efforts, each one leaving him more depleted than the last.

"So we may need to go to D.C. next week," Roger said.

Andre came to a dead stop. "Wait—what? I've taken next week off."

"We'll know more on Tuesday. Enjoy Memorial Day. Just don't do anything to put that prized brain of yours at risk. Depending on what we hear, we may need to get flexible."

"Roger, I've made plans. And what's with 'we'? You never go to D.C. and furthermore, even if you did, you're not allowed to enter the facility—you're not classified." Andre spun in the opposite direction. Other passengers stared at them.

"Where are you going? We're boarding."

"I need to get something first. You go ahead." If he stayed, he was bound to say or do something he'd regret.

The Illy Cafe was a short walk away. He ordered a double espresso, then slumped down on a stool. He studied a couple who appeared to be on vacation. A novel concept. Seven years with the company and he had yet to get one week to himself. Every vacation had been interrupted by some important engagement. Initially he'd felt compelled to put his life on hold and prove himself. Then it was the greed. His commission payments were astronomic, and the correlation was direct—the more he pushed himself, the more he earned. But when a year ago, one of his closest friends died of cancer at the age of twenty-three, he knew he needed a drastic change in his life.

In a few months, once he received his retention bonus, he'd walk away from all of this.

He sipped the rest of his espresso, then grabbed his bags and headed to the terminal. Something tightened in his neck. Another headache. He eyed the spa store, wondering how quickly they could massage his neck. Then he caught a whiff of a jasmine-scented perfume.

Gemma.

He realized a silly grin had reshaped his face. Probably looked goofy, but he didn't care. He conjured the memory of her eyes, her lips, her voice. Immediately, raw energy added a bounce to his steps. He would find a way to get in touch with her again, to know the inner Gemma he saw behind those eyes. He had many contacts, particularly in England.

At the priority gate, he handed his boarding pass and passport. He was one of the last to board.

"*Bonjour*," the attendant said.

The machine yelped and the screen flashed *erreur.*

"Is everything okay?" he asked.

"One moment please," she said, typing feverishly on the computer. "Ah, you have a new boarding pass. Seat change."

"That's odd. I reserved the seat I wanted yesterday."

"I don't know, sir," she said as she handed him the new boarding pass.

The new pass said *First Class,* which didn't make sense. M&T's contract called for the client to pay for business class. Maybe Air France had upgraded him? Or had Roger upgraded their tickets to make up for the canceled vacation plans? If so, it was pitiful and transparent.

Andre stepped onto the plane and turned left, passing through business class. But Roger was still there. Odd.

"Where are you going?" Roger asked.

"I've been upgraded."

Roger's mouth slackened. Upon reflection, Andre was glad Roger wouldn't be next to him for the next eleven hours.

His boarding pass identified his seat as 2B. When he turned, he noticed the passenger occupying seat 2A and froze in place.

Gemma turned toward him. "Hope you don't mind the upgrade."

Words didn't register on his lips fast enough. "Wait, you upgraded me?" he asked.

"Guilty." She produced a shy smile. "If you're going to fly to Los Angeles, you might as well have a proper seat."

He transferred his bag from one hand to the other. "Are you sure you're ready to spend the next eleven hours with a stranger who may sell you out to *People* magazine?"

Her angelic eyes brightened. "I'm willing to take a chance on you."

PART II

SERVE

The presumption is that the person serving has an advantage over the receiver. Therefore it is only possible to win the match by breaking, or defeating, the opponent's serve. The service must be broken at least once, if the opponent has any hopes of forcing the match into a tiebreak.

~Tennis Basics

CHAPTER EIGHT

"All the events of your life are there because you have drawn them there. What you choose to do with them is up to you."

~Richard Bach

Gemma studied Andre as he put away his bag in the overhead compartment then tugged his jacket over his head. His shirt slid up, exposing his abs. Her eyes froze on his chiseled body. That alone was worth the price of admission.

"It's warm in here," he said as he adjusted his shirt. The scent of his cologne drifted.

"Yes. Yes it is."

He sank into his seat. "I'm starting to enjoy this stalker thing. Thank you, Gemma."

"My pleasure, but there is no free lunch, I'm afraid. I fully expect free advice from the master problem solver."

His mobile rang just as he was about to respond. He studied the display. "Sorry. I have to get this."

She waved him on.

"*Hola Gustavo, cómo estás?*" He spoke in Spanish for a couple of minutes with a perfect Castilian accent. She understood Spanish fairly well and eavesdropped shamelessly. Andre was apparently approving some construction work in his home.

"How do you know Spanish?" she asked once he hung up.

"My father's family is from Spain."

A Spaniard, like me. Another coincidence, she mused.

"So, back to where we left off at the lounge. Do you like what you do?"

"Mmm…" She hesitated.

"That's not a trick question," he added.

"No, but difficult to answer. My first memory is tennis. In fact, I can't say I have any independent recollections of events in my life that exclude the game. My life is completely intertwined with the matches, the tournaments, the training, the sport, the travel, the competition. It's like asking a bird if she likes to fly. Is there anything else? Do I like it? It's the only thing I know." She glanced at him, reading empathy in his eyes.

"Does this bird fly because she can or because she loves to?"

"Both," she said with no hesitation.

"I'm no expert, but I can see your talent spills through your pores. Your fans clearly see that."

"Sometimes I wonder. Is it really my talent my fans appreciate?"

"Gemma the athlete or Gemma the celebrity?"

"Precisely."

"That bothers you?"

"I couldn't care less about being a glassy-eyed celebrity. It's what I do on the court that should matter. Absolutely nothing else." *Calm down.* This was not the time or place to lose her wits.

"I don't see how you can separate the game you play from the business of tennis. The sport needs celebrities to sell expensive advertisements. They are inseparable. Success in one means success in the other."

"Unfortunately, I understand that," she said. Her short fuse flirted with her clenching fists, while at the same instant, the airplane accelerated and lifted off the tarmac.

"Then you must also see your stock value is directly proportional to the amount of time you're in the spotlight, for good or ill."

"What if I don't want that? What if I just want to focus on the game and nothing else?"

"If that's what you want, then your career choices would be consistent with that. Yet here we are."

"It's not that simple."

"It's always simple, it's just hard to do. I'm curious now. How did you get to where you are? You must have gotten your fame because of the way you play."

"Yes, I did. Well, when I first turned pro. But I've sputtered since. In general I do well, but my albatross remains. Until I win a Grand Slam, I will not be considered amongst the elite players. I may go down as a celebrity athlete, instead of the athlete who also happened to be a celebrity."

"Grand Slam?"

"There are four tournaments that propel a career, sustain it, or define it. The first is the Australian Open, then the French Open, followed by Wimbledon, and finally the U.S. Open. I choked at the Australian Open, and you just saw me drop a solid chance at the French. Wimbledon is next, in a few weeks." She studied the shrinking world from her window. "So, Mister Problem Solver, how would you solve my problem?"

"This is a no-brainer. I won't even charge you." He glanced both ways conspiratorially.

Gemma drew near with hesitation. She could smell his cologne. Her feeling of weakness when near him was palpable.

He whispered. "All you have to do is *win* a Grand Slam." He gave her a wink.

Her mouth dropped open.

"But you can't share this groundbreaking advice with anyone else," he whispered. "I make a killing selling my consulting services."

"That is brilliant. Absolutely brilliant. Right. Just win the bloody thing. And, forgive me for asking this, do people pay in hard currency when you provide this type of... what did you call it? Groundbreaking advice?"

He smirked. "Sometimes they even give me kick-ass seats to tennis matches."

Gemma burst out laughing at the absurdity of his silly—but accurate—advice. She studied his eyes. She saw softness, endearing him to her a bit more.

"Since you so quickly solved that little irritant," she said as she reached into her carry on bag, "maybe you can explain this Sudoku thing." She handed him Tish's booklet.

His eyes lit up. "Gladly." Like an excited young boy, he explained the game. She watched him, barely hearing a word he spoke. She studied his hands. Powerful. Dangerous.

She had needed this, someone to chat with. Tish was her friend, but with her there was no access to new ideas. Andre was new, smart, funny, and she felt good talking to him. Sure, she was attracted to him. But she wasn't a child who didn't know how to manage these types of situations. She was surrounded by good looking people all the time. But... none quite like Andre.

"Are you listening?" he asked.

"I'm sorry, were you talking to me?"

"Ohh... good one," he said, nodding in approval. "Gemma one, Andre zero."

"I didn't ask for a doctoral dissertation. Just solve a few pages so I can win a wager, and we're good to go."

"So you want me to cheat? Is this what you're used to? Give someone a first class upgrade and they'll do your homework?"

"After that crap advice you gave, the least you can do is help."

One eyebrow arched before he winked. He clicked open his pen and started. "The advice I gave was not crap," he said, rapidly filling cell after cell.

"Please, that was bollocks." She watched him with curiosity.

"Do you agree the problem will be solved if you win a Grand Slam?" He continued to complete cells rapidly, now on the third page. As if he was jotting in random numbers.

"Well, yes."

"So the solution is easy. Execution is the challenge." Another page done. "Do you believe you're good enough to beat anyone you face?"

"Yes," she said, amazed at how quickly he tore through the pages, limited only by how fast he could write.

"Good. Then the question is, what has stopped you? Was it your opponent, the environment, or something else? You have to think about that carefully."

He had completed ten pages, maybe more.

"The best place to start is with ourselves. Usually we are our own worst enemy," he added. "Have you considered—"

"Stop."

He froze. "What?"

"Are you writing gibberish?"

"No." He seemed hurt. "I'm completing the puzzles for you."

"But that's impossible. You're not even paying attention to what you're doing. How is that possible?" She was confused, on the verge of giggling with hysteria.

He flipped to the back of the book. "You can check the answers if you want."

"Are you fuc—" She bit her tongue, glanced around and tried again. "Seriously? I've never seen anything like that."

He hesitated. "It's my talent, my curse."

"Explain." She leaned in close, grinning ear-to-ear, amazed.

"Once I know the rules—that is, once I understand the way to solve something—the answers become obvious. They show up, and all I have to do is trace the answer in the proper cell."

She blinked.

"If you saw one plus one, would you hesitate in writing the answer?" he asked. "That's how it is. For me, a lot of things are one plus one."

Her mouth was partially open. "Have you always had this... gift?"

"For as long as I can remember. I'll quote a profound statement: My first memory is this ability. In fact, I can't say I have any independent recollections of events in my life that exclude this ability. My life is completely intertwined with it. It's the only thing I know."

She saw what she thought was sadness in his eyes. "Photographic memory also? You are amazing. A phenom. A—"

"Freak?" he said.

"Why would you say that?" She pulled her legs up beneath her.

"I've always been 'that' kid. The one who was different. *He's a genius* eventually turned to *he's a geek*, and then *he's weird*. I didn't feel different, and my friends didn't treat me differently, but the fact is I was different. And some people were just weirded out by it, while others wanted to study me. From the ages of four to eleven, I tried to hide it by disappearing, but my buddies wouldn't let me. The school knew, my parents knew, but I just wanted to be a kid—ride my bike, play basketball with my friends, try to impress the girls. You know, just be me—a kid."

"So what happened at eleven?" she asked.

"Pressure from my school, my parents, and everyone who wanted to get their hands on me. A university professor convinced them my ability needed to be harnessed. They agreed. So I attended USC in Southern California and earned my bachelor's degree by fourteen. Then they whisked me away to MIT for another four years."

She clenched her legs to her chest, stunned. "How was MIT? Were you socially accepted there?"

"Sure, somewhat. But I was an outlier. An oddity. I was a fourteen-year-old working on two Ph.D.'s alongside twenty-five-year-olds and older who felt they were the best of the best. I didn't have to try, while they killed themselves. I killed the curves wherever I went, so my presence became an annoyance. I was always surrounded by people, but I was never with them. Do you know what I mean?"

She nodded, almost in a trance. "Smiling and talking to the people, but never truly present."

"Exactly. You nailed it. Every day, all I wished for was to go back home. To see my friends who had been there for me since we were toddlers, to see the girl I loved. But I had to live out someone else's plan."

"Bloody hell, Andre."

"Hey, it all turned out for the best," he said with a strained smile. "Look at me now, I hang out with Gemma Lennon." He shrugged. "A normal life is all I wanted. Just a normal life."

The young boy had aged before her. Gemma took his hand. A beat, then her breath caught and the world transformed.

Her posture straightened as electricity swam through her hand. He must have felt something too, because his grip tightened, and in that moment, she wanted to put the world on pause. His hand in hers felt like what had been missing. It felt perfect.

CHAPTER NINE

*"Love's greatest gift is its ability
to make everything it touches sacred."*

~Barbara DeAngelis

Their hands did not separate. Gemma expected the current of warmth to disperse, but it didn't. She stared at their intertwined fingers and allowed her gaze to travel to his. Their eyes locked for a long moment.

He turned her hand and studied her palm. She held her breath as an electric current reverberated along her skin.

"Your hand has adapted into the perfect mate for a tennis racquet," he said as he traced the calluses on her fingers and palm. "I once heard that when you are committed, wholly and completely, you build scar tissue. Whatever you dedicate to that passion absorbs the weight of the damage."

A small sound escaped her mouth. She swallowed. "I imagine it's the price we pay."

"Sometimes the price may be too high."

"Excuse me, Dr. Reyes?" someone said from behind them.

Gemma pulled her hand away as they both turned to a woman who had appeared in the aisle next to them.

"Stella, right? Stella McCormack from TeraVision." They shook hands as he rose. The woman didn't let go of his hand.

"I'm sorry for interrupting," she said as she glanced at Gemma, then did a double take before turning back to Andre. "I just wanted to say hi."

As they spoke, Gemma pretended to read a magazine, but she caught every detail. Stella leaned on the seat, shifted her weight, touched his hand, placed her hand on his chest, giggled, and seemed amused by his wit. He answered her questions, explained, and motivated her. She seemed very motivated. A little too motivated for Gemma. Also, she was a little too old for him, if you asked Gemma. And now she was writing her phone number on the business card that had been conveniently tucked in her pocket. *Of course he'll call you next time he's in Seattle*, Gemma thought. After a few moments the woman stretched and kissed his cheek. *Must be nice.*

"Sorry about that," he said as he sat.

"No worries, Dr. Reyes," Gemma said, still flipping through the pages of the magazine. "She's pretty."

Andre glanced at Gemma. "You want me to introduce you to her?"

"Don't be daft. She's definitely interested in you."

"Hmm."

"Not interested?"

"Not remotely interested."

She laughed a little too easily. "Why's that? Do you already have someone special?" As soon as she asked, she mentally kicked herself for being so transparent.

"I have a few special people in my life. But I think you're asking if I have someone special-special."

"I feel like I'm in grade school again. Do you like her, or like her-like her. Yes, are you in a relationship with someone?"

"No."

"Too busy?"

Andre nodded. "With my schedule, it's a non-starter."

"Rather sad our life, no?"

"You too? I considered picking up a tabloid to learn about your love life, but thought better of it."

"Argh! Those parasitic magazines. Everyday there's new rubbish about me."

"Did you see today's headlines? Seems like you don't need to worry about winning a Grand Slam after all. You're quitting tennis."

"I'm what?"

"Also, you're a complete mess and are escaping the country because of your depression."

"Unreal." She wanted to break something.

"So… is there someone in your life that helps you maintain sanity?"

"I prefer insanity. Makes for much better headlines."

The plane jolted violently for a few seconds. A patch of turbulence. Gemma squeezed her temples and fanned her face, suddenly feeling warm. "Shit! I forgot to take my airsickness medication." She fussed through her bag and found two pills. "I'm supposed to take them one hour before the flight. I'll be a basket case now." What if she puked in front of him? *Dear Lord.*

"Here," he said, "give me your wrist."

She studied him, then at his inviting hand. "What are you going to do?"

"Trust me."

Trust? That was difficult for her to hand out. She scanned from his hand to his eyes, calm and in control. She hesitantly offered her hand.

"Close your eyes and relax," he said. With both hands, he applied light pressure at different points on her hand and wrist. "Your eyes," he said. "Close them."

She did.

"Take a deep breath in, then release slowly," he said, as he expertly touched and squeezed. "There are a couple of pressure points—nerves—that once excited, will bring equilibrium back and eliminate nausea."

She pictured his face, listened to his voice, and focused on his touch, which drove her weak with pleasure. His touch traveled from her palm to each finger as he gently, but firmly, massaged her hand. A stirring sensation sparked in her navel. Not nausea. Raw pleasure. After a few minutes, the lightheadedness disappeared and the nausea vanished, replaced with glee.

"I feel much better now," she said once she opened her eyes.

"Good." He did not release her hand. "By the way, what I just fed you was a bunch of crap. I had no idea what I was doing. I just wanted to touch you some more."

She broke into a belly laugh. Gemma knew then she was in trouble.

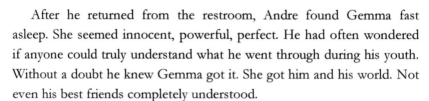

After he returned from the restroom, Andre found Gemma fast asleep. She seemed innocent, powerful, perfect. He had often wondered if anyone could truly understand what he went through during his youth. Without a doubt he knew Gemma got it. She got him and his world. Not even his best friends completely understood.

He glanced toward the partition separating first and business class. A few times during the flight, he had felt the unsettling feeling of being watched. He thought it may have been Stella, but she had been asleep most of the flight. He wondered if it had been Roger, snooping. He hoped not because if he had seen Andre with Gemma, life would get more complicated at work.

Whatever it was, most of the passengers were out now. He opened his blanket and gently placed it across Gemma's body, then lowered her seat to flat. She stirred, but did not wake. He reclined his chair also and turned toward her. He was tempted to make a noise, so she'd wake up and they could talk some more. Instead he thought of this woman, trapped in a world she had not created. He understood that situation all too well.

She shifted, now facing him. Strands of hair covered her face. Gently, he brushed her hair back. His fingers grazed her forehead, causing the tight skin to loosen and ease. Her eyes fluttered momentarily. Suddenly, her hand emerged from beneath the blanket and took his hand in hers, tight against her chest. He felt her heartbeat and gentle breathing. He studied her face, wanting to remember every detail, knowing for once he could use his photographic memory for something he actually wanted to commit to memory.

With her face etched in his mind, he drifted.

"*Mademoiselle. Monsieur.* Please put on your seat belts," someone said. "Heavy turbulence." It was the flight attendant.

Gemma rose slightly, trying to remember where she was. Her neck was tight, and a heavy headache weighed her down. Medication always disoriented her. She noticed her hand. That wasn't her stuffed dog... that was his hand.

Andre woke up. "What's going on?" he asked, but did not release her hand.

"Turbulence," she whispered.

He nodded then squeezed her hand. "We'll be fine."

Their chairs rose while the plane jolted. Gemma rubbed her temples and turned her head this way and that, hoping to release the tightness in her neck.

"Are you okay?" he asked.

"Ugh. I think so. My neck is frozen stiff and I have a headache."

"Face me and scoot closer."

She did without hesitation.

He laid his hands on her temples and applied a gentle pressure. First light, then stronger. Her eyes did not break from his. His long fingers slid down her jaw, to her neck. She blinked and leaned a bit closer to him as his hands found the back of her neck, then the base of her skull. She was no longer sure if her head hurt, or if her neck was tight. What she wanted was to grab his face and press her lips to his.

"Gemma?"

"Yes?" she muttered.

"You're drooling."

"So are you, love."

He laughed then pulled her into his chest, embracing her completely.

"This is a good day," she whispered just as the plane shook again.

When breakfast was served, Andre glanced at his watch. They had less than two hours before landing. He thought carefully about what he wanted to say next. He wanted to see her again, but his life was too complicated—and so was hers—and, in any event, that's not what he wanted. Truth be told, he wasn't sure what he wanted. But he loved talking to her. Well, maybe love was too strong a word. Really liked? Really-really liked? Whatever it was, he knew he could talk to her freely, because like him, she had also given up youth. Like him, she was trying to make sense of the crazy world they now lived in. They were more alike than different.

"Are you staying in L.A., or is this a layover for you?" he asked.

"Staying for a few days, then I'm heading back to London," she said, forking her fruit salad.

"Are you here for a match or an appearance?"

"No, nothing like that. I just needed to get away for a couple of days. Needed to collect myself before my upcoming matches."

"So the tabloids were right. You are having a nervous breakdown."

She poked his hand with her fork. "Careful. I can get nasty."

He rubbed his hand. "Clearly. So, you're staying at a hotel, a resort—"

"My home in Malibu."

"You have a home in Malibu?"

"Yes, Malibu and London. When I'm not traveling, that is. I stay in L.A. maybe six weeks out of the year. About the same in London. The rest of the time I'm in hotels or on planes."

"Then your travel life is as bad as mine. That must take some of the fun out of the game. I know it kills me," he said.

"The travel is dreadful. Absolutely hate it. Some months, like this one, are criminal. French Open, then to another match in the U.K. next week, then possibly the Netherlands, followed by the big one, Wimbledon. Back to back."

"How does your body hold up with this type of grind?" he asked. When his words registered, he turned beet red. "Wait. What I meant..."

"Very well, thank you very much." She punched his shoulder.

It was now or never. "Look, since you're in L.A. for a couple of days, maybe we can catch up again. I don't know, maybe get coffee or something, if you have time."

She stopped eating. "Your bastardized, savage English confuses me. What are you asking?"

"I was just saying that—you know—we should hang out while you're in L.A."

"So you're asking me to hang out? On a proper date? With you?"

"If you want. If you have time." Sweat broke out on his forehead. He picked up his coffee and drank it all.

"I'll think about it. After all, the way you put it sounded so enticing, I fear my stay in L.A. would be dreadfully dull if I don't take you up on that offer."

"Nice. Laugh at the geek. What's the score? Gemma two, Andre one?"

"Pitiful attempt, really. By the way, you haven't scored any points yet."

He eyed her. She smirked.

"I'll try harder."

"I'm sure you'll try."

"Well, if you want to break away from your solitary confinement, give me a call." He wrote his cell phone number on the Air France napkin and handed it to her. "I'm no Leonardo DiCaprio, but I have watched most of his movies."

She almost snorted again. "That nearly sounded like a normal invitation." She took the napkin. "I'm curious. That last pitiful invitation notwithstanding, for someone who is a certified geek, you are a balanced chap. I would have thought someone with your background would have been... what's the word? Less social?"

"Wow. Hold on, I'm updating the scoreboard. If you have any more insults prepared, this may be the time to deliver them."

"I meant that in a positive way."

"Obviously. Excuse me while I call my therapist. Note to self, do not accept her Facebook invite."

"There's nothing wrong with being a geek. It's just that you're an atypical geek."

"There's another one. Gemma fifteen, Andre zero. Will I score any points?"

"Doubt it." She sank deep into his eyes. "By the way, it's love."

"Sorry?"

"In tennis we don't have zero. We have love," she said as she lay her hand on his. "Gemma fifteen, Andre love."

At the plane's final descent, Andre stole glances, anticipating the end. The flight had been the best eleven hours he had ever spent. But she would be gone soon and like it or not, he'd have to accept the impending emptiness that would follow her departure.

When the plane landed and reached the gate, Gemma turned to Andre. "I'll be escorted off first. Part of the celebrity thing. So let me say bye for now," she said.

When they rose, she kissed his cheek and then hugged him. "I'm sure we'll talk soon." Her soft lips were like a whisper on his skin. Her body warm and strong. He didn't want to let go.

She pulled away, her eyes trained on his. "Bye." She gave him a warm smile, slid on her sunglasses, and followed the flight attendant.

In that moment he had a distinct feeling he understood how sunshine impacted plants. He felt rejuvenated and unstable all at the same time. But he was certain this instability was the source of life. The uncertainty made life worth living.

He wanted the warm pressure of her hand on his again, the hand he held during the flight. He pictured her holding tight, not letting go even during turbulence.

CHAPTER TEN

*"We're born alone, we live alone, we die alone. Only through
our love and friendship can we create the illusion for the
moment that we're not alone."*

~Orson Welles

The Customs agent processed Gemma's entry quickly. He also took a picture with her and asked for, and received, her autograph. When she arrived at the gate, an explosion of yells and flashbulbs disoriented her. Gemma froze, scanning for her security. Had they not been told? The crowd converged on her, and she took a tentative step back.

"Out of the way," someone commanded. The sea of bodies parted as her security staff closed around her, building a protective human shield. They marched her through fans, reporters, and paparazzi.

She was inundated by the voices, the inane questions…

—*Is it true? Are you quitting tennis?*

… Odd requests…

—*Can you sign my car?*

… Pleas for surprising details.

—*Is it true you and Johnny Flauto have rekindled your romance?*

On that one she wanted to deliver a few choice words, but she kept her composure and maintained a steady gait until she slid into her waiting car. The locks engaged.

"Xavi, you didn't have to pick me up."

"I wanted to pick you up," he said with a warm smile. "To welcome you home."

"It's lovely to be back."

"The bastards got word about your flight hours ago." His eyes hardened. Always her protector and guru.

With the help of her security team and airport police, the car rolled away.

"How's Mari?" she asked.

"Now that you're home, she is happy. She is preparing *Crema Catalana* for you."

The mere mention of the Catalonian dessert made her salivate. "I can't wait."

"We will eat, then over coffee and dessert, we will talk."

Finding Xavi and Mari three years earlier had been serendipitous. She had been searching for information on her birth parents when she'd met them. Like her birth father, they were also from Spain. They had been friends with her birth mother before the tragedy that left newborn Gemma an orphan. In no time, they became part of her extended family, and when Xavi and Mari's son started college in Los Angeles, Gemma purchased a home in Malibu and transplanted them there. She trusted them with everything—home and soul. They offered unconditional love and respect. When she came to Malibu, she was home.

"Yes, there is plenty to talk about," she said. But the urgency for visiting seemed to have vanished. After the French Open loss, she'd felt dizzy again and her insides churned, just like in Australia. She had wanted to curtail the anxiety before it spun out of control. But somehow, it was all but gone. Was that because of Andre? In so many ways, his story was her story. Had she found her kindred spirit?

She removed the napkin with Andre's number from her purse and took a whiff, hoping the scent of his cologne was still detectable. She wanted—needed—to see him again.

Andre didn't wait for Roger. He rushed off the plane and practically ran to the Customs gate, beating the large crowd. He walked past the awaiting company car, toward the taxi station. He was in a great mood and didn't want Roger to irritate him.

"Where to?" the taxi attendant asked.

"Santa Monica."

He rolled down the window in the cab. The dry afternoon heat rushed in, practically choking him. And although the air-conditioner blew cool air, he needed real air. Each city had its distinctive smell, but all airports and the surrounding areas smelled the same—like fuel. He longed for the scent of the ocean.

He texted Roger. *"Sorry, had to run. Talk to you later."* He hoped that would keep the man at bay.

Andre entered his condo with a singular goal in mind—get fresh ocean air. Fast. After a quick shower, he took Pacific Coast Highway. Convertible top down, he inhaled the warm rush of the air and exhaled slowly. The scent of the sea always took him back to his youth in Spain. His safe haven.

He parked his car at Zuma Beach, the north end of Malibu. It was early Sunday afternoon and beach-dwellers littered the coast, sunbathing and swimming. Farther north, a film crew marked off an area. A typical day at the beach.

He sat on the sand, absorbing everything around him. A large wave crashed, and the white wash came up to his feet, sinking his toes. Seagulls drifted overhead, their cries hoarse. After a few waves, his feet were completely submerged in the wet sand. One wave at a time, he was sinking deeper and deeper. In trouble—on many levels.

He wanted to spend more time with Gemma, but time with her meant time away from work, jeopardizing his contract, his bonus, his sanity. None of which he was willing to risk. Not after all this time. But she was different than all others. She understood him and his chaotic life.

He studied his cell phone. Five missed calls. One text message. All from Roger. Andre willed the phone to ring, willed her to call him. As if on cue, the phone rang. Not Roger. Not Gemma. But a call he would gladly take.

"Hello, sir," he said.

"After all these years, will you stop with the 'sir' business? Just Jeffrey," the man said.

"Some habits are hard to break," Andre said. Since the passing of Andre's uncle, this man had stepped in to fill the gap in Andre's life.

Jeffery was more than just a close family friend—he deserved all the respect Andre could give.

"I understand you were in Paris. Why didn't you fly up to London to visit?"

"I apologize. Something happened that I couldn't pass up."

"Let me guess, another critical project that could not wait?"

"No, a personal break. I actually had fun."

"Well, call the Pope and have the bells rung at the Sistine Chapels. This is fantastic news," Jeffrey said. "Speaking of chapels, why haven't you confirmed your attendance for my daughter's engagement?"

"I'm sorry, I won't be able to make it to Emily's engagement. I'll be on a classified project during the same time."

"Another classified project. Can't you schedule a few days off? We are practically family. It would mean a lot to have you with us."

"As much as I want to—"

"If you wanted to, you would. You are driven by the wrong motivational forces. You need to pace yourself. Take the foot off the accelerator."

"The finish line is near."

"That's rubbish and you know it. The finish line is not real. Enjoy life. You're young. Your uncle would have told you the same. I realize I'm not your uncle—no one is—but someone has to tell you."

"Six more months and the worst will be over."

"And then what happens? Does M&T actually let you walk away? Even if they do, how much of your life will you have forsaken in the process?"

"I need to see it through. I want my bonus."

"Forget the bonus. It's just money."

"I've worked too hard to leave that on the table."

"And if you burn out before that? I hear things, Andre. And I worry about you."

"I'll be fine."

"I hope you're right."

A beat. "I do apologize."

"Don't apologize, use your brains to find a way to join us."

How much more would he have to forfeit from life? How much had he lost already?

Thirty minutes later, he took the winding canyons through the Malibu hills to Agoura to his parents' home. He didn't visit them often, but felt the need today because his uncle was on his mind. He helped himself in. Good to see his key still worked. The house was silent, which meant they were in the yard.

He found his father on his knees, tending to his tomatoes.

"*Hola, flaco,*" he said even though his father's midsection hadn't been *flaco* in more than a decade. But that was his nickname. The one his uncle had always used.

Gabriel straightened. "Your mom's not home. Yoga or Pilates or something like that." He rose slowly and turned to face Andre.

Typical. The dry business executive through and through. *Hi Dad, I missed you too.* He brushed it off. "Will she be long?"

"Don't know," he said as he tugged at his soiled gloves. "When did you arrive?"

"A couple of hours ago."

"Came for Memorial Day?"

"Came to spend time with Linda. To be here for her."

Gabriel was about to say something, then the significance of the weekend registered. His eyes dropped. "I'd forgotten. Tomorrow would've been their anniversary."

"That's right. Have you called your niece or sister-in-law lately?" Andre asked his dad.

Gabriel opened the outdoor fridge and got two bottles of beer, offering one to Andre. "Your mom has, I think."

"I didn't ask about Mom. I asked about you."

Gabriel stared into Andre's eyes. "I'm not going to get into this with you again."

"This has nothing to do with me, Dad. It's about you and your late brother. It's about—"

"It was always about you, Andre. You can't be so naive to not see the issues my brother and I had were always about you."

"Your brother didn't have any issues. You were the one with a chip."

Gabriel guzzled half the bottle. "That's right. He had no issues. He just felt it was okay to parent you and go against what we wanted for you."

"He wanted me to choose."

"You were too young to make good choices. A gift, Andre. You were born with a gift and he was trying to talk you out of using it."

"He wanted me to be happy." A foreign concept for his dad. Happiness meant wealth. Andre had that, and what brought him joy was not his bank statement.

"That's right—happiness. That's what he called it. 'He's a kid, he needs to experience youth and be happy.' What he was trying to create was division between us."

No, they had done that all on their own, he thought, but didn't say.

"I didn't come to argue about the past—"

"That's exactly what you're doing," Gabriel said, then drained his bottle. He grabbed another one. Andre had yet to take a sip of his.

"It's been five years since he passed. Almost six. You need to remember you still have one niece left and a sister-in-law. You need to get over yourself."

The sliding door opened. They both turned. Andre's mom. As fast as his dad seemed to be aging, she was somehow turning back the clock. She looked great.

"Andre, why didn't you tell me you were coming? I would have prepared something." Which actually meant she would have ordered delivery or made reservations somewhere.

He rose and kissed her cheek. "Didn't want to create work," he said.

"What's wrong with your dad?"

He turned to face him. He wore a scowl, accented by a flushed forehead and cheeks.

"I pissed him off. Again."

"You didn't piss me off," Gabriel mumbled.

"Well then I will definitely piss you off when I remind you Linda is your niece. You are her uncle. Consider acting like one."

CHAPTER ELEVEN

"Life is too short for bad coffee."

~Author Unknown

Andre woke at 5:30 a.m. ready for some quality time with his friends. He hadn't seen them in nearly two months and once Project Sunrise started, he wouldn't be able to speak to them, much less see them, for months. They were his clan, his circle. The same kids he'd known since they were in diapers. The same ones who kept him sane and true no matter how much he wanted to withdraw from the world that wanted to poke and prod him.

They were to meet at the beach at 7:00 a.m. and other than the headache that greeted him, nothing would derail him.

His cell rang. It was his cousin. He grabbed the earpiece and answered the call.

"Linda, how are you, *chica?*"

"Good morning, sunshine. Welcome home," she said.

"Good to be back. Are we still on?"

"Yeah, wanted to make sure you didn't flake on us."

"When have I flaked?"

"Let's see, how about every planned vacation since you started with M&T."

"Yeah, well, I'm coming. What should I bring?"

"Just your sunny disposition. By the way, Jeffrey called me."

"He called me too. Let me guess, he's worried?"

"Yup."

"I hope you set him straight."

"Yes. I told him we're all worried about you."

"Great. You know, he's a fairly important guy and has his hands full with matters more significant than my well-being."

"Somehow I think he'd argue that point."

"I'm fine, just a bit worn out. But that's what little breaks are for—refueling."

"Speaking of fuel, get some carbs. I think Chris plans on putting us through the grinder on the rock he wants us to climb."

"Does he ever relax?"

"In one word, no. And for the record, you should go to Emily's engagement."

"You too?"

"Go get ready. I'll see you soon."

"*Ciao.*" He ended the call.

If he could find a way to make it to the engagement, he would. He wished everyone would just accept his situation.

The phone rang in his ear again. He pressed the button on his earpiece. "You forgot something?"

"Sorry?"

"Linda?" he asked, unsure.

"No, it's Gemma."

"Gemma." A smile rose. "I'm sorry, I thought you were someone else."

"I can see that—a *Linda* no less. That means *pretty* in Spanish, doesn't it? Is she another one of your many stalkers?"

"Sadly, no. Linda Reyes is my cousin."

"Oh, okay. In that case she may call you this early."

"Thank you, dear. Speaking of which, it's barely past 5:30 in the morning. Is it customary for you to call at this hour?"

"I couldn't sleep. You should thank me. I almost called you at 3:00 a.m."

He moved to the living room sofa, sitting with elbows on knees, hands to his face. A man in prayer. "I'm glad you called."

"You didn't have a choice, love," she said, her voice warm. "I'd like some coffee. What do you say?"

"Yes, absolutely. When, where?"

"Meet me downstairs, outside your building."

"What do you mean? You're here now?"

"Yes. Don't take long." She hung up.

How the hell had she found his home? In the bathroom, he checked his hair. His bed head was nearly presentable.

When the elevator opened, the doorman stepped out to get the lobby door. "Morning run?" the doorman asked.

"Not today."

"Then the black Porsche must be here for you."

Andre stepped outside. A heavily tinted Porsche idled in front of his building. The passenger window rolled down.

"Hop in," Gemma said.

He leaned against the door and studied her. She wore a black FC Barcelona cap, her ponytail snaking through the opening. Sunglasses hung from her white tank-top. She wore short denim jeans, exposing her tanned kill-me-now legs. The scent of jasmine was mixed with something else—body lotion. For a moment he visualized Gemma applying lotion on those legs. That image would last a couple of decades.

"What are you waiting for? Get in before someone sees us." She slid on her sunglasses.

"It's not even six in the morning. Who's going to see us? Let's walk. There's a nice cafe a couple of blocks from here."

She peered over her sunglasses. "Walk? Are you mad? The bloody paparazzi will be on us in no time." Her fingers tightened around the steering wheel.

Andre scanned the street, looking for patterns, anomalies. "I don't see anyone. You're safe. Come on, you can leave your car here. The doorman will keep an eye on it."

She hesitated then murmured something as the passenger window rolled up. She stepped out, still murmuring.

"Come again?" he said

"You better be right," she said, and marched southbound.

"Where are you going?" he asked.

She paused. "The coffee shop."

"We're headed that way," he said, pointing north.

"I did some research before I came. There's a coffee shop in that direction."

He strode up to her. "Relax."

Her jaw pulsated.

He held her shoulders and squeezed. "You don't have to be in control of every detail. I've got your back." After a few moments, her tense muscles relaxed.

"Fine. Let's go please, before someone sees us."

"Two things—you haven't said hello yet."

She frowned then gave him a hug. She was warm and smelled like an orchard. Her body was hard, electric. Like in the plane, he didn't want to let go. "Good morning," she whispered, then stepped back. "And the second thing?"

"I never gave you my home address."

She grinned. "All information is available if one wants it."

"You *are* stalking me. This is awesome."

"Don't get too happy. My cook found your address," she said, then spun and walked toward the cafe.

What kind of cook did she have? He noticed a tattoo of a black bird on her left shoulder blade. He caught up to her. She wore a poorly disguised smile on her face. "Don't get too close in public," she said.

"Right. Am I allowed to look at you? Should I refer to you in third person?"

She glanced at him. "You're asking for it."

"I am. And I'm ready when you are."

Minutes later they were at the cafe. Gemma found a secluded corner table on the patio while Andre placed their order. He wore board shorts and a t-shirt, which accentuated his physique perfectly. Like a boxer, he had dense muscles and a wiry frame, barely any sign of fat.

He approached their table with coffee and pastry.

"Were you headed to the beach?" she asked.

"Yes, I'm meeting my friends in about an hour."

"That sounds lovely."

"It is. Haven't seen them in weeks."

She removed her sunglasses. "You look happy."

"Yeah, I guess I am."

She had woken up lonely and sad this morning. And in some ways, she had hoped he felt the same. They were the same after all. But he wasn't sad at all.

"In fact," he said, as he placed his hand on hers and squeezed, "with the exception of the first time we met, every time I see you, I feel that way. I'm glad you called."

An uncontrollable smile crept over her lips. "I'm glad I called as well."

His eyes suddenly widened with excitement. "Do you want to join us at the beach?"

"Oh no, I couldn't."

"Why not? They're not weird. They're cool and down to earth. We're going to Point Dume in Malibu. You should come. You'd have a blast."

"It's not that easy." How could she explain it to him? "I couldn't." And who knew what his friends would do when they saw her? Maybe snap a picture or two? Sell the story to the newspapers? She was just beginning to trust him. She couldn't jump in blind—she didn't need another mess on her hands.

"What's the worst that can happen? Someone takes pictures of you and posts them?"

"It's not just the pictures. It's the stories they write, the assumptions they make, the incriminations. Not interested in any of that."

"Is it odd for celebrities to hang out with friends?"

Friends.

She had to explain—at least try. "Ever since Australia, I go out of my way to avoid the paparazzi. Lately the pictures they have of me are boring: I'm leaving a hotel, I'm entering a hotel, I'm attending a match, I'm leaving a match."

"What if they took a picture of you at the beach, or at a coffee shop?"

"Who is Gemma dating? What is Gemma eating? Has she gained weight? She has lost too much weight. She's more interested in partying. She needs to focus on winning a Grand Slam. She's all hype. She's a nothing." Gemma nearly bent the spoon she was holding. She collected herself then whispered. "It's none of their fuckin' business." Her heartbeat thrummed in her ears.

"But aren't you letting them win?"

She frowned, confused.

"You can't go to the movies, or to a party, or to the beach. You can't be you. You've allowed them to dictate your life."

Her eyes narrowed, wanting to lecture him on how ugly, hurtful, and debilitating some of the things they wrote could be. But she didn't. "That's the price I must be willing to pay to do what I do."

"I see." Silence hung between them. Something shifted on his face. "What's wrong?" she asked.

"Nothing. Give me a sec."

She watched him walk back into the coffee shop and say something to the kid behind the counter. The same kid she had noticed taking a picture of them on his cell phone moments earlier. Had Andre also seen that? She had elected to pretend he wasn't there and not do anything that would be material for the rags.

She wished she could hear what he was saying. The kid's tanned face lost color, and his mouth hung loose. Less than ten seconds later, Andre left the stunned-looking kid. Andre, on the other hand, looked very calm when he came back out.

"What happened?" Gemma asked.

"Just wanted to know what espresso beans they use. I'm a bit of a coffee snob."

Interesting. Was he trying to shield her from the situation? "I saw what he was doing," she said, and focused on his eyes. "Is that why you went in?"

"Maybe."

She grinned. "What did you tell him?"

He shrugged. "Just that I have a lot of friends at the FBI and CIA. So if I saw pictures from this morning anywhere, I'd make sure my friends looked into his background." He drank the rest of his coffee.

"Can you really do that?"

"I guess he'll find out if he posts anything."

"So whatever we do here, we'd be safe."

"Theoretically."

"Then I can do this…" she stretched her leg and dropped it right next to his thigh.

He glanced at her shoe then peered up, a smirk on his face. "I suppose you could."

"When you're born with long legs like mine, you need to stretch them regularly." She rolled her toe, flexing the muscles, rubbing against his thigh.

His eyes did not leave her leg. "By all means, stretch on." Andre cleared his throat then focused his attention on the pastry plate. He spun it, like a sculptor studying a slab of clay.

"Is this pastry appreciation day or are you planning on eating it?" she asked.

"No need to rush this," he said. "The trick is to spread the Nutella on the inside of the croissant." She studied him as he took the knife and first cut the croissant lengthwise, then with an artist's touch distributed the hazelnut spread inside the pastry. "Some people put a dab on the outside. Amateurs. On the inside, you get balance and proportion." He took a bite with his eyes closed. "Heavenly."

A smile cracked her face. "That does look good."

"No way, you didn't want any. I asked. Didn't I ask you? And you said 'no, thank you,' in your polite accent."

"I have the right to change my mind… I am a woman."

He placed his hand on her shin, sliding up toward her knee. His fingers curled around her calf and squeezed. "A badass one at that."

She would have smiled, or said something, but she was focused on moderating her breathing. His hands were like fire on her skin. The muscles spasmed, her toes curled, and her heartbeat danced. But that is exactly what she had wanted. His touch on her skin. She dropped her other foot on his other side.

"My other leg is getting jealous."

He grinned.

This day had the potential to turn great.

Gemma didn't notice the van until she saw Andre's eyes darting around. The same van passed by a few minutes later, driving a tad slower. She took her feet down, just in case. Soon after, one man hovered near the street corner. Another man waited at another corner. Both wore sunglasses and appeared to be eyeing the cafe.

She hoped they weren't paparazzi, but their behavior was suspicious. On the streets of Santa Monica only the usual suspects were out so early—runners, power walkers, bike riders, the homeless, the street cleaners, and of course the runaways with their dogs. Not men in wrinkled clothing standing around.

She studied Andre, whose eyes scanned and searched, calculating, trying to find an answer to this problem of hers that had no solution. They would have to leave soon. She would have to go into hiding because anywhere she went, the leeches would follow. Maybe she could invite him to her place?

No, too soon. She had to be smart and not let her emotions drive her actions.

"I have to get back home in a bit to grab my gear. I promised my friends I wouldn't flake. But maybe we can see each other later?" he asked. "We can put on disguises and eat a meal. There's a Halloween store down the road. Hey, I have an even better idea: why don't you join me and my friends at the beach?"

"You are one persistent nag. Let me see. My handlers have been trying to call me. They didn't know I was coming to L.A. So I may have surprises waiting for me."

"Give me your number. I'd be happy to surprise you also."

She considered his question. "It's best I call you instead. I don't like surprises."

They headed back to his condo, a silent stroll through the streets of Santa Monica. All morning, their words had flowed with ease. No hesitation, no pretense, just two people enjoying each other's company. But what Gemma really loved was that each moment she spent with him, she slid further away from her other world.

She thought about it for an instant, scanned around, then reached out and grabbed his hand. They glanced at each other then allowed their arms to swing.

"Are we going to skip?" he asked.

"You won't look graceful. You'll cramp my style."

"I thought Brits were polite."

"I *was* being polite."

If someone saw them now, they could have been mistaken for high school kids. And in that moment she was a kid, with no pressures or burdens from the tennis world.

He tugged her in closer, then released her hand and wrapped his arm around her waist. His hand resting on her hip, his thigh rubbing against hers. Tremors burst along her skin.

When they reached his building, she turned to him, her body tight against his. She studied his eyes then fought the urge to study his lips. "We'll talk later," she said then placed a soft kiss on his cheek, barely missing his mouth. She let the kiss linger, long enough to feel his chest tighten.

Too soon, be smart, she thought then stepped back, avoiding eye contact. She turned and quickly slid into her car, and sped away. The pressure in her lungs made breathing nearly impossible.

CHAPTER TWELVE

"Freedom is nothing else but a chance to be better."

~Albert Camus

From inside his car, Andre watched the coastline and studied the fifty-foot cliff named Point Dume, wondering if it had really meant to be spelled "Doom." The climb would prove formidable, having seen others scale her before. Most ascended the north face, overlooking the sand, but the more daring took on the west face, overlooking the ocean, high above the jagged boulders littering the base. He looked forward to the challenge. When he scaled, the world and the conversations in his head came to a hush. Instead he focused on negotiating a peaceful climb with nature—not debating the future, exhaustion, or Gemma.

She was causing a commotion in his head. That was the only way he could describe it, because he wanted to be with her.

All.

The.

Time.

He had never felt this before. If he didn't hear from her soon, he'd have to track her down. She was unhealthy for him. But somehow also breathed life in him.

Just as he stepped out of his car, his phone rang—Gemma? No... Roger. He pressed *Ignore*. Why was the concept of a day off so difficult to grasp?

His friends were already making camp. Chris had prepared the north face with hooks and two rope lines, ready for parallel climbs—maybe even a couple of face-offs. Chris's fiancée, Sandy, the architect, was assembling their poor-man's cabana because she was an architect, after all. Dan fiddled with the boom box while his wife, Dina, was applying suntan lotion to their two-year-old daughter, Haley—Andre's goddaughter. He scanned around and found his cousin, Linda. He admired her. How she found the power to fight even when life dealt her one misfortune after another, he'd never understand. Today was for her. On Memorial Day, they remembered a fallen friend—Linda's fiancé. Today would have been their one-year wedding anniversary. But the wedding never happened. His flame had been extinguished by the hands of an invisible assassin: cancer.

"How are you slackers doing this fine mornin'?" Andre asked.

"*Andre!*" Linda yelled. She sprinted toward him. The others released a primal grunt and followed her.

"Wait, wait!" Andre said, his hands up, hoping to thwart the attack. "Be gentle, I've—" The gang tackled him to the ground. In the pile-up, they punched him, poked him, and even kissed him. "Okay, enough!" he said, chortling through the persistent tickling. He sat up. "Really, guys?"

"It's your fault," Chris said, and offered his hand to Andre. "You're always with your uppity friends. How else are we supposed to keep you grounded?"

"Yes, I feel grounded all right. My ass has a lot of ground in it."

"Too much information," Sandy said.

"Was that my outside voice?" Andre asked.

Minutes after she had left Andre's, Gemma had changed her mind. She would join him and his friends. She pulled into the parking lot and saw them—they were the only ones there. She stared in wonder as Andre's friends helped him to his feet, then hugged and kissed him. *How beautiful.* She wondered if he realized how lucky he was to have so many friends. She had Tish, full stop.

What are you doing here? You don't know them. You don't even know him. But she wanted to know him better. And on some level, she felt she did know him and understood him.

One of the women there wrapped her arm around his waist then leaned her head on his shoulder. *Who is she?* Gemma took a deep breath, drank her water bottle empty, then raised her chin. "Right. Let's do this."

She stepped out of her car and with a jolt of adrenaline inadvertently slammed the door. One of the women, with medium-length, dirty-blonde hair, turned. Gemma's chest tightened. *Just keep walking… left, right. Do. Not. Trip!*

The rest of the group turned.

Andre swiveled slowly, then paused. She focused on him, his eyes. "Gemma," she saw him mouth. His smile broadened as he let go of the woman he was holding and plowed through the sand toward her.

His body pressed into hers when they hugged. "Thank you for coming," he whispered. The wind rustled through his hair. "Glad you changed your mind."

She beamed. "Me too." Her voice cracked.

"You're safe here. Just be you," he said then paused. "The one I met on the plane—not the one at breakfast in Paris." He winked then peered at his friends. "Family, I want you to meet my friend, Gemma. Please behave yourselves."

Gemma shook hands with the men, received a kiss on the cheek from the ladies, and was hugged by his cousin, Linda, the woman who had been holding Andre so tightly.

Gemma felt torn, unsure how to act. Which Gemma? The reserved one who obsessed over everything that was said about her, or the Gemma who had let loose the day before? She had heard Andre, but it was hard to drop her guard.

They sat under the canopy, and while the men studied the cliff, the ladies lay out snacks and drinks. Then she caught sight of the little girl—platinum blonde with hazel eyes and the cutest round belly.

"How do you know Andre?" Sandy asked.

"We met in Paris," Gemma said.

"As in, last week?" Linda asked.

"That's right."

Linda appeared to be studying Gemma. "You have such lovely eyes," she finally said.

"Thank you." For an instant Gemma relaxed, but just as quickly she was worried again. She glanced over her shoulder, expecting the worst.

"Don't worry," Linda whispered. "No one but surfers show up this early. You'll be safe from wandering eyes."

"Do you climb?" Sandy asked. "My fiancé, Chris, may try to work you."

"Climb what? That?" Gemma asked. "Is he serious? That's a flat wall."

"Dead serious," Dan said as he slid under the canopy. "The good news is he also claims he's a survival expert, so if you fall and break something, he'll help you survive."

"As reassuring as that sounds, I'll have to skip this go," she said.

She was nearly certain they recognized her, but beyond Linda, no one made reference to it. They treated her like a normal person. Gemma's armor lowered.

She watched Andre play with little Haley, who appeared to be taken by him as well. Haley giggled and snuck little peeks. A toddler being coquettish.

"Okay, we're ready to climb," Chris said, calling the group into action. "Sandy, will you get the camera? Andre climbs first."

"Andre?" Gemma asked. "Are you insane? That looks awfully dangerous."

Andre winked. "I should be okay."

"Should?"

Andre took off his shirt and tossed it on the sand. Her face went slack. Like the rock he was about to climb, he was made of stone. An absolute perfect structure.

"Andre, what happened to your chest and shoulder? Are those burns?" Dina asked.

"These things? Nah. They're my beauty marks." He eyed Gemma.

Andre and Chris were adjusting their gear when Linda tugged on Andre's elbow.

"Should you be doing this?" she asked, concern etched on her face. "Why don't you climb the other side instead?"

He frowned. "What's on your mind?"

"Your contract. What if you get hurt? You know you have a no extreme sport clause. Should you be doing anything to jeopardize the contract? After all this time, is this worth it?"

"Don't worry. This is a simple climb. I'm not free-climbing it. I'll be strapped in."

A beat. "Please be careful," she said then stepped away. Andre considered Linda's advice as Chris cross-checked Andre's gear. She was right, of course. Even if only an infinitesimal chance of injury existed, climbing was not smart. What if someone from the office saw him?

"You're good to go," Chris said.

Andre placed his hands on the cliff's face, feeling the cool surface. A damp rock was riskier. He'd need to use more chalk. He was being bull-headed about this. He didn't need to climb.

"You okay, bro?" Chris asked.

Why did he have to second-guess every aspect of his life? M&T controlled everything—even his latest vacation was on the verge of being cancelled. It was time to live the life he wanted. He'd climb if he wanted to climb. "Yeah, I'm great," Andre said.

But a knot at the base of his neck tightened. The morning headache was back.

The waves crashed against the jagged rocks. The electrifying dissonant sounds of the waves and the howling wind replaced all other sounds. Gemma sat on a boulder and watched Andre.

"He'll be fine," Dan said. "He's harnessed in. If he loses a hold, the worst will be a five-foot slip. He may get bruised, but not much more. The difficult part is that point up there." He waved his hand toward a protrusion of rock near the top. "When he gets underneath that lip, he'll have to leap to catch it before he can summit."

"That does not sound safe," she said.

"That part can get a bit ugly. If he doesn't catch the lip, he'll swing in an arc and hit the rock face. I'm sure he'll protect his vitals."

"Dear Lord, I'm going to vomit."

"Nah, he'll be fine," Dan said as he took a hesitant step away, but stopped. "By the way, I hope you don't mind me saying, but your match against Sonia was some of the best tennis I've seen in years. I'm looking forward to Wimbledon."

"Thanks… I appreciate that. But who were you cheering for?"

He smiled. "I've always been partial to southpaws."

They do know me. Yet, they were comfortable with it—not star-struck at all. She was not used to this. But she could get used to it very quickly.

Her mobile rang. It was Tish. What now? She considered answering it, then pressed *Ignore*.

She trained her attention on Andre as he carefully placed his hands on the flat wall. Like a human spider, he grabbed the face of the rock and without hesitation climbed. Fast. Practically leaping from one hold to the other. She'd seen rock climbers on TV, but what he was doing was different—as if on fast-forward.

"He's a natural speed climber," Linda said.

"Speed climber?"

"When these guys climb, their goal is speed. Beyond physical strength, he's like a chess player planning multiple moves ahead. As Andre climbs, he's planning the path that'll lead him to summit with the least effort."

"Is this related to his gift? The fact that he sees patterns?" Gemma asked.

Gemma noted a hint of surprise in Linda's eyes, but then a smile emerged. "Yes, exactly. Pattern recognition. He sees all the possible patterns then eliminates options. You should try a parallel climb with him on the north face. You will not regret it."

"I have this little issue with heights," Gemma said then bit her lip. She didn't want this information to end up on a newsreel.

"I understand, but maybe heights don't have an issue with you."

Gemma grinned, then turned back to Andre. Right there at the beach, with the smell of the ocean, the scent of suntan lotion, and the sounds of the waves, seagulls, and wind, she was mesmerized by Andre, unwilling to take her eyes off him. He was amazing. She studied how his arms stretched, the way his legs spread from one foothold to another. He was magical.

Just then, he stopped climbing.

Linda straightened.

"What's wrong?" Gemma asked.

"I don't know."

She watched him twirl his head, as if relaxing his neck muscles. Then with the free hand, he squeezed his neck.

"Oh, God," Linda said. "I hope it's not another one of his headaches."

Headaches? Gemma took a few steps toward Andre.

"Are you okay?" Chris yelled up. Gemma stood next to Chris, watching intently.

Andre turned to respond, but at that instant she locked eyes with him. He was a good thirty feet up, but she was certain he was locked on her. She wanted to help, she just didn't know how. So she smiled up at him.

Two, maybe three moments later, he shoved his free hand in the chalk bag, switched grips, chalked his other hand, and then yelled, "Climbing!" as he leapt to the next hold.

He continued up as if nothing had happened.

Gemma took a few steps back, next to Linda. "Bloody hell. What was that?"

"Not sure."

Gemma held her breath when he reached the complex point Dan had identified, but Andre didn't miss a beat. Another leap. With both hands he managed a wide grip on the lip, then pulled up. His muscular shoulders and back gave him the appearance of a bird spreading his wings. The rest was child's play. He summited gracefully, then waved down at them.

He rappelled in a few successive hops. Once down, he unhooked before jogging up to Gemma. His body shone like mist on a bronze statue. "Well? What'd you think?" he asked, slightly out of breath.

She wanted to grab him, touch his body. Instead, she said, "Intoxicating. Simply intoxicating."

"It's your turn."

"Are you mad?"

"No, I'm quite happy."

"Bloody Yank. You know what I mean."

"Yeah, but I love it when you get irritated. Reminds me of the first time I met you. When was that? Six days ago?"

"A lifetime," she mused. "What happened to you up there?"

He hesitated. "I thought I couldn't go on."

"Yet you did. What changed?"

"You. I saw your eyes. You're like a shot of adrenaline."

She beamed.

CHAPTER THIRTEEN

"Love all, but trust a few."

~William Shakespeare

Through the early morning, the others climbed the north face. Each tried to convince Gemma to give it a try, explaining it was a simple climb, unlike the other one, but she wouldn't bite. It was silly to even consider. She was a professional athlete. A cut on her hand could devastate her performance, much less something more significant, like a head injury.

They were seated on towels under the canopy when Andre shuffled over to Gemma.

"Gemma," Andre said, his hair a bit messy. "Climb. I'll climb next to you. Move for move, I'll be there with you. Trust me."

She brushed his hair, her eyes trained on his. "I don't trust anyone," she said, then rose. "But I'll trust you."

"Yes!" From his seated position he catapulted to his feet. "Chris, Linda, you're on belay."

Those were not the words she meant to speak, but she couldn't deny him, particularly when she was drowning in his warm, glistening eyes.

Andre walked Gemma to the rock face. "The person at the base is your belayer. You and Chris are connected by the rope harnessed to you. It's like an umbilical cord. The belayer is your anchor and watches you move-for-move to ensure you have enough rope and support. Most important, if you slip, he holds the rope tight, not allowing you to drop."

"Right. Good thinking. Dropping is not good."

"Let's harness you in," he said. He knelt on the sand and held out the harness. "Step into it."

She placed a hand on his head for balance and considered grabbing a handful of his black mane. As she stepped through each loop, his fingers dragged across her legs. Goose bumps ran up her back. He lifted the harness to her waist then circled behind her. Gemma's will weakened. He put his hands around her waist, tightening the harness and looping the rope through. The contrast of fear and Andre's hands on her body wreaked havoc.

"You're good to go," he said as he tightened her helmet. "Let me grab my gear and we're ready to climb."

"Are you ready?" Chris asked Gemma.

"No. But to hell with it. Let's climb this bastard."

"That's the attitude." Chris fist-pumped.

With that, they started to climb.

Andre was on her left, moving up together. He remained close, carefully explaining where to place her hands and feet. He leaned in when he needed to point to good holds—meatballs as he called them.

She was an athlete. She knew how to use her body and execute on any challenge. But the truth was she wanted him close. As close as possible, so she could breathe his scent, feel his graze, and touch the veins that swelled with his muscles.

Things were progressing well until her foot slipped. Both hands maintained a solid grip with one foot still planted, but none of that mattered. She broke into full-body perspiration and did the worst thing possible. She peered down. They were over twenty feet up. One knee shook uncontrollably.

"Tight!" Andre yelled down. "Talk to me. You okay?"

"Frightened out of my fuckin' mind. I want to go back down."

He moved in close and touched the small of her back. "I'm here. I won't let anything happen to you."

"I'm freaking out."

"If you want to go down, we'll go down. But before we go, look toward the ocean. Take it in. It'll be yours to keep forever."

Gemma's face was plastered against the rock, her hair clung to her sweaty face, her helmet askew. He brushed her hair out of her face.

Summoning courage, she turned toward the ocean. Her breathing labored, but one look and she discovered an overwhelming surplus of untapped oxygen. The ocean was an infinite pool of melted silver. For the first time, she appreciated the insignificance of man in the hands of nature. She was on the cover of every magazine, but she was nothing compared to what she was witnessing. The wind picked up, pulling her body away from the rock. She tightened her grip, allowing the breeze to swirl around her, dissipating her sweat and anxiety.

She faced Andre. "Let's keep climbing."

He smiled his lovely, encouraging smile. "Climbing!" he yelled down.

His instructions came as if from a conductor leading instruments into a crescendo. But she was getting the feel of it now. They were in perfect harmony with each other, and within moments, reached the summit and burst out laughing.

The gang below cheered, though Gemma could barely hear them over the sound of surf and wind.

"I can't believe it. I actually climbed this monster!" She threw her arms up in victory. "Not in my wildest dreams. This is awesome!" Unadulterated joy took over mind and body.

She turned to Andre and without thought or consideration, pulled his face to hers.

Their lips melted in the midmorning sun. They bodies clung against each other as Gemma's body hummed. For a moment, they were alone in the world. Their lips unwilling to part. Then her eyes popped open and she pulled away slowly until their lips separated. "I'm... I didn't mean to..." She took a step back, but he held her hand.

His eyes were alert. "If we climb again, will I get another?"

His smile melted her. She wanted nothing more than to give him another. And another.

Gemma sat on the sand, thinking of that kiss. As wonderful as it had been, she had made a grave mistake. What part of kissing him on a public beach had sounded like a good idea? Thankfully, no one had been up there and it was still early. At least that's what she hoped.

A week ago she was in Paris playing for her life. Now, she was in Los Angeles, living for once. Life took such quick and drastic turns sometimes.

Under the canopy, Andre was talking to Linda, who then nodded and went to a large beach bag. From there she pulled out a blue jacket, then jogged over to Gemma.

"In case you're cold," Linda said, the smile on her face making it clear there was more to the offering.

"But I'm not cold."

Linda leaned down. "He's worried someone will notice you or your tattoo, then ruin your day. He's being a protective ape-man."

Gemma grinned. "I've always had a thing for primates."

Linda, looking content, practically skipped away. Gemma slid on the hoodie then glanced at Andre who was jogging over.

"You look good in blue," Andre said.

"Is that your new pickup line?"

"Yes. I hope it worked. Let's take a walk."

She scanned the coast then rose. 8:30 a.m. was too early for most. Only surfers graced the beaches. She considered holding his hand, but thought better of it. One snap of the camera and that picture would go viral.

"Remember, we're in public," she said.

"Right. Public. Got it."

Andre moved increasingly closer. She eyed him. "What are you doing?" she asked.

"Nothing," he said.

"Good," she said, then trained her eyes on the distance.

He bumped her elbow with his.

"What was that?"

"I tripped."

They walked a few more steps. He shouldered her, knocking her off her path.

She spun to him. "Seriously? You'll regret this when we're alone."

He took a step closer. "That's what I'm counting on."

Uncontrollably, she grinned.

He glanced over his shoulder, watching the ocean. "I love watching surfers," he said.

She studied them, noting the few who tried to catch every wave. Invariably failing more often than not.

Andre planted himself on the sand. "Look at that one." He pointed to one surfer who floated, waiting. "He gets it. He understands."

She sat next to him, watching the same surfer. "I think he's lounging."

"He's patient, waiting for the right one. Not like the others, who'll try everything that comes their way. But not that guy. He's not a wave slut."

"A what?"

He grinned then scooted closer, his legs nearly touching hers. "A wave slut. Not any wave will do. But look at him now. He waited for the right one."

She watched as the surfer paddled effortlessly. In one swift move, he was up on his board.

"He's commanding the board, not the wave, following the wave's lead. He's in the moment. Some try to force the wave to be something it's not. The real surfer knows the wave will do whatever the hell the wave wants to do."

"I like that," she said.

"When I was a kid, my grandfather took me to a bullfight in Spain. Before you get offended, it's a cultural thing."

"I'm not offended." How could she be? Spain was her paternal land.

"My grandfather explained the graceful dance of the matador. The successful matador has tremendous presence on the field, but must exert the least amount of effort. He stands, gracefully awaiting the charging bull. He keeps himself planted like a statue until the last instance, where with the slightest movement on his part, nearly imperceptible, the bull runs past him. They are close enough to smell each other, but far enough that the bull never touches the matador. It requires the greatest amount of concentration, focus, and presence. You have to be comfortable with yourself, and know yourself so well that a charging bull, ten times your weight, won't even get spit on your shoes. That's the graceful dance of the matador."

"I suppose a good surfer knows how to dance with the wave. While the others are trying to wrestle the bull."

"Exactly. They're fighting the wave, not riding it."

A few moments passed. She shifted toward him, eliminating the space between them. His warm legs leaned against hers. "By the way," she said, "just wanted to take back an earlier apology."

Andre faced her. "You can't take back apologies."

"I understand the outrage, but if you really aren't sorry, you can't just pretend like you are, can you?"

He seemed to consider the explanation, then peered up at her. "Which apology are you taking back? Not the scorching business I hope."

"Oh no, I do feel sorry about that bit. It was when I kissed you at the top of the rock."

"Oh." He grinned. "That one."

"The thing is, I'm actually quite proud of that one."

He leaned into her ear. "I think that's some of your best work."

"Thank you," she whispered, feeling heat across her entire body.

"I am hoping for an encore performance, though."

She leaned her head on his shoulder. "The day is fairly young. So if you behave yourself—"

"I don't think you really want me to behave, do you?"

She pulled back, studying his eyes. "No, I really don't."

By mid-morning, crowds had filled the beach. Gemma was huddled with the ladies under the canopy. Andre was talking to Dina and the guys. And just like Linda had a while back, Chris and Dan nodded then ran off to a truck parked in the lot. A minute later they ran back with some material in hand and started making modifications to the canopy.

Dina dropped on the towel next to Gemma.

"What are they doing?" Gemma asked.

"Creating privacy, to keep the gawkers at bay."

In her other world, she had to pay people large sums of money to think ahead. With this group, they thought ahead for her. Andre was doing everything he could to protect her.

Sandwiches, salads, and drinks occupied the center of their world. Gemma watched this group in wonder. They were completely free and always in action. There was no waiting for something to happen—they made it happen. And in this circle she felt as unchained as the rest.

"Who plays the guitar?" Gemma asked, pointing to the guitar case.

"You'll have to be loose with your definition of *play*," Dina said.

"Thank you, honey. That's my wife," Dan said, reaching for his shoulder blade. "Excuse me while I remove the knife from my back."

"Can you play for us?" Gemma asked.

"I want to state for the record the lady asked me to play."

Dan grabbed his guitar then tuned it for a few seconds. She now understood why he was partial to southpaws—he was one himself. "Okay. What do you guys want to hear?"

"'Hotel California'."

"Something by Chris Isaak."

"Anything by the Beatles."

"Something from this century, for cryin' out loud."

"If he plays Justin Bieber again, I swear I'll leave."

"Can you play 'Black Bird' by my countrymen?" Gemma asked. "Do you know that one?"

"Are you kidding me?" Dan strummed a chord for emphasis. "One of my all-time favorites. By the way, when someone requests a song, they have to sing backing vocals. Come over here." He tapped the blanket next to him.

"But there are no backing vocals to that song."

"Details. Details. Come over here m'lady. You can't hide in this group."

Gemma scooted over, and when the team cheered, she nearly giggled.

Dan's fingers maneuvered the fret board with ease and precision while his voice mimicked Paul McCartney's. Behind the shelter of her sunglasses, Gemma closed her eyes. Memories of the past, the pain, and the threat of tears returned. She sang along, her voice swimming in the canopy. On the last verse, she opened her eyes and eyed Andre. He was in an unblinking daze.

When the song ended, there was a momentary silence. Then they all erupted, leaping toward her and high-fiving.

"That was perfect," Dan said to her.

Gemma leaned over and kissed him on the cheek.

He blushed. "That happens to me all the time," he said. Immediately the gang jeered and threw carrots at him.

Gemma was beside herself. She could not believe what she had just done. The adrenaline rush was fantastic, but... what had she been thinking? If anyone had recorded her, it would be all over the telly, day and night. People analyzing her voice, making fun of her.

But when she studied each of them, it was clear they had moved on. What she had done was merely a contribution to the day. She wasn't the main attraction. The group, the circle, the memories were the main story, not Gemma. She allowed herself to relax as more songs came from Dan's guitar. A sense of melancholy had joined the tent, though. Maybe it was the selection of songs. She doubted it.

She leaned over to Andre. "This isn't just a regular day at the beach, is it?"

He shook his head. "We're here to remember a friend who passed away just over a year ago. He was Linda's fiancé."

Gemma's face froze, and a combination of grief and shame overwhelmed her. She did not belong here. She needed to say something to Linda, to apologize. Instead Andre spoke.

"Dan, play 'Empty Space'."

Silence draped the canopy. Andre held Gemma's hand. They focused on Dan, who after a moment's hesitation played an airy guitar intro, transporting her somewhere in the heavens. Then he sang:

Can we walk away, pretending not to see the empty space?
We don't give reasons why, the gleaming tears flow gently from our eyes.
Miss you so, dear friend—fly, to your cloud, dear friend.
Lamenting what's too late, we never talk about the tears we cried.
It comes to us all, we're bound by the time that keeps us here for a while.
And I miss you so, dear friend—fly, to your cloud, dear friend.

When the song ended, Gemma came out of her trance and saw everyone hugging Linda. Red swollen eyes and wet cheeks reshaped the faces of the clan. She wiped her own tears. Maybe she didn't belong, but she wanted to.

Minutes later, after Dan retired the guitar, Gemma watched Dina playing with Haley. Dina was maybe a few years older than Gemma, yet she was married and had a child already. She wondered when she would be able to plan for a family.

"Hey you, what's on your mind?" Andre asked.

She snapped out of it. "Nothing. A bit overwhelmed, I suppose. Also, I think I've fallen in love with Haley."

"She became more adorable after I became her godfather. This is documented fact."

"I'm sure it is. How long have you known Dina?"

"Since second grade. My first love."

Gemma spun to him. "Dina? She's the one?"

"Yup, until I was fifteen," he said, smiling in reflection.

"What happened?"

"She and my best friend, Dan, fell in love."

"No, I mean what happened with you two? Did you separate when you went to MIT?"

Andre turned to Gemma. "Oh no, you misunderstand me. I was in love with her, but she had no clue."

Gemma stared at Andre. "Why didn't you tell her?"

He shrugged. "Too young, too dumb. Then my world turned upside down."

Silence. "Sorry for diggin' up old memories," Gemma said.

"Don't be. All those memories make me who I am and give me what I have today. It may not be a perfect tapestry, but it's mine. I continue to believe—I have to believe—things will turn out in the end." He faced her. "It'll all turn out in the end, right?"

"Yes." She put her hand on his. "It always does."

CHAPTER FOURTEEN

"Sports do not build character. They reveal it."

~John Wooden

B y noon, the heavy crowds had confined Gemma beneath the canopy. She watched the gang clear their possessions, and as the items were hauled to the cars, Gemma's heartbeat raced. She didn't want to be harassed, but she also didn't want the day to end. It was ending, though, and little could be done. Probably for the best. Time to go back home and find out why her team had been calling and texting her all day.

She held Andre's hand. "I better leave also. I had a great—"

"Leave? We're heading over to Dan and Dina's for a BBQ. Come with us."

That sounded nice, so different. She had never been to a proper BBQ. But joining them was like petting a tiger.

"It's a brilliant idea," Dan said in a pitiful British accent. "Admit you want to be with us. The sooner you admit it, the sooner the healing begins."

Gemma laughed. "Are all your friends like you?" she asked Andre.

"How so?"

"Smartasses."

"Sadly, yes. But they're trying to behave—this being the first time and all."

She wondered if this would also be the last.

"I tell you what—I challenge you to a tennis match," Andre said.

"Ooh," Linda cooed.

"That's right. And I guarantee I'll win. If I lose, I'll take you back home. But if I win, you stay with us the rest of the day."

"And am I allowed to use my arms and legs?" Gemma asked.

"All of them."

"The gauntlet has been dropped," Dina said.

"This is going to get ugly," Chris added.

"Five bucks Gemma creams him," Sandy said.

"Well?" Andre asked, and crossed his arms.

She studied him, wondering what he was up to. She'd have to find out. "Challenge accepted."

"Are you sure this is a good idea?" Xavi asked Gemma.

"Yes. It's a brilliant idea," she said, using Dan's earlier line. "They'll never see me." She was in Xavi's truck, lying flat in the rear king cab section, so when he drove through the crowd outside her home, no one would see her.

"No, I mean going with these people you just met."

"Stop talking. People will see your mouth moving and know someone's back here." A few moments passed. "And yes, they are good people."

He mumbled something in Spanish. She could hear the crowd now. He must have been passing through them. She remained frozen solid. Then the truck picked up speed. She sat up.

"There, that's his car," she said, pointing to Andre's car some one-hundred yards away.

Xavi pulled ahead of Andre's, then stepped out. "I am not crazy about this," he said as he opened the rear door. "That is a fast car."

"I'll tell him to drive slowly. He'll listen to me. He's a good bloke."

"I have memorized his license plate, just in case."

She leapt out, gave him a kiss, then ran to Andre's car. He was waiting, passenger door open. "I told you it would work," she said.

"Very cloak and dagger of you."

She hopped into the car. "We have to get creative sometimes." He shut the door and jogged around to his side.

"The guy who drove you is giving me the eye," he said as they drove off.

"Xavi? He's a puppy. Then again, you could be a mass murderer."

"True."

"Bugger. I forgot my racquet."

"Fret not, m'dear. Racquets will be provided."

"Does my racquet include the strings?"

"Your racquet will be as good as mine."

"How in God's name do you plan to beat me at tennis?"

"You forget—I'm a genius."

"An arrogant one at that." Her phone rang. She studied it.

"What do you say if for one day we leave that other world behind?"

She turned off her phone then dropped it in her bag. "What other world?" She fiddled with the radio, hoping to find some decent music. They came to a red light.

"I love this song," he said. The station was playing a Muse song. The same one had been blaring in Johnny's car when they had the accident in Australia. All those dark memories came at her.

"Do you mind if I change it?" she asked.

She could feel his eyes on her. "No, of course not. Something wrong?" he asked.

She turned off the radio. "That song brought back bad memories from an incident in Australia. It's sad how a song I used to love now reminds me of bad memories."

"It can go the other way too," he said. "From now on, each time I hear 'Black Bird', I will remember how you spent the day with me at the beach."

He lifted her hand then kissed the inside of her wrist. Butterflies, millions of them, flapped through her fingers and arm. His lips lingered for a moment before placing another peck on her. He laid her hand on his leg, squeezing it. He glanced at her.

She was trying to focus, trying to control the urge. "That was lovely," she whispered.

He slid his hand through her hair to the back of her neck and brought her lips into his. She was addicted to his taste, his scent, his warmth. She could do this forever.

A car horn blared.

He pulled back. She wobbled.

"Damn green light," he said then accelerated away. He gazed at her. "Are you okay?"

"Shh," she said, "give me moment to control my heart rate."

Fifteen minutes later, they reached Venice Beach, thick with crowds.

"We're going to play tennis here? I can't play in a public—"

"Patience," he said as they got out of the car.

"Did you say Dan and Dina live here? This must be expensive." She slid on a beanie and raised her jacket's collar.

"They rent here, and you're looking at the landlord."

"This is yours?"

"Bought it a year ago and rented it to them. I am robbing them blind though. I make them pay for their own groceries."

"Helping the girl who broke your heart? How noble."

"Just giving my friends a helping hand. We all could use a little help." He put his arm around her shoulder and brought her close. She breathed in his scent. She felt drunk on how good he smelled and how complete she felt in his arms. "Come on," he said. "I need to whoop your British arse."

Gemma was immediately taken by Dina and Dan's vibrant home. Through the large vertical windows, sunlight drenched the living area. Mosaic-adorned Spanish tiles paved the floors. Black and white photographs accented the walls. The house was simple, pure, perfect.

"I got you something," Linda said to Andre. She handed him a plastic bag.

He dug in quickly. Gemma could imagine that same look of excitement on a young Andre come Christmas Day.

He pulled out a black t-shirt. "Ms. Pac-Man? I can't believe you found it." He gave Linda a bear hug.

"I saw it at one of the street vendors here in Venice. I had to grab it."

He was thrilled over a five dollar t-shirt. He drove an Aston Martin, yet a t-shirt stole his heart.

"Ms. Pac-Man? Weren't you addicted to that game?" Dan asked.

"No," Linda said, "not the game as much as—"

"Don't—" Andre tried to interrupt.

"—addicted to *Silvia*," Linda continued.

Andre reddened while the others laughed. "It had nothing to do with her. I loved that game."

"Sure," Linda said as she turned to Gemma. "We were twelve, vacationing in Spain. Mister Andre here had a major crush on this redhead, Silvia. He literally stole money from my dad and shared quarters with her. It was pitiful."

"I was trying to be neighborly," he said.

"Each evening, we went to the cafe in the center. Like us, Silvia was a fixture there. One day, before heading to the cafe, Andre rushed into the bathroom. He was there much longer than normal. When he came out—"

"Will you stop already?" he said.

"When he came out," she continued, giving Andre the evil eye, "his hair looked odd and smelled weird. Our own child-genius here had used Vaseline on his hair."

The room exploded with laughter. Through tears, Linda went on. "He had slicked back his hair, this afro of his, with Vaseline to look handsome for her."

Gemma was wiping her tears. "Vaseline? Andre, what were you thinking?"

He dropped his head for a few moments. Eventually, he peered up. "But she was so pretty. I had to try something."

Gemma placed a hand on his shoulder. "You are a geek."

"I need a drink." He went to the refrigerator and grabbed a Corona.

"Beer will slow you down. I don't want to hear excuses afterwards."

"We'll just have to see about that. Dan, are we ready?"

"Nearly."

"Come on." Andre walked her to the den. "Time to be taken to school."

The television screen lit up. Gemma was confused for a moment, then it all made sense. "A bloody video game? Wii Tennis? Seriously? This is what you're challenging me to?"

"Is Miss Tennis Star afraid of playing?" He whipped the motion-based controller in air. "Are you going to bring your A-game or what?"

She stood, studying him. "That's the only game I bring."

Gemma loved watching Andre panic—he had miscalculated. He clearly had not considered that she was also an avid gamer. Even so, the battle was epic in its own right. Not because it was a close match, but because Andre, who fancied himself "the man" at the game, was being trounced. He had yet to earn a point and she liked it like that.

Match point. She glanced at him. Perspiration dripped down his forehead.

"Are you ready to be a man of your word?" she asked.

He spun to argue, to renegotiate the terms, discuss, which is exactly what she thought he'd do. With him distracted, she served.

"Wait—" he yelled out, but it was too late.

Ace.

He collapsed to the floor. The audience cheered, while Sandy took her winnings from Dan.

"You cheated. You distracted me," Andre said.

"Yes, I did." She twirled the controller like a gunslinger. "Well?"

He rose and tossed the controller on the couch. "I'm a man of my word."

She didn't budge. "And I say we stay."

He beamed. "Best of three?"

CHAPTER FIFTEEN

"The moment of victory is much too short to live for that and nothing else."

~Martina Navratilova

Everyone tried to beat Gemma at Wii Tennis, all hoping to be able to loosely declare they had defeated Gemma at tennis. But they all lost. Badly.

Lunch, board games, early dinner, and dessert—it had been a full day of bliss. She met Andre completely by chance—a coincidence. But here she was, spending the day with him and his extended family, and loving every moment of it. With each passing minute, her feelings grew stronger. Like a tree, his roots were taking hold.

Andre was on the balcony with his friends, while she was at the kitchen table with Linda. Dina and Dan were putting Haley to sleep. Gemma and Linda were nearly inseparable. As improbable as it was, they were already building a solid friendship. Linda was honest, a straight shooter, and easy to talk to. Gemma was saving Linda's contact information on her mobile when she noticed that Linda's email address was from a well-known high school in an affluent Los Angeles neighborhood.

"How long have you been teaching?" Gemma asked.

"Three years. I must admit, my kids have taught me more than I've taught them."

"High school students? Hard to imagine"

Linda sipped tea. "Has Andre told you about Rob?"

A beat. "Was Rob your fiancé?"

Linda nodded. "He was one of Andre's childhood friends. We fell in love in high school and went to college together. We had recently graduated, getting into our careers. We were also planning our wedding on a detailed spreadsheet he maintained with the diligence of a squirrel. It was his way of contributing to the chaos called wedding planning."

Gemma instinctively placed her hand on Linda's.

"One evening, when I came home after a parent teacher conference, all the lights in the house were still off. When I flicked the switch I found him curled up on the couch in the den. He'd been crying. He was unable to talk, despondent. The results of his routine tests had come in. He was told he had melanoma. And it had spread. He was given months. Just like that, everything changed."

Gemma's tears streamed uncontrollably. Why was life like this? Unfair and random. Just like her birth parents, they had found love, the perfect love. And in an instant they were torn apart.

"Four months was all it took. This young, vibrant, powerful man was taken away from me." Her voice was hoarse. "I had my friends and family, but it wasn't until I went back to school that I found the healing power of love. My students came to my rescue. Surrounded by their love and energy, I made it."

Gemma thought of the passion and electricity she experienced when surrounded by her fans in the stadium. On some level she understood. The game was her sanctuary.

"We were to marry on Memorial Day weekend. Today would have been our first anniversary."

Gemma's throat constricted. "I can't find the proper words. All I feel is loss and profound sadness. Like a hole in my chest." Her words choked in her throat.

Linda took Gemma's hand and held it tight. "I didn't mean to make you sad. You're comfortable to talk to. It's your eyes I think—you disarm the most guarded person."

"Both you and your cousin seem to be under the spell of my eyes," Gemma said, smiling through tears.

"What's that saying? 'With great power comes greater responsibility.' Use it with care."

Andre and Chris were outside cleaning the grill when Dan showed up.

"Is Haley asleep?" Andre asked.

"I hope so," Dan said. "Dina told her if she doesn't sleep soon, I'd go in there with the guitar and sing all night."

"That's cruel," Chris said.

"Thanks, bro."

Andre glanced inside. Dina joined Gemma and Linda.

"So…" Dan said.

"Yeah…" Chris added.

Andre glanced at them. "What's on your birdbrain minds?"

"Nothing. We're good," Dan said. "Everything's the same, right Chris?"

"Yup, all's copacetic here. Just like you, right, Andre? Nothing new with you?"

"Yup, you got it," Andre said. "Nothing new. Just hangin' out—"

"Dude," Chris nearly yelled. "How could you not tell us about Gemma? For the love of all that's awesome, how did this happen?"

"Nothing has really happened," Andre said. "We're friends… or something."

"Is that right?" Dan said. "So what happened when you guys summited? Why did you both suddenly disappear up there?"

"I have no recollection of said events," Andre said, dropping his eyes to the grill, a stupid grin burst out.

"I told you," Chris said to Dan. "Einstein here had us all fooled. I'm too busy, I'm flying, I'm in meetings, I don't have time for a personal life. Yeah, sure looks like it." Chris bore into Andre's eyes. "You know what, bro? I'm so freakin' happy for you." Chris dropped a hand on Andre's shoulder.

"Hear hear," Dan said. They all clinked their near-empty bottles. "You are finally with someone who puts a legit smile on your face."

"We're not together, guys. We're just starting to know each other."

"No, it's more than that. You two look like you've been friends for a long time. Even with us, it's so natural. Like she was always here."

That's exactly what it felt like. Like they'd always known each other and were somehow separated. "She gets me. It's like she's always been a part of me."

"From the way she looks at you, I bet she feels the same way," Chris said. "I am so glad you and I are best friends."

"Hold on," Dan jumped in. "Andre and I were best friends first. You were an afterthought."

"Too much time on the beach has softened your brain…"

The guys went on, but Andre turned his attention to Gemma, sitting with Linda and Dina, smiling and chatting. She was what had been missing in his life. A partner.

Gemma watched the sun as it danced with the ocean. Nearly sunset. The shadows grew long and the air turned cool. One by one, the friends left. The next day was a work day. When they hugged Andre, they held on, as if unsure of the next time they'd see each other again. It seemed this circle of friends had always been, and would continue to be, each other's support structure.

"When will we see you next?" Dan asked Andre.

"Soon. The worst is almost over."

Gemma wondered what he was talking about.

"What's going on?" Dina asked. "How can we help?"

"Don't worry. It's all under control."

Dina frowned then extended her arms to Gemma who leaned down to embrace her. "Thank you for trusting us," Dina said. She whispered into Gemma's ear. "He'll move mountains for us, but won't ever let us help him."

"I didn't realize he was so stubborn," Gemma whispered back.

"Like a mule."

"Hey, what are you two whispering about?" Andre asked.

"You," Dina said.

Gemma's eyes opened wide. "You're honest to a fault."

"That's the only way this group operates," Dina said. "Always the truth."

They drove with the top down, the cool air soothing.

"Slowly," Gemma said then glanced at him. "Drive slowly."

Andre reduced speed, the car practically gliding through Pacific Coast Highway.

She placed her hand on top of his. He glanced at her.

She mouthed, "Thank you."

"Maybe you can have a normal life after all."

For the first time, she had tasted the possibility. "Today was lovely."

"Nearly perfect," he said.

"Nearly?"

"It had to end."

She reach out and caressed his hair. "Then don't let it end. Take me somewhere you'd want me to see."

They drove past Santa Monica into Malibu, farther north than her home. Some time later, he pulled a U-turn and parked on PCH on the ocean side.

"Leo Carillo," he said. "Have you been here before?"

"Never."

He grabbed a blanket he had from the beach, took her hand, and found their way to the sand. "To the lifeguard shack," he said.

"Are we allowed to do that?" she asked.

"Yes, absolutely. So long as nobody catches us."

They climbed the ramp and leaned against the rail in front of the vacant lifeguard's viewing tower. He draped the blanket across their shoulders.

Gemma hooked her arm through his and squeezed tight into him. She laid her head on his shoulder, certain the warmth of his body would stop her from shivering.

"During the day," he said, "if the skies are clear, you can see Point Dume from here. At night, it's just serene. The ocean is lit by the moon and the stars. Unfortunately we already missed the sunset."

"It's so beautiful here," she said, but the cold was a bit too much. Her teeth rattled for a few moments. The minutes drifted while they listened to the crashing waves.

"It was near that cave," he pointed to some boulders in the distance. "I was visiting from MIT. Dan drove me out here to catch up. We were hanging out when Dan told me he and Dina were dating. I told him I was happy for them and even told him I had been over her for years."

"You lied to him."

He nodded. "I had to. I wanted him to be happy and chase his heart."

"Then this place doesn't hold fond memories for you."

"I'm about to change that," he said.

His lips met hers. His mouth thawed her trembling lips when his warm tongue found hers. She grasped his face as she tasted his mouth forcefully and backed him against the rails. She stepped into him, sliding her leg between his, pressing tighter. His hands slid into the back pockets of her shorts. She needed air, she needed him.

What are you doing? You're in a public place.

Between kisses she said, "Wait."

His lips latched on to hers again, but she took a small step back. His eyes opened. "What's wrong?" he asked.

"Not here. What if—?"

"What are you doing up there?" A booming voice startled both of them, and a flashlight beamed in their faces.

Andre spun around, keeping her behind him. "Good evening, officer," Andre said. Gemma put out a hand to stop the blinding light, but also to hide her face from the officer.

"What the—?" the officer said. She was done for now; he had recognized her. "Is that you, Dr. Reyes?"

Gemma's eyes widened. *What the hell?*

"Yes?" he said cautiously.

"Oh, sorry," the officer said as he dropped the light and lit up his face instead.

"Sheriff Bonelli. How are you?"

Andre walked down the ramp and shook hands.

"I'm fine," the Sheriff said. "Didn't mean to startle you. The park is closed, so when I saw a parked car near the entrance, I came to investigate."

"We didn't realize the park was closed," Andre said. "We'll leave."

The Sheriff waved his hand. "You don't have to. It's a beautiful night. Just mind the path in the dark." They shook hands again, then the Sheriff tipped his hat to Gemma as he left.

Andre started to climb up when Gemma met him half way. "Can you take me home?"

"Sure. Did the cop freak you out?"

"A little. I'm worried. I don't want to be found here."

"Right. Pictures and newspapers."

"I'm sorry," she said.

"Don't be. I get it. I want you to feel comfortable, not scared or worried."

As they strolled the path back to the car, she squeezed into him. "How did you know the officer?"

"I've done plenty of work for the various police agencies here. I am connected, my dear."

"CIA, FBI, Sheriff... who are you?"

"To protect the innocent, it's best we leave some secrets unearthed."

Once inside the car, he blasted the heater, but it didn't seem to warm her fast enough. "Bugger! It's freezing!" she yelled. "Look at my legs. I have gooseflesh all over."

He laid his hand on her knee. "I can help with that," he said then slid his hand along her inner thigh.

She gasped and slammed her hand on his. "You better not do that," she whispered.

"Do what?" He squeezed.

"That!" She closed her eyes. "Take me home before something bad happens to you." She wrapped her hand around his.

"I was only trying to help," he said as he pulled the car out of the parking spot.

"I bet you were," she said. Her body rumbled. She wanted more of him. All of him. "What am I doing with you?" she asked through a flirtatious smile.

"Anything you want."

She gave him a sly look and nodded. "I'll keep that in mind."

They fell silent for a few minutes.

"Come over tomorrow," he said as they neared her home. "Breakfast, lunch, dinner—anything. I'll prepare us a meal."

"You cook?"

"I make a killer *paella*—my grandfather's recipe. What do you say?"

"I'd like that. But to be clear, were you inviting me to breakfast, lunch, *and* dinner? Or were you giving me an option?

"You can have it all."

The crowds were long gone by the time they pulled up to her private gate. Security opened the doors, but before they were fully open, she stepped out of his car.

"Let me drive you in," Andre said.

She jogged around to his side and leaned on his door. "What you did for me today I will never forget. I am indebted to you. Go home. We'll talk tomorrow."

He put his hand on hers. "Tomorrow."

Her eyes faltered. "I'll call you," she said, then quickly ran up her driveway as the gates closed. If she hadn't run, if she had hesitated, she would've dragged him out of his car and into her room. What was wrong with her? With him, her self-control was anything but. She wasn't ready to make the same mistake she had with Georg and Johnny. Even with Johnny it had taken weeks to open up. She had to be smart this time.

As he drove back home, Andre pulled his phone from his glove compartment and studied the missed calls and messages. Practically one per hour. The convertible's top rose as he listened to his voice-mails. Ten from his assistant and the last two from Roger.

"Roger here. We need to talk. You have to be in D.C. Wednesday morning. That means you have to leave tomorrow. I'm looking at the 9:00 a.m. flight. I need to hear from you so we can book the trip. Call me."

The last one concerned him.

"I don't know what's going on, Andre. This is odd behavior. You don't answer my calls, you don't return my calls. I can't help but wonder if something else is on your mind. Please call me."

Andre wanted to see her again. He didn't want to leave. He would push the trip out by a day. He'd call the client directly and work something out.

His phone chimed. A text message from Gemma.

"You can call me with surprises. This is my mobile. Sleep well."

After she sent the text, Gemma sank in her bed, thinking of Andre and what he had in mind for the next day. She knew she wanted to be with him. But they were moving too fast, too soon. What would be the appropriate time to wait, she wondered. A day? Two?

Her mobile rang. *Andre?* She grabbed it and studied the display. *Tish? At this hour?*

"Isn't it early in London?" Gemma said.

"She's alive! Bloody hell, Gemma. We've been trying to find you all day. Where have you been?"

"I've been about," she said, disturbed at how quickly the day's freedom disappeared with just one call. With one question, her dream day was replaced by her other life. She felt stuck between two worlds. "What now?"

"You need to get back to London ASAP. We dropped the ball fantastically. Your agency arranged for your appearance with Johnny for the UK premiere of *Triton Warriors*. It's on Wednesday night. You need to come back."

"No! No fuckin' way. The agency screwed up. Let them find some other imbecile who'll smile for the cameras. I'm in L.A. and can't leave."

"G, be reasonable. You've never broken a commitment. They can't just send anyone. Johnny's expecting you. This was the plan, remember? You both agreed you would keep up appearances of friendship and not let the media create alternate interpretations of what happened with you two."

Silence. Of course she remembered the plan. After she broke it off, the false rumors spread. Who dumped whom? Who cheated on whom? Wesley had advised them to maintain their "friends" story so that no one lost face in the chaos that followed. This premiere was part of the plan.

"Even the Prime Minister will be there. His people have asked us to set up a meet and greet. And let's not forget you're in the film, after all. You should be there."

"This is ridiculous. Can I have some time for myself? Any consideration for what I may have been planning? You're supposed to be on my side."

"Believe me, this will be a disaster if we don't correct it now. I am absolutely looking out for you."

She wanted to scream, yell, and curse.

"G?"

"Arrange the goddamn flight." And although tears shimmered in her eyes, her voice did not falter. "Then on Thursday morning I want Wesley to show me all the planned appearances, so I can cancel as many as I can get my hands on. Good night." She hung up and nearly threw her mobile against the wall.

Gemma squeezed her fists into her eyes and cried. She cried because she did not value her personal life as much as she valued her career. She cried because she wanted to see Andre again, and she cried because when the moment of truth came between her two worlds, she knew which one would win—which one had to win. And it was this fact she held on to. She reminded herself if she pursued anything with Andre, it would always lose to tennis.

She wiped her tears and picked up her mobile.

Andre was pulling into his parking lot when his phone chimed again. A new text message from Gemma. "*Bad news. Must go to UK asap. I leave tomorrow morning. I'm sorry. I'll call you as soon as I can.*"

He froze. Read and re-read the text. After a few moments, he sent a text to Roger.

CHAPTER SIXTEEN

"The next point—that's all you must think about."

~Rod Laver

A ndre arrived at the departure gate with less than an hour to spare. His head was full of scattered thoughts and a headache. He was supposed to simplify his world, not complicate it. What was happening with Gemma was an improbable relationship, and he had gotten what he deserved—she'd blown him off within thirty minutes of accepting his invitation.

He needed to cool things down with her and stay focused on the task at hand. If she wasn't going to make an effort, then neither would he. He had nearly postponed a client engagement, which would have immediately alerted M&T of his lack of commitment to the future. *Six months and you're free. Get your house in order first.*

On second thought, the first thing he wanted to do was hear her voice. He found a quiet spot and called her. One ring, two, three. He was about to hang up when she answered.

"Andre, can I ring you right back? I'm leaving for the airport now."

"Of course."

"Cheers," she said, then the line disconnected.

That confirmed it. She was definitely trying to create distance and he wasn't getting the message. Too much, too soon. He leaned against the wall and tried to remember how he had gotten in this mess. It was her

118

fault. She had come to his home. She did that—not him. Yes, he had asked her to go to the beach and then conned her into going to Dina's house, but she's the one who had first kissed him. *Man, what a kiss.*

Andre's headache deepened, inching its way into his skull. He needed his meds. He dropped his bags and just as he sat, his phone rang. It was her.

"Hi, Gem."

"Ooh, I love that nickname. Sorry about earlier. Didn't mean to brush you off. It's been crazy."

"Don't sweat it. Are you on your way to the airport now?" He rubbed his temple.

"Yes. Where are you? The beach?"

"LAX, waiting for my flight to D.C."

"What? You're leaving on a trip as well? I didn't know."

"I wasn't, but when you sent me your travel update, I decided to take the customer's call."

Silence. "Well, at least now I won't miss out."

"Miss out?" He closed his eyes and shoved a fist into his neck.

"If you did something fun and I wasn't there, I'd feel a bit left out."

"When will you return to L.A.?"

"I don't know. No specific plans as of yet."

"We'll just have to plan on that *paella* some other time then," he said, wondering when that day would come. "What dragged you back so soon?"

"That's how my world is sometimes. My agency made commitments without realizing I was out of the country."

"Something fun?"

"Something dreadful."

"*We are now boarding priority—*" the intercom announced.

"My flight's boarding. Text me when you land. Let's talk once you've settled in."

"That'll be lovely."

They hung up and Andre made his way toward the gate. He reached inside his bag for his headache meds, but paused. The tension, the tearing sensation of the headache was nearly gone. His shoulders were loose, his neck muscles were no longer tight. It was her voice. It had to be.

In about four weeks Project Sunrise would start, and for three to four months he would not be back home. He wanted to see her again before that project. He had to see her again.

Gemma slid on her sunglasses and leaned back as Xavi drove her to the airport. She liked predictability and discipline in her life. What she was experiencing right now was a roller coaster. Roller coasters made her vomit.

With all the rumors printed about her, one could have naturally assumed she was well-experienced and would one day write a how-to book. But she wasn't experienced, not really. Yes, she had dated a handful of people, which made for exciting articles, but truth be told, she trusted very few and had only been intimate twice before. The first could not count and the other had been years later with Johnny.

With Johnny, she thought she had been in love. But when they finally made love, it became evident he was not a lover. He was an animal claiming his possession. Johnny was not someone who could understand the fear and inadequacy she experienced when with another. So she never told him of her scars from years earlier. Now she understood she had been going through the motions of a relationship with him. In retrospect, the incident in Australia may have been heaven-sent—a gift from her father.

With Andre, she was experiencing a unique emotion. Trust. And passion. Maybe one day she could possibly tell him everything, because on some level she thought he'd understand without judgment. But how could she really know after this brief friendship? More time was what she needed with Andre, but she also understood duty, responsibility, and sacrifice.

Maybe it was for the best. Distance and time provided perspective. She could get this stupid appearance out of her way, closing the chapter on the whole Flauto mess. Then she'd go to Birmingham to prepare for the Aegon tournament.

Objectively, this getaway had been perfect. She had gone to L.A. hoping for time to get her mind off the French Open. Done, with Andre's help and that of his friends. Now she had to focus on the work ahead, because that's what mattered. So then why did her thoughts continue to drift back to Andre?

What did she think would come of it? Dating? A relationship? They both had to appease very demanding gods. She scolded herself for allowing her feelings to blossom for him. She couldn't afford another media circus.

Then why had she messed it all up by kissing him? She melted at the memory, at the tenderness he had shown when he kissed her. In retrospect, and if she was going to be honest, her only regret was pulling back.

Her heart beat with an irregular cadence. She rubbed her face. For now, she had to remind herself her objective was the game. In four or five weeks, after Wimbledon, maybe she could think of other matters. One thing was for sure: she couldn't drop another Grand Slam.

CHAPTER SEVENTEEN

*"The trouble with the rat race is that even if you win
you're still a rat."*

~Lily Tomlin

As soon as the plane lifted off, Gemma popped sleeping pills, reclined her seat flat, and slept on the makeshift bed. A seasoned traveler.

When she awoke, she was groggy, her head heavy and her mouth dry. She dragged herself to the restroom and washed her face. Inches away from the mirror, she analyzed her eyes—the crystal blue eyes that had hooked Andre.

My mother's eyes. A mother she had never met.

She collapsed on her seat and shut her eyes. She missed Andre. For that she hated him. How had he, in such a brief period of time, hooked his talons so deep? She could not dwell on that. Not now.

When she landed at Heathrow, the press, paparazzi, and fans waited for her. How the hell did they always know? And where was her team? She took a tentative step forward.

The overlapping questions and cheers were like simultaneous slaps. Did they honestly think she could understand a word they said?

Just then, a diaper was shoved into her chest.

"Can you sign this? It's clean!"

She let it drop to the floor and kept walking.

"Bitch!" someone said. There was no winning this game.

She reconsidered her earlier thought. No, the paparazzi did not always know where she was. While in L.A. with Andre, no one had found her. She was shielded from the madness.

The crowd of people suddenly flew apart as her security detail fought their way to her.

"Sorry, ma'am," her lead said.

She was practically lifted off her feet until her car appeared in front of her. As she slid in, her mobile chimed. A text message from Bedric. She braced herself.

"Dearest Gemma, we must speak."

Each word spoke volumes. He was not happy. She would have to call him. Later, definitely later.

She was taken to her Chelsea home, although the word "home" may have been an understatement. Like her place in Malibu, this mansion was built for a family of twenty. Maybe one day she'd visit all the rooms.

When she had purchased it less than a year ago, she knew she had made the big time. Chelsea was where the who's-who in London lived—from Russian oil tycoons to rock legends. And now she lived in a place that could be confused for an empty hotel.

She stepped in and was greeted by a lavish arrangement of flowers. She read the card. *"Looking forward to tonight - Johnny."*

She crumpled the note. She didn't want to see him, be with him, or talk to him. Why had she agreed to this plan?

She never should have gotten involved with him. But at the time, the thought that someone as famous as Johnny would have been interested in her was flattering. Maybe she had been a little starstruck. Johnny was named one of the sexiest men alive, the most eligible bachelor, and his last three movies had been undisputed blockbusters.

She had been a blind child, yet again.

As was typical with most high-profile relationships, they had tried to keep things private. Also like with most high-profile relationships, rumors spread. And with rumors came more paparazzi. They both had done a good job of calling their relationship, "a friendship." But the press never bought it.

As for the other problem, she should have recognized the symptoms earlier in the relationship. Instead, when she kissed him and smelled alcohol on his breath, she pretended the smell and taste didn't raise bile to her throat. Alcohol and Gemma did not mix. Never had.

Then Australia happened.

He had rented a private home. It should have been safe. But the pictures of her in a bikini, lip-locked with him in the hot tub, proved nothing and nowhere was safe. The next day, the paparazzi barraged them.

She could still remember the smell of the burning tires. The song that played on the radio. The fast corners. The yelling and screaming in the car. The accident. The bleeding.

He had overreacted. He had been drunk. Again.

The next evening, Sonia trounced her.

Minutes after the loss, she broke it off.

They had agreed to tell everyone they were still friends. Days later, word spread she had been dumped. Then the rumors evolved. She was accused of cheating on him. Although Johnny swore he had not been behind the rumors, she never trusted him again.

"Keep on making appearances together," Wesley had advised. "Keep the friends thing going and the press will eventually back off. No drama, no interest."

That had been months ago, and the '*Triton Warrior*' premiere was the planned fixer event, to prove the existence of a friendship. Of course, Johnny was still interested in her and Wesley loved the idea. "It's a match made in heaven. The publicity you two can generate will be unimaginable."

That was the first time she had come close to punching Wesley. It would not be the last. She knew what Wesley wanted. He represented both of them and was always ready to find cross-promotional opportunities.

None of that mattered now, because they were done.

Her shoulders ached. A solid workout would do her good. She would stretch her limbs, get the blood flowing, and prepare for the circus that would be the main event of the night.

When she entered her home gym, she stopped cold. On the floor, a few hundred new tennis balls awaited her. Next to them, a table, a chair, and black markers. Was she supposed to autograph these?

She pressed the intercom bottom. "Who placed the tennis balls in my gym?"

"Wesley had them delivered yesterday."

"I want them removed."

"Very well, ma'am, but he did mention these are gifts for the Children's Hospital."

Silence. "Never mind."

Typical Wesley. Exercise would have to wait.

Two hours later, her hand ached, but only a handful of balls remained. Her mobile rang. It was Wesley.

"What?" she said.

"Is that any way to talk to the person who'll have your face on the front page of every newspaper?" Wesley was far too jovial, as if unaware of the personal sacrifice she had just made.

"Sorry. Let me try again. What do you want?"

"Well, aren't we a bit pissy?" Silence. "Anyway, the promoter is sending a car to pick you up at 18:30 sharp. Also—"

"Wait. Will Johnny be in the car?"

"I think... umm. Well. Not sure. I think you'll be taken to him."

"Is he the princess? I'm picking him up, then? Fix it."

"Not sure if I—"

"I know you can. Just fix it. Anything else?"

A beat. "An impeccable Donna Karan dress is being sent to you as we speak. Makeup and hair will be at your home by 14:00. Be your radiant self."

"Fantastic, I can't wait."

"On the red carpet, be sure to mention Karan, Cartier, and Ferragamo. In that order."

"If that's all—"

"One more thing. At the theater, the Prime Minister and his wife want to meet you."

"Does he know I didn't vote for him?"

"Well, of course not, you silly thing. And he won't find out either, because politics don't sell commercials. But we want to leverage national pride for Wimbledon."

A walking billboard, that's what she had become. No longer a tennis player, but a living, breathing advert.

She allowed herself to smile. Studying her reflection in the floor to ceiling mirror of her master bedroom, she had to admit she looked damn good. Her boyish figure was all-woman now. She wondered what Andre would think if he saw her.

Tish walked in. "Okay, gorgeous, Johnny is here. Ready?"

"I suppose so. Let's get on with it." But before Tish left, Gemma held her arm. "Tish, stay close to me, okay?"

"Don't worry. You'll be fine."

Johnny and his crew waited in the entrance. "Hello, John," Gemma said as she swept down the spiral staircase.

"Will you take a look at her?" Johnny said, his Hollywood smile unmistakable. "No one will notice me." He strode up, held her hands, and gave her a peck on the cheek. He seemed hungry—like a wolf. "I'm glad you agreed to do this," he whispered. Her eyebrow rose when she picked up the scent of alcohol.

During the ride, Johnny recounted stories—all selected to impress her. She watched his lips move and wondered how much whiskey sloshed inside him. What a donkey. Words continued to dribble out of his mouth, and when his eyes indicated an 'impressive' part was coming, she lobbed him an obligatory, "Oh, wow."

He was still talking when he placed his hand on her thigh. She glanced at his hand and then at him. Her eyes penetrated his drunken mind, and he slowly pulled his hand, letting his fingers run on her thigh momentarily. *I will have to kill him. If he tries anything, I will drive his head into the wall.*

Through the tinted windows of the limousine she glared at the spectacle that awaited them. Flashbulbs lit the dark streets like strobe lights. "Christ," she said.

"Worry not, Gemmy," Johnny said. She hated that nickname. "Hold on tight and I'll get you through the sharks."

How comforting.

The doors opened and the screams escalated. Security guards stood on either side as Johnny stepped into a deafening burst of cheers. He waved to both sides of the red carpet.

Here we go. When she stepped out, she was struck back by the invisible hand of the crowd's erupting cheers. She was dazed, not expecting this type of reception. She settled and waved to the fans. No doubt, her star was at its height. At least for now.

Johnny grabbed her hand and led her down the red carpet. The questions came at them in rapid fire. The flashbulbs exploded faster.

The routine on the carpet was familiar. Stroll from one media outlet to the next. Smile, pose, answer the same questions, and move on.

Are you ready for Wimbledon?

Was that a tough loss?

Who are you wearing?

The questions didn't bother her. What bothered her was Johnny holding her, his arm across her hip, and the pictures that would be produced. Pictures that would make news.

At the next outlet, just when he tried to grab her hip again, she shifted, facing him. Smile on her face, she whispered. "Hands. Off."

He nodded, but at the very next stop, he did it again. He held her close and tight. Was he too drunk to understand? His behavior was bound to raise more questions. Friends don't hold each other that way.

They moved on, and when he touched her, her body shook, disgusted. Memories of her long-forgotten past gnawed at her. Sixteen, another drunk, another deep cut.

Tish ran up to her. "This way, G. The Prime Minister is waiting for you."

She rolled out of Johnny's hold, grateful when she entered the theater—five more minutes and she would have broken his hand.

"Gemma," Prime Minister Beckford said, "it is a distinct pleasure to meet you, my dear." He held her hands and kissed her on both cheeks.

"Thank you, sir. It's an honor to meet you," she said, surprised that she was awestruck by him. He was taller than she expected. Also, he was relaxed, not in a sleazy politician way, but like one of the lads at the pub. She turned to his wife. "Good evening, ma'am," she said, and shook hands.

"My dear, you are more beautiful in person," she said.

"Don't embarrass her," the Prime Minister said, reeling the conversation back to what must have been on his mind. "I know you have a busy evening ahead. But I wanted to wish you luck for next week, and also say a word about Wimbledon."

"Sir?" What could he possibly have to say about Wimbledon?

"We invented the sport," he said, "but our ladies have disappeared from the face of the championships. It is about time Great Britain raises the trophy in victory. This is our soil, our game. You are this country's favorite daughter, and I'm certain you will make us all proud."

"You are being ridiculous," his wife said, rolling her eyes. "His competitive nature makes him talk this way. Just play your heart out."

"And while you're at it, win it all for your country," he added.

A sinking feeling overtook. "I will do my best, sir," she said, managing to shoot him a smile.

"I'm certain of that. Here are the photographers. Shall we?"

More pictures. She did her best to show her happy face, but she was reeling. As if she didn't have enough pressure, now her country was depending on her too?

She pivoted, and was relieved to see Tish nearby.

"You okay?" Tish asked.

Help me, she wanted to say. Instead she said, "I think so."

Tish nodded, then grabbed Gemma's hand and walked her back into Johnny's needy arms.

He took her by the waist again as they were escorted to prime seats. Gemma's fingers felt numb and her feet weighed tons. She wanted safe hands—she needed Andre. She needed someone she could trust, certain no one really cared about her. Maybe they cared for her *interests*, but not her.

When the movie started, she drifted. She thought of the beach, the rock climbing, Andre, and his friends. She thought of his lips and his fingers intertwined with hers. His world was so different from this one. She wanted to be a part of that world.

When she came back to the present, she realized two things. She had missed her scenes and more alarmingly, Johnny was holding her hand. When had that happened? She snatched her hand away.

When the movie ended, more pictures and interviews followed. Throughout, she controlled her breathing, moderated her temper. She had to hold on a little longer. The evening was nearly done.

"Ready for the party of the century?" Johnny asked once the interviews were done.

"Sorry?"

"The after party. It'll be a blast. Don't know about you, but I intend to get properly pissed," he said, pulling her by the arm.

"Stop. I can't. I need to get back. I have an early trip for my match." She waved Tish over.

"Yes?" Tish asked, as she reached Gemma.

"I need my car to return home."

"What about the after party? Wesley told me that we should—"

"No," Gemma said, "I have an early trip. Remember?" She needed Tish to be quicker to the take.

When the car came for Gemma, she marched out with her security guards, but someone pulled on her elbow.

"Wait," Johnny said. Her security held back.

"What is it, John?" she asked, exasperated.

He grabbed her face and kissed her hard.

A million thoughts exploded in her head. *Pull away? Push back? Bite his lip?* Instead she froze, her eyes wide and her lips sealed. She stopped breathing. The putrid smell of alcohol, forced on her lips, sparked flares of violence.

When he let go, he stepped back and winked. "Sorry, love," he mouthed, and swaggered backward with a triumphant grin plastered on his face. He spun and strutted back to his entourage.

She kept her face stone-cold, aware the cameras were having a seizure.

Same bedroom, same dress, same floor-to-ceiling mirror. This time Gemma didn't feel beautiful. She felt cheap—used. *I've sold my body and soul.* And for what? This had nothing to do with the game. She was trying hard to focus on the game, but the celebrity world she had walked into was spiraling out of control, with no end in sight.

She undid her hair and stepped out of her dress. She continued to watch her bare reflection in the mirror. The body of an athlete, the life of a runner-up. Tears rolled down her cheeks, smearing her mascara. She didn't utter a sound. Tears streamed, collected at her chin, and dropped one by one.

Gemma stepped into the shower and scrubbed—over and over again, hoping to erase any trace of her past, until her skin felt raw.

CHAPTER EIGHTEEN

"Believe me! The secret of reaping the greatest fruitfulness and the greatest enjoyment from life is to live dangerously!"

~Friedrich Nietzsche

Andre wrapped up the first day of analysis early at Homeland Security. They had made significant inroads in deciphering the latest terrorist communication streams. This would be a critical piece of information once Project Sunrise started in a few weeks.

As grueling as the work was, he liked these types of assignments, because he understood the value. Innocent people's lives depended on them. And even though he dreaded the start of Project Sunrise, deep down, he felt honored to have the intellect and the ability to help the good guys.

He decided to walk the two miles to his hotel to loosen his stiff limbs and induce blood flow. Stagnation was the lightning rod for his headaches. Soon the headache's fault lines would be triggered and eventually debilitate him. Like potholes on the face of the moon, his brain was pockmarked and bruised. He couldn't take much more.

Once in his hotel room, he ordered room service, collapsed on the couch, and took out his phone, searching through his personal e-mail. There was one from Linda with "Gemma" in the subject line. He went to it immediately.

Gemma will be on Access Hollywood at 7:30 p.m. She was at a movie premiere in

London. Didn't realize she was heading back so soon.

He checked his watch. 7:28 p.m. He clicked away at the remote until he found the show. The preview was on, and there she was, a teaser clip. He froze.

Who the hell is that guy?

During the commercials, Andre undressed, eyes fixed on the television set. Anticipation and dread built an unfamiliar sensation in his gut. More teasers came at the end of the first two segments. The second teaser caught him off guard.

"Is it official? Are Gemma and Johnny back together?" the hostess said. A picture from an askew angle of a guy with greased-back hair holding Gemma's face and kissing her.

Blood drained from his face. His heartbeat drummed loudly, muting all other sounds.

He had a sudden warm sensation, which delivered a cold shiver up his spine. He ran his hands through his hair. Was he really surprised? Of course she would have someone. Why wouldn't she? But why lie about it?

He paced the room. Opened his laptop, then closed it. Studied his wallet, then threw it on the bed. He stopped pacing and placed both hands on his temples.

"Is this why she left early?"

He heard the theme music for Access Hollywood and marched back to the TV. On the floor, he crossed his legs, hands to his face, awaiting the worst.

"At the UK premier of Triton Warriors, *box office sensation Johnny Flauto appeared hand in hand with tennis superstar and sex symbol Gemma Lennon..."*

They showed images and video footage of them walking and smiling. He held her. He touched her. Andre felt his face flush.

"Gemma also had an opportunity to talk with the Prime Minister..."

More images followed. He focused on her face and felt somehow detached from the rest of his body, as if coiled in numbness.

"For months we were told Johnny and Gemma were no longer together. Given Gemma's small role in the movie, we wondered if she would make an appearance. Last week, speculation ran rampant when rumors swirled that Gemma would attend the premiere. Instead, she surprised us all when she not only showed up, but showed up with Johnny, hand in hand, appearing very much together. It wasn't until Gemma's departure that we got a glimpse of this breaking news. Cameras captured the two

kissing before she left."

And there it was. Pictures from different angles. A definite kiss.

But something caught his attention. He scooted forward, studying the montage of pictures. The same moment in time from various angles. In one picture, a portion of her face was visible. Her eyes were open.

Why were her eyes open?

Were they open in all the pictures or just this one? Was it because she wasn't expecting him to kiss her in public? Did he catch her off guard, or was it because she was shocked by his action? Andre needed to see more pictures, get different angles, read blogs, analyze the information, and—he spun away from the TV.

What was he thinking? Even if he were willing to fight for her, with everything that was going on, it would be a fool's errand. Definitely best to leave it alone. He would have to get over it. She didn't owe him a thing. This must have been why she held back when they kissed.

He decided to send her a text. That's what a friend would do.

He wrote, *"Saw you on TV. You looked amazing."*

After reviewing the message, he tapped *Send*. He stared at the screen for fifteen minutes, distracted only when room service arrived. His meal sat cooling while he meditated his migraine away.

It was 2:00 a.m. when Gemma received Andre's text. She was awake. Although exhausted, she could not sleep. She read the message over and over again, considering its implications.

What had he actually seen? She didn't dare watch TV, dreading the trash that would be produced. That last kiss—she should have slapped him. That would have made for great TV.

Why had Johnny kissed her? That git had now incited a new round of speculation.

Did Andre see the kiss? The holding? Maybe all he saw was her in that dress. Maybe, but she knew better. This would be the talk of the shows and magazines for days.

What should she do? She cared about what he thought, but it sure didn't sound like he was upset or jealous. He must have seen the whole thing and wasn't fazed by it. Which meant he didn't care.

CHAPTER NINETEEN

"You only live once, but you get to serve twice."

~Author Unknown

Wesley's spacious Chiswick Park office had always been a place of rewards and accomplishments. Today it stood for everything that was wrong with Gemma's life. She shifted slightly in her seat and held Wesley's gaze. "How did this happen?"

Wesley didn't blink, while Tish dropped her gaze to the floor. Gemma wanted to say plenty, but needed to remain calm and measured.

Wesley cleared his throat. "Gemma—"

"I'm struggling to understand," she interrupted, "how this event that was carefully orchestrated by you turned into such a disaster."

"Please calm down," Wesley said.

"I am calm, Wesley. I'm just confused. You're my manager, aren't you? You're supposed to protect me—my brand, as you call it. How could this happen on your watch?"

He blinked.

Her hands threatened to tremble while her left knee shook. Her voice was on the verge of cracking.

"You're jumping to conclusions—" Wesley said

"The only thing I'm jumping to is the front page of the newspaper."

She had woken to a copy of the morning paper with her picture on the cover and Johnny kissing her. It read, *"Love Made in Hollywood Heaven."* A phrase that sounded ominously like Wesley's past proclamations.

Wesley was the one who had put her in this situation. With a drunk in the equation, anything could happen. Anything. He knew that better than anyone else.

She squeezed the armrests of the chair and attempted to speak calmly. "Please cancel all appearances that have nothing to do with tennis. I can't—" the words choked in her throat. She squeezed the bridge of her nose and breathed out slowly. "I can't do this anymore."

"I understand," he said.

"Do you? I'm not so sure. You dragged me back from my vacation for this event that was supposed to fix things. Instead it has put me right in the middle of a public embarrassment." She glanced at Tish. "You guys are my team, right? Mine. If I can't count on you to protect me, then who?" She recalled Andre's words. *If not me, then who?*

"What he did shocked all of us. I called him and gave him a piece of my mind."

"Please don't patronize me."

Wesley flinched. "He was drunk. Maybe a bit more than just drunk. He has issues," Wesley said.

"I don't care about him and his issues. I want my team to focus on one thing. Tennis. No more appearances. No more anything with Johnny. No more making me look like the prized idiot. Please."

Tish's eyes remained downcast, while Wesley stared directly into Gemma's eyes.

"Wesley, crush the innuendoes. Do whatever it takes."

"I'm all over it," he said.

That's exactly what she was afraid of.

Tish and Gemma left Wesley's office together. "Please watch my handbag for a minute?" Gemma asked as she went to the loo.

She just needed to clear her head before facing Tish again. Tish had failed both as an assistant and best friend. Gemma had asked Tish to join her team to avoid these types of situations. She had hoped Tish would know where to hold the line. So much for hoping.

Gemma splashed water on her face, dried off, and then stepped out into the hallway. Tish jumped to her feet and handed Gemma her bag.

"Here you go," she said.

Gemma studied her friend, who was acting erratic. She took her bag and entered the lift without exchanging words.

Gemma hated conflict. She had plenty on the court. She didn't need conflict with her team. She felt an equal measure of anger and regret as they drove to Birmingham. Tish wasn't to blame—not fully. Yet if Tish had considered things from Gemma's perspective, she could have minimized the exposure.

"How was L.A.?" Tish asked.

Tish was trying to break the ice that pervaded the backseat of the car. Gemma would accept the olive branch. "It was nice."

"Do anything interesting? Go anywhere?"

Gemma glanced at her. Tish seemed a bit too interested. "Went to the beach."

"The beach? Wow, that's a personal breakthrough. Thus far, a beach home hasn't meant use of the actual beach. What brought this on?"

Something was definitely up. "I met up with some people and hung out with them."

Tish shifted in her seat. "You? Met some people and hung out? Who?"

"Friends of someone I know."

"In L.A.? Anyone I know?"

"Yes."

"Who?"

"Andre. From Paris, last week." There, she said it. Saying his name sparked a cut in her. She wanted to be with him. Right now.

"Andre? The 'Merican?"

"That's the one."

"You barely know him. Did I miss something?"

"We happened to be on the same flight to L.A. and we spoke. So we hung out." It felt like months had passed since she had spoken to him last. She had to explain Johnny before Andre assumed the worst.

"He happened to be on the same flight with you? Interesting coincidence. G, it's not like you to meet someone and then go off with them. Please be careful. A lot of suspicious people out there will want to use you for their personal benefit. You know this."

"Not him. He's not that type."

"And you think you can identify *that* type?"

Gemma faced Tish and peered directly in her eyes. "I'm learning to read people. I'm getting pretty good at it."

Gemma leaned back and pulled her mobile. Something was wrong. She had been reading an article before the meeting with Wesley. But her phone was now on the calendar app. She glanced at Tish. Had she been snooping through her e-mails and texts when Gemma went to the loo? That was nothing new. Tish regularly cleaned up the mess in Gemma's contacts and calendar. Tish must have read her texts. She scanned the ones she had exchanged with Andre. Nothing juicy, but enough to possibly pique Tish's curiosity. Which explained her earlier interrogation about L.A. She had been fishing for more.

"Bedric is pissed, by the way," Tish offered.

Gemma could only imagine. "Did he say something specific?"

"When I told him we're driving down together, he said he was happy for us."

"Ugh. I may have to listen to all his coaching advice for the next couple of days to win his favor again."

Tish faced Gemma. "I've noticed sometimes you argue with him over tactics or training."

"Sure," Gemma said. "He's not always right."

Tish went silent. "How do you know? What I mean is, when do you take his advice, and when do you listen to your instinct? He's the expert after all, isn't he?"

Gemma glanced at Tish. "The truth is you don't know."

"Then how do you choose if you should listen to him, or tell him to bugger off?"

"Sometimes the only way to know is to try it on. Sometimes it's listening to your gut because logic and planning are not always right." Andre's face, his smile clouded her vision. "Sometimes you have to go with your heart."

Tish leaned back. "Try it on. If not, listen to your heart. And then have the courage to say he's full of crap if you disagree," she recited, almost to herself.

"And if that doesn't work, I use guerrilla tactics. Which I may need to resort to with Bedric. Do you recall which Belgium chocolate brand he fancied?"

Tish grinned. "All taken care of. I have half a dozen of his favorite bars in my bag."

"Brilliant. I need more of that type of thinking from you."

Andre studied the flight schedules to Heathrow. He had attempted to convince himself that this turn of events was for the best. But he was far too smart for that. He knew without Gemma, there was an absence in his life. It seemed improbable that after only a few encounters he felt so strongly about her, but there it was. She'd screwed it all up. She had dug a space for herself in his life, and the thought of some nitwit, greasy-haired actor spending time with her was—to be blunt—annoying.

He would not be a spectator. He could wait it out, but he had an uneasy feeling about the effects of time and distance, particularly with his upcoming assignment. It was not like him to take a backseat and let things happen. But he wasn't a pest either, running after the girl. He would be patient for a day or two. She was preparing for her tournament. Better than most, he understood the space a professional needed. He would give her a couple of days. For now.

His cell phone chimed as if in response to his sentiment. A reply text message from Gemma to the text he had sent the night before.

"*Thanks.*"

That's all it said. That's all she gave him.

Gemma wrote various drafts before she sent the text.

"*Call me, I want to talk,*" and, "*I miss our time at the beach, call me,*" and, "*I've fallen for you, you American bastard.*"

But when she caught sight of Tish's wandering eyeballs, she had written the first thing that had come to mind and hit *Send*. Now, in retrospect, she hoped the message wouldn't come across as dry or crass.

She dropped her phone in her bag and decided a few days of silence would be good for both of them. Sometimes distance and time clarified things. And sometimes they screwed up everything.

By early afternoon, Andre's migraine had gotten progressively worse. His doctor had told him to manage the pressures surrounding his life. Great advice.

The phone call with his dad earlier had also contributed greatly. Another head-butting session over his deteriorating relationship with his niece and sister-in-law. The man was as obstinate as a cinder block.

But the good news didn't stop there.

He stepped outside the Homeland Security facility to catch fresh air and try to understand what he had just heard over lunch from the director of the department.

"Your office insisted on an early start. We were told you had another engagement at the end of the week."

Andre didn't have any other engagements on his calendar. That had been a lie. It was at best two days of work, unnecessary for an immediate start. He could've had one more day of rest. Why had Roger forced the issue?

Andre's phone rang. It was Gemma.

Here we go. He wanted to show detachment and lack of care, but when he tapped the *Answer* icon, the smile that broke out on his face was uncontrollable. "Hi, Gem."

"Did I catch you at a bad time? Are you busy?"

"Perfect time." Urgency laced her voice, but she hesitated, the silence spreading like an unbreachable crevasse. "How are you, Gem?"

"I guess it depends. The movie premiere... how much of it did you catch?"

He closed his eyes and spoke. "Are you and Greasy-Hair-Guy together?"

"If I just said no, would you believe me? Would that be enough?"

"You don't owe me an explanation—"

"Please answer me. If I said no, would you believe me?"

"Of course."

More silence, then a muffled sound. "In that case, I'll tell you everything."

She told him about their past relationship, about Australia, about their breakup, and the plan to appear as friends to minimize the media fall-out.

"And the kiss?" he asked. "I can't imagine that was part of the plan."

"That was not a kiss. That was a drunk who caught me off guard."

"Why would a prominent actor do something so careless?"

"I don't know. Publicity? Fried brain cells? Who knows? What I do know is I felt humiliated, betrayed."

"Betrayed? By him?"

"By him, by my team, by everyone who's conspiring against me. And now the press are having a field day. The celebrity rags love it because it's fresh content, and the sports press are browbeating me because it's more of the same."

"They're all idiots. If they'd been looking, or if they cared, they would've seen something was wrong."

"Okay, what are you talking about?"

"When we kissed, your eyes were closed, you were in the moment. With Greasy-Hair-Guy, your eyes were wide open. Definitely not in the moment. Your eyes showed no joy."

Silence. "There is no joy when a drunk forces himself on me."

"Next time, consider kneeing said drunk in the balls."

A delicious laugh escaped her. "I'll keep that in mind."

"Forget him. What's the situation with the paparazzi?" The story about Australia had put a new fear in him. They were not just a nuisance; they were dangerous.

"I've had to increase the security team around my home. They found some asshole living in one of my trees. Can you believe it?"

"I'm thinking of taking a trip to the UK—for just a couple of days. What do you think?" He wanted to be there, to shelter her like he had in L.A.

She sniffled. "I'd love to see you again, but please don't. I need to focus on the tournament. These are critical days as I prepare for Wimbledon. With the right momentum, I should be able to peak at Wimbledon. I love that you would do that for me, but I need to focus on what's really important."

His chest went warm.

"Wait. That came out wrong. What I meant—"

"You don't have to explain. I understand what you meant."

He should not have been surprised or hurt. Tennis was the priority, not their silly little nothing. He would have to understand. As much as the words stung, he would accept it.

"Look, I'll return to L.A. soon after Wimbledon. Let's plan for that, okay? We'll get coffee again."

But would he be there? "Sounds great," he said, knowing he'd probably be in military headquarters in various locations around the world. "Coffee, croissant, and Nutella. But no sharing this time. We'll get two." That breakfast would not happen for a good four months from now. How much would have changed by then? "Go and rest. Win, and the sports press will pipe down quickly."

"Thanks, Andre. For being there."

"I'm only a call away."

"You know, you're not bad for an American. I may need to reconsider my long-held beliefs."

"Gem, knock 'em dead."

"I'll knee them in the bullocks, as you so aptly recommended. Cheers," she said, and hung up.

"I miss you," he told the dead connection.

CHAPTER TWENTY

"I let my racquet do the talking."

~Pete Sampras

On Friday morning, Gemma woke determined to win the Aegon Classic.

She could have been smart and sat out this tournament, waited for Wimbledon, saving her strength and minimizing the wear and tear. But she had been out of tournament play for months, and her mental agility and timing improved by continually competing against those who wanted to defeat her. Practice was never enough. She needed to be on the court, fighting the fight, absorbing the strong serves, returning, and digging out the impossible plays.

Aegon and Topshelf Open were the path to winning her first Grand Slam. Unlike the Australian Open, where she had choked, in the French she had fought a good fight. The game turned with momentum. And momentum was on her side.

Wonder what he's doing now? She wished thoughts of Andre wouldn't just creep up on her. One day with him had left a permanent mark on her.

The first round match ended faster than it started. Gemma's warm up with her hitting coach had proven to be more challenging. The match ended in less than forty minutes. She won in straight sets and felt stronger than ever.

"We should withdraw from the Topshelf Open," Bedric said when she wrapped up interviews. "You don't need to compete in back-to-back tournaments before Wimbledon."

"You may be right. Ask me again if we win the third round match."

But the second and third rounds were barely competitive. She was a machine, breaking service against her opponents, not allowing them to win points even when they served. Grass was her favorite court surface. And it showed.

"I am going to withdraw you from Topshelf," Bedric said.

"Let's discuss it if I win the quarterfinal match."

She put on a clinic at the quarterfinal match, not conceding one game. She won 6-0, 6-0 and the buzz in the circuit was that Gemma had the potential to be the spoiler or dark-horse at Wimbledon. She didn't care for what the odd-makers had to say.

"Gemma, about Topshelf—" Bedric started.

"I was going to ask you about that. When were you planning on withdrawing me? You are my coach after all. You should be the one thinking of these things." She grinned. Bedric didn't bother arguing.

The night before the semifinal match, an interviewer stumped her.

"What do you think of Johnny Flauto's comment? Do you want to say something to him?" the interviewer asked, then flashed an all-tooth smile.

Gemma blinked. "Since I don't know what you're talking about, I'll have to say no comment."

"Would you like me to tell you?" More all-tooth smile.

"No, thank you."

Although she won the semifinal match, for the first time in the tournament, she had to work a bit harder to break service against her opponent. She did win, and that's what mattered, but she committed over two dozen unforced errors. She knew her final match against Petra would not be as forgiving. Gemma would have to be at her best.

During the press conference, a question stopped her in place.

"Gemma, rumors are that Johnny will be coming to your final match. Anything you'd care to share?"

She hesitated, wishing she could throw her water bottle at the journalist. Instead she said, "It is always a treat when my friends come to my matches."

Once in her room, she searched the net and found an interview with Johnny.

"No, I've been staying away from her matches. Focus is key for her as you can imagine. I don't want anyone to blame me if something goes wrong. Particularly Gemma. She would hurt me." Then he laughed like a hyena.

She slammed the laptop closed. Now was not the time to get angry. She would not get derailed.

Her concern was Andre. How would he interpret this news? She had not spoken to him in days. She had planned to talk to Andre after the tournament. But she felt it important to talk to him now in case he was getting suspicious. If she was being honest, she also wanted to call because she missed him and his calming voice. Like an addict, she wanted to feel his energy again.

"Hey you," she said.

"Hi, Gem." God, how she loved that nickname. "Is everything all right?" he asked.

"Just wanted to say hi. How are you?"

"Livin' the dream."

"That good?"

"Not just good, fan-freakin'-tastic. Never mind. I've been watching your games. Did you know there's a channel just for tennis? It's called the Tennis Channel. Did you know about this? Because you're on it all the time."

"Welcome to the modern ages, love."

"You're kicking some major ass out there."

"I've done well, but tomorrow's match will be tougher."

"Can't wait. I love watching you fight like that. The grunts, the screams—"

"You enjoy that do you? Grunting and screaming."

"Ahh—wait—I mean the... you know—the fighting spirit, and—"

"Oh, shut it. You can't even clean up properly."

"How's everything else? How are you holding up?"

She closed her eyes, convinced he would ask about Johnny. "I don't have a donkey's care about anything else. I have a tournament in my hands. All the other shit is created solely for the entertainment of daft monkeys. Those cur dogs can entertain themselves with their own filth like the git pigs they are."

"That was the cleanest cuss out I've ever heard. You Brits are so civilized. I sometimes think you wish you could curse like a drunken sailor with the exception that you probably don't get drunk, nor much of a sailor given your seasickness issue."

"You'll need to visit my hometown someday and hear how my mates curse. Your cute little ears would turn red."

"You think my ears are cute?"

"In a not-large-like-an-elephant's sort of way. Sure."

"I see. English is obviously not my strongest language. That sounded like a veiled insult. It must be a Brit thing."

"Must be." Silence. "Andre, thank you for being there. It means a lot. Your silly jokes, even those that aren't funny, help."

"There it is again. It's almost a compliment. Amazing how when a Brit puts you down it sounds so pretty and benign."

"It's the civilized English versus what you call American."

They both laughed, and when the laughter ended a comfortable silence hovered. Gemma was lying on her bed, her stuffed dog in hand, the phone gently resting on her ear.

"You sounded a bit tired when you answered the phone, Andre. Are you well?"

"Headache. I have too many things on my mind, and my brain is fighting back."

Too many things on his mind? Like maybe Johnny?

"I'll be fine."

But she didn't hear a lot of resolve in his tone. "You need a vacation."

He laughed dramatically. "Yeah, one of these days. Don't worry about me. Keep your focus on the game. Speaking of the game, I've noticed an interesting pattern with your style of play."

"Oh?"

"You are an aggressive player. You strike with a killer's instinct, always going for winning shots. Down the line, or one ace after another."

"I'm proud of you Andre. You've learned a lot. And they say TV has no redeeming value."

"Here's what's interesting to me. You go for perfection. Highlight type of footage. Do you have to go for the winning shot?"

"Is there another option?"

"Make your opponent make a mistake. Unforced errors seems to be a critical indicator. You are far more powerful and considerably more fit than the opponents you play. You can probably grind them, exhaust them, frustrate them into making mistakes."

"Interesting."

"Anyway, what the hell do I know, right? Just something I thought I'd share with you. Go. You need to get rest. And remember I'm watching the games live. Smile once in a while, so I know you're not a machine."

"I do too smile."

"I mean smile externally, so the rest of us can share your joy."

"Okay, fine. And you get off your 'too many things on my mind' story. It's unbecoming for a handsome man to sound so drained."

"You think I'm handsome?"

"Cheers," she said, and ended the call. "I think you're very handsome, you silly man," she spoke to her dead phone. "And thank you for not asking about Johnny."

Game day. And for once, with Andre's voice still warm in her ears, she was not nervous.

"Miss Lennon, it's time," the tournament coordinator said.

She drained her water bottle then tossed it into the waste bin. The crew in the locker room jumped into activity around her. She moved through them and observed how they moved, fidgeted, got something, got nothing. Time seemed to slow. Her stride was both long and purposeful.

When she stepped onto the court, the roar lifted her hair. When the cheers finally subsided, she noticed a television camera directly on her. She peered into the lens and delivered her best smile and winked. The crowd erupted, but she had only one thought on her mind as she took her side. Were that smile and wink good enough for Andre?

Today she felt rested, mind and body—and heart. But before the match started, she saw a familiar face sitting next to Wesley and Tish. Johnny Flauto.

Fueled by anger, Gemma fought mercilessly in the first set. She hit harder than she had to, she yelled with more aggression than was typical for her, and she went after every ball like it was her last.

She won the first set 6-1.

With a 4-1 lead in the second set, the tournament championship was in hand.

Petra delivered a precise and flat cross-court return on Gemma's first serve.

Leave it, Gemma thought for an instant, but a burning drive told her to leave nothing out there. Gemma sprinted and stretched to slap the ball quickly off the rise. When her right foot hit the grass, something popped in her leg. Her knee buckled, and she collapsed to the grass. With both hands, she squeezed her right leg, writhing on the floor, vacillating between pain and fear.

A jolt of sharp pain shot through her inner thigh, up her spine to her neck and then back to her ankle. Like an electric shock, the shooting pain ping-ponged through her body. She whimpered, trying her best to subdue the agony.

A tendon? No! No! Don't let it end like this.

Sweat broke out across her body, and warm numbness danced in her toes. Tears and perspiration were one and the same.

The stadium's collective voice silenced. She shut her eyes and heard the commotion around her, but her entire focus was on not letting the pain and fear defeat her. *Not like this.* In that instant, voices converted to waves. One wave after another, breaking against the coast, against the jagged rocks. Then she pictured his smile.

She opened her eyes. The match medic was talking to her. With his help, she hobbled over to her seat. The medic taped her thigh as tight as possible without constricting blood flow.

"You need to have this examined. It is probably best to withdraw—"

"Thank you. I'm fine."

After a brief hesitation, he nodded then walked away.

She squeezed the towel into her face. Was this it? The injury that would forever remove her chances of winning a Grand Slam?

She rose and limped to her baseline. The crowd applauded and cheered. *Gemma! Gemma! Gemma!*

She had to somehow make it through the match. She recalled something Andre had told her. *The Graceful Dance of the Matador.* The utmost amount of presence with the least amount of effort. Control, focus, and ball placement. She had to treat each shot like it was the last shot she'd take.

She had to hold her serve twice to win the match. The utmost amount of focus on the perfect serve and the least amount of effort on the court. She had to plan ahead. Like chess, she had to consider all the options and possibilities, taking advantage of her ability to play with both left and right hands. One of her gifts she seldom exploited.

Gemma! Gemma! Gemma!

Then another thought. *Force them to make mistakes.* She would ride the wave, step around the bull. She was channeling Andre to get her through the match. His voice was in her head.

She scanned the fans, all on their feet, cheering for her. She felt... love. She soaked it all in, then studied Petra, awaiting Gemma's serve.

Done.

The chatter in the stadium and in her head disappeared. She received three balls, chose the right one, then stepped up to the baseline.

Focus. Toss. Hammer.

She bounced the ball five times—always five—then tossed the ball high above. The next thing she heard was the sound of her racquet cutting through the air.

Every point was fought with the determination of a gladiator—neither willing to concede anything. Petra, like a shark, tasted the blood and fought harder than ever. Drop shots, slices, side to side, anything to force Gemma to move. But Gemma didn't bite on those. She let them go. She had the lead. All she had to do was hold the serve twice to win the match.

Thirty excruciating minutes later, she had squeezed out one more game, but had conceded four games to Petra in the process. Leading the set at 5-4, she was winning the sixth game, 40-30. Set point. Match Point. Championship point. It was her serve.

She closed her eyes, the cheers reverberating throughout the stadium.

Done.

She thought of Andre and breathed deep. Her eyes still closed, she tossed the ball up, popped open her eyes, and bore in on the spinning ball. She yelled louder than she had ever yelled and tore her racquet through the wind. The ball left an explosion of yellow fur in the air before it went straight down the middle, caught the outside line, then curved away from Petra's outstretched racquet.

Ace.

"Game, set, match, and championship," declared the umpire.

The crowd erupted.

Gemma collapsed on the grass in tears, pumping her fists.

The standing ovation and cheers went on for what seemed like days. The raw emotion drowned out everything else. This was the best she had felt throughout a tournament. A bittersweet victory. She didn't know the extent of her injury, but the pain was real. Could she pull this off at Wimbledon? She knew one thing for sure; Andre was with her. He had been her inspiration—her lucky charm.

The camera was on her. She stared straight at the camera lens and sent a message she hoped both Andre and Johnny would understand in no uncertain terms.

She pointed to the camera, kissed her fingertips, then blew the camera a kiss. She was talking to Andre, not Johnny fucking Flauto.

CHAPTER TWENTY-ONE

*"The time your game is most vulnerable is when you're
ahead; never let up."*

~Rod Lever

The traditional champagne celebration followed the award ceremony. Gemma wanted to respect the club's tradition, but all she thought of was getting home and calling Andre. While here, she would address a few open matters.

"Tish," she said, "do you have a minute?"

"Miss Champion," Tish said, "what can I do for you?"

"Defend me from the sharks, don't feed me to them."

Tish's face went pale. "What are you talking about? I—"

"I need you with me. Don't get wrapped up with the celebrity bullshit."

"What—?"

"At the premiere with Johnny, I needed your help, I didn't get it. Wesley has a million ideas, but they are not consistent with what I want. I need you to stop things before they spin out of control."

"Sorry, G."

"Also, why didn't you warn me about Johnny coming to the match?"

"I didn't know. I found out when he showed up in our seats."

Gemma wanted to believe her.

"It's the honest truth, G. I am sorry."

149

"Friends should never have to apologize," Gemma said then hugged her and prayed Tish was still salvageable. Once one had tasted what was available in the circle of the rich and famous, letting go was difficult. And it was harder to remember what grounded you in the first place.

Minutes later, Bedric approached Gemma. "You need to get off your feet," he said.

"I'm nearly done here."

"I have contacted the best therapist. We will start tomorrow morning."

"Couldn't we take a day off?"

"Do you trust me?"

She studied his eyes. "Yes, of course."

"Then just trust me. There is no time to waste. We have only one week. You need to start tomorrow morning to understand if it is a strain or more serious."

"Fine, tomorrow morning."

She heard the commotion then saw the source. Johnny and his crew had made a grand entrance. When they made eye contact, he flaunted a big Hollywood-smile and walked toward her, his arms outstretched.

"Keep your distance from him," Bedric whispered. "You promised me when you decided to return."

She studied him. "Do you trust me?"

"Most of the time."

She winked then strode toward Johnny, producing a faint smile. Just as he prepared to embrace her, she held him back with an outstretched arm. Smile on her lips, she leaned in and whispered in his ear.

"If you kiss me, touch me, or give another interview where you imply there's something between us, I'll drive your balls up into your throat."

She stepped back, shook his hand and spun away. She strode up to Bedric and squeezed his arm. He almost smiled.

One conversation left. She found him at the bar just as he received a glass of champagne.

"Wesley, can we talk?"

"You don't need to ask. I'm at your disposal."

"I love you like a brother, but if you ever pull something like this Johnny shit again, that'll be the end of our relationship. I want to be clear. I am indeed threatening you. Don't fuck with me."

The celebration was over. She was done with the interviews, the pictures, and the handshakes. She was finally home, tucked in bed and slowly drifting, while talking to the one voice that was her sanctuary.

"What are the doctors saying?" Andre asked.

"We'll know more tomorrow, but initial prognosis is a strained hamstring. I need rest and physical therapy."

"But when…?" he started then stopped.

"Will I be ready for Wimbledon? I think I'll be ready. With proper rest and therapy it should all work out. I have a full week to dedicate for rest and rehabilitation."

"Listen to your body. It never lies."

No, she thought, *my body does not lie.*

"By the way, I loved the little message you sent after you won. It made my day."

"Glad you caught that. The TV shows were thrown for a loop with that one."

"How so?"

"They were confused. After all, if that idiot Flauto is in the stadium, *to whom did Gemma send a kiss?* Bloody morons."

"So you admit you sent me a kiss."

"I'm not admitting anything.'"

"You can't concede anything, can you?" He chuckled. "I have a theory about you."

"And what's that?"

"For you, everything looks like competition."

She went silent. Her immediate reaction was to refute it, but isn't that what a competitive person would do? "Hmm," she said instead.

"And I get that. All these years you've focused on winning. You've had to beat both your competition and your own objectives. Things are either going to end in a win or a loss."

"True," she mused.

"Just know this: when it comes to me, you can't lose. I'm here for you whenever you need me."

The excitement of the championship match in the morning and the conversation with Gemma in the afternoon left Andre drained. He wished he had been there with her.

An early morning meeting had been scheduled for the next day at M&T. The thought of yet another unplanned trip somewhere in the world drained him of the joy he was feeling. There were no breaks. In three weeks, Project Sunrise would begin. But for M&T, every day was an opportunity to cash in.

His phone rang. It was the doorman.

"Courier for you Dr. Reyes," he said.

"Courier? On a Sunday? I wasn't expecting anything. Legitimate?"

"Yes, sir."

The courier handed him a manila envelope, then left. Andre opened the envelope and placed the contents on the kitchen counter. He stared at them for a few moments.

His cell phone chimed—a text message from Gemma. He read it, then studied the papers splayed across his countertop: Virgin Atlantic tickets to Heathrow, hotel confirmation at the Kensington Hilton in London, and an all access pass to Wimbledon.

He read her message again. *"What do you say? One week with me, then two weeks at Wimbledon. You said you'd be there for me if I ever needed you. I need you."*

PART III

ACE

Recreational tennis players use the serve simply to initiate the point. For advanced players, the serve is a declaration of power. Aggressive players will often attempt a winning shot with their serve. A winning serve, untouched by the opponent is called an "ace."

~Tennis Basics

CHAPTER TWENTY-TWO

"Do what you feel in your heart to be right."

~Eleanor Roosevelt

Roger Trutt's office would've been the envy of any Fortune 100 CEO. Each time Andre entered, the panoramic 270-degree view of Downtown Los Angeles caught his breath. The floor-to-ceiling glass walls invited natural light, accenting the cherry wood furniture, which glistened like fine china. The office epitomized power. Just over a year ago, Andre had dreamt of the day this would be his office. So much had changed in twelve months.

"But I don't understand. Is everything okay?" Roger asked.

"Yes, everything is fine. I need some personal time before the start of Project Sunrise. I'll be available for calls, but for the next three weeks I'll be out of the country."

Roger loosened his tie, walked over to his fully equipped bar, and prepared a scotch on the rocks. Interesting choice for breakfast.

"I'm not comfortable with this. I was about to discuss a new project, send you to a site visit for tomorrow, and you drop this. Frankly, this is unprofessional and poorly timed."

Andre uncrossed his legs and straightened, no longer comfortable in the plush leather sofa. "Unprofessional? Just last week you asked me to cancel my vacation because of the Homeland Security project. A project we didn't need to rush, as it turned out. But we rushed it anyway."

"I explained the reasons. We expected another engagement at the end of the week. I thought you understood."

"I did. I do. I've always understood. To date, I have yet to take a vacation because they all had to be adjusted."

Roger sipped his drink as he strolled toward Andre, his eyes shifting, calculating. Then the corner of his lips lifted. Roger sat next to Andre. "Andre," Roger said as he placed his plump fingers, riddled with age spots, on Andre's shoulder, "look here, son. You have my word as soon as this next engagement is complete, we will honor your vacation plans. In fact, you can use the company yacht. Maybe take a trip to Mexico? You and your friends? Rest for a few days before Project Sunrise."

"I don't need the company yacht. I don't see why this is an issue. I have to leave, but I'll be available for urgent calls. I have never abandoned clients in need, and I'm not starting now. As for this new client, there are other consultants here. Some who I've personally trained."

"This change will place M&T in a bad predicament with this client," Roger said as he wiped his brow. "Let's get the initial discussion taken care of this week. Take next week off and then we can regroup the week after. What do you say, son?" Roger showed his unnaturally white teeth.

"As reasonable as that sounds, it is impossibly unreasonable. My flight leaves in a few hours."

Roger's face froze. Andre would wait it out. The best negotiation tactic was complete silence.

"We need this client. And with Sunrise coming, we will not be able to address their needs for three, four, maybe five months. We may even lose the client, but I will call them and explain." He squeezed Andre's shoulder.

"Thank you," Andre said as he rose, then walked to the door.

"Andre," Roger said.

Andre turned, facing Roger.

"I hope whatever you're doing is worth it. I don't have to remind you that you have an obligation to this company. A contractual obligation."

"I'm taking a vacation, not quitting."

Roger chuckled. "I'm sure you wouldn't do that. You have a good thing here—and we do too, admittedly. All I'm saying is, stay focused. Don't get distracted. Particularly now, weeks before a critical project. It's in all of our best interest."

CHAPTER TWENTY-THREE

"God will not look you over for a medal, degrees or diplomas, but for scars."

~Elbert Hubbard

Passengers flying upper class on Virgin Atlantic quickly forgot they were in a tin box flying over the Atlantic, lugging 20,000 gallons of fuel. Everything was designed with comfort and luxury in mind. But Andre was restless and spent the first five hours at the bar. He expected to arrive in London by early evening. He should have taken a nap, but too much was on his mind.

Roger's reaction bothered him. He had expected a bit of hesitation, but Roger came out swinging, confirming Andre's suspicions. M&T would play hardball now that Andre had shown lack of commitment to his career. He'd seen it with other consultants. They were placed on back-to-back flights, assigned to impossible projects, pushed to the limit until the consultant quit or failed, breaching the contract. Was that why Roger had insisted on a trip to D.C. even though Andre had a planned vacation? Had Roger already been suspicious? If so, these tactics were too little too late. Six months was nothing. Of course, they could fire him if they showed cause, in which case Andre would forfeit his bonus. But Andre was too smart to do something stupid.

A car service greeted Andre at the airport. As he entered the car he scanned around, capturing and etching all the faces around him. He committed crowds to memory, particularly when traveling. Last time he'd been in London, things had gotten a bit dicey. His work on tracking terrorist cells had earned him a tail. With the help of the Metropolitan Police Service, better known as New Scotland Yard, all had ended well, but he was advised to be cautious. That had been six months ago. But the unsettling feeling of being stalked had not left him.

A light drizzle gave the world a fresh and clean look—a new beginning—and the ever-present London traffic confirmed some things would never change. Double-decker buses, most half-full, filled the streets. Bicycles raced through the tight paths, snaking between cars, through traffic, cutting off buses, and endangering pedestrians. Thousands walked, going somewhere—getting nowhere.

Nothing had changed.

When he checked in at the Kensington Hilton, he found a sealed envelope in his suite.

Andre,

If you're up to it, text me and we can meet.

Cheers,

Gem

He grabbed his cell phone and wrote, *"Give me thirty to shower and change. Send me your coordinates. I'll meet you wherever."*

After the shower, he read the new message:

"Wrapping up interviews. I'll send my car to get you."

Andre stepped off the elevator and approached the front desk. He automatically ingested the scene in the hotel lobby. He did a double take on a man who whirled and walked away. Andre tried to see the man's face, but an older man in a suit walked up to him.

"Mr. Reyes?" he asked.

"Yes?"

"I am Glen Aldridge. Miss Lennon asked me to collect you. Are you ready, sir?"

Andre glanced once again, but the man was gone. *Coffee shop, Malibu, now here. I'm officially losing it,* he thought.

They went to the mecca of tennis and entered the All England Lawn

Tennis Club through the special access entrance. When they parked, Andre grabbed the door handle, ready to step out.

"Sir," Glen said, "Miss Lennon asked us to wait for her in the car. They will join us momentarily."

"They?"

"Yes, Miss Lennon and her assistant, Miss Nigist."

Too bad. He would have preferred some alone time. Andre considered the light drizzle for an instant before he opened the door. "I'll be outside."

"Sir, shall I get you an umbrella?"

"No, thanks." He stepped out.

He faced the sky, welcoming the mist. He took a deep breath and exhaled, arms hanging at his sides. Fresh air always released the tension. Tension meant headaches.

"What the hell do you think you're doing?"

He opened his eyes and saw Gemma walking toward him, Tish next to her.

"I'm enjoying the fresh air."

"It's raining." Her smile brightened her eyes.

He opened his arms wide. She hesitantly stepped into his embrace, which covered her completely. Her body language communicated the unstated—be careful when we're in public. "It's great to see you," he whispered. His heartbeat picked up, playing a rhythm he had been looking forward to.

She pulled back a little and gazed up at him. "Thank you for coming. Now get in before you get pneumonia."

"Hello, Mr. Andre," Tish said, squinting through the light drizzle, "I hope the details of your trip were handled to your satisfaction?"

"Thanks for arranging everything. It's been perfect."

"Come on you two," Gemma said.

"Well, well, well. If it isn't the world famous Gemma Lennon." A voice with a Germanic accent came from behind them.

They all spun. A tall man in his mid-to-late twenties stood with arms crossed, his sweat pants and jacket practically spray-painted on his hard body. He smiled, but his eyes betrayed him. He was not a friend.

"Oh no," Tish whispered. "Georg."

The guy took a step toward Gemma; Andre immediately moved to intercept.

"Aren't you going to say hello?" Georg asked.

"No," Gemma said, her voice steady, but tension strained the corners of her eyes.

Andre stepped between them. He and Georg were the same height. "Do you know him?" Andre asked, his eyes trained on the man.

"Of course she knows me, pal. We go way back." He smirked. Two feet separated them.

Andre studied Georg, awaiting any movement he perceived as threatening. Instead, Georg's eyes widened. At that instant, Andre sensed motion from his left side.

Gemma delivered an unforgiving uppercut directly to Georg's chin. The animal strength behind the punch lifted Georg off his feet. He stumbled back, then slipped on the wet floor and fell.

Andre first grinned with absolute excitement. Then he stepped in front of Gemma, stopping her from going after Georg for more. She struggled behind Andre's extended arms, while he tried to keep an eye on Georg.

"You bitch!" Georg yelled.

"Gemma, get over here," Tish demanded as she and Glen grabbed Gemma's flailing arms and pulled her toward the car.

Andre moved toward Georg, who spat blood, then charged forward.

In one motion, Andre crouched and struck Georg's solar plexus with an open palm. The wind whooshed from Georg's lungs. Andre grabbed Georg's hand and spun him around. Now behind Georg, he locked his arm at an impossible angle and squeezed the man's neck. Georg's knees buckled. He dropped to the floor.

Georg knelt on the floor, his head bowing down to Gemma.

Andre stooped and spoke in Georg's ear. "Keep your distance. Next time, you'll eat cement."

Georg remained on the wet floor, unmoving.

Andre stepped up to Gemma, who pulled her arms free of Glen and Tish.

"You okay?"

Venomous anger poured from her bloodshot eyes. Her breathing labored. She nodded.

"Nice upper cut."

"I kicked his ass, didn't I?" A tear slid down her cheek.

"Come on, let's get out of here," Andre said, holding her tight as they walked back to the car.

Tish was not smiling. "I hope no one got this on film. Wesley will croak over this one."

Glen opened her door. "Can I get you anything, ma'am?" He seemed shaken up.

"Ice," Andre said as he studied her reddening knuckles. "She'll need ice for her hand."

Within seconds Glen prepared an ice pack, then they drove off.

Gemma shifted toward Andre and grabbed his hand. "Did you break him?"

"No, just made him wet his pants."

"Good," she said. A small shiver shook her. "I don't know what it was you did, but that was some serious crap."

"Who was that guy?" he asked.

"An asshole," she said.

"Anything you want to tell me?"

"No, not now." Gemma dropped her eyes, adjusting the ice pack on her knuckles.

"Let me look at that," he said and took her hand, lightly touching the swollen areas. "You'll survive. But I'd recommend a cooler head. Does she always get into fights?" he asked Tish.

"No, absolutely not. I don't know what the hell came over her." She spun to Gemma, glaring. "Do you know the media mess this could cause? The press will have a field day. You don't need this, G."

"No one saw anything," Gemma said.

"She's right, Gem. You don't need this."

Gemma rolled her eyes.

Glen opened the privacy window. "Where to, ma'am?"

"I'm famished," she said, turning to Andre. "Do you want to eat?"

He shook his head in disbelief. "Sure, why not."

"Take us to Maurice's," she said.

"Again?" Tish said.

"Bad food?" Andre asked.

"It's best we pretend Tish isn't here. Maurice has the best pizza in London. More importantly, he lets me in from the back entrance and has a private room."

"Yes," Tish said, "like criminals on the run."

Andre studied Gemma. "That bad?"

"It's almost comical now. Particularly with my injury. There's apparently a large bounty for any photographer who can get a picture of me in a wheelchair. And if I had been in one, someone would have been wealthy by now because those bastards seem to know where I'm going even before I've decided."

"How's that possible?"

"She's exaggerating," Tish said.

Gemma glared at Tish.

"Okay… how's your therapy coming along?" Andre asked.

"Fantastic, thankfully. The injury was significantly less traumatic than originally diagnosed. I'll be able to play a few practice rounds tomorrow to test my strength."

"That is excellent news."

"She's a machine," Tish said. "She'll fight through anything. Stubborn as a mule, this one."

Gemma turned to Andre. "If you're looking for a smartass assistant, please tell me. This one," she said, pointing to Tish, "will be available very soon. Although I must warn you, she is more ass than smart."

Gemma had been right—the food was divine. An exquisite blend of French dough mastery, Italian sauces, and Asian spices. This restaurant had it all. They even had fresh *Lahmajoun*, or what his grandmother, who was of Armenian descent, called Armenian Pizza.

"Small world, isn't it?" Tish said, glancing at Andre. "You two bumping into each other at the airport and then on the same flight to Los Angeles?"

"I still think she's stalking me. On the other hand, maybe it was predestined. Depends on what you choose to believe," Andre said.

"What do you believe?" Gemma asked.

"I believe all the planning, preparation, and dreaming sometimes makes no difference. In other words, anything can happen at any time.

Does that mean everything in life is random? Is coincidence a way of life? Maybe. Then again, in chess, the masters know how the game will end after the first few moves are played."

"I've heard that before. Why's that?" Tish asked.

"In chess, each move has a finite number of counter moves, and most are predictable. The great ones can practically fast-forward the game through its various permutations and predict what will happen next. In life, as in chess, we can also guess what our actions may cause down the line."

"But chess has rules," Gemma said.

"You're right. And typically, unlike in the game of life, no one makes unreasonable moves. The challenge is everything we do sets off countless events, building on trillions of events that happened in the past, unnoticed or forgotten. But for argument's sake, imagine if we could calculate and track every little detail, then maybe we could fast-forward to see what would happen next. Of course, we don't have the intellect, or the technology, so we can't predict it. Yet. But just because *we* can't do it today, doesn't mean it's not predictable. So, having said all that, who knows what this little dinner may cause?" Andre speared a forkful of sun-dried tomatoes and goat cheese. He glanced up. "Any guesses?"

"The way you're putting away that cheese," Tish said, "I predict heartburn and gas."

They had polished off the pizza and were waiting for their desserts. Tish typed away on her phone.

"How long have you known each other?" Andre asked.

"We met at tennis camp when we were ten," Tish said.

"You play also?"

"*Played.* I got tired of getting embarrassed by the great one. Would it have killed you to throw one lousy match?"

"I took pity on her and now I don't know how to get rid of her," Gemma said.

"Bollocks!" Tish said, grinning ear to ear, still looking down at her phone. "You're lost without me."

Andre eyed Tish. "Were you born in Ethiopia or North Wales?"

Tish's jaw dropped slightly, and her eyes rolled up to meet his. "Ethiopian parents, born in Wales. How'd you manage to figure that out?"

The waiter brought the coffee and tiramisu. Andre took a large serving. "Shot in the dark—lucky guess."

"Bullshit. Explain."

"Your last name is a dead giveaway—Nigist means 'queen' in Ethiopian. Also, your narrow and long facial features are regal. High cheekbones, long neck. Classic Ethiopian. Then there's your accent. The Welsh have a melodic way of speaking. When you speak, you're practically singing. The Southern Welsh accent is barely English."

Tish considered him for a moment then brightened. "So you think I'm regal and sound melodic? I'll take that compliment."

"Now she'll think she's the Queen incarnate," Gemma said, shaking her head. "But don't hesitate to ask Her Majesty for anything you may need. Tomorrow's a bit of a mess for me. I'm booked with therapy, training, and interviews."

"It's not a problem; I know people in London. I wasn't expecting you to take me sightseeing. I'm here to watch you win the whole thing."

Gemma blushed. "Don't hesitate to call Tish. She can arrange anything for you."

"Don't worry about me. I'm fine. In fact, there's a couple who I have to visit while I'm here, otherwise they'll disown me. I'll see if they're free tomorrow night." He would visit Jeffrey and also apologize to Emily in person. Just because he couldn't make it to her engagement didn't mean he couldn't take advantage of the situation and visit them.

"Oh," Gemma said, a ring of disappointment in her tone.

"Which of course can be changed instantly if you had something else in mind."

"There's a little celebration tomorrow night. I thought maybe you'd like to join me."

"She's being elusive," Tish said. "The Prime Minister has invited her and a few others to celebrate her Aegon championship. It's a big deal."

"The Prime Minister? Well, that's perfect. I'd be honored."

"Okay," Tish said, "I'll call the PM's office and let them know you'll be joining. Any instructions?" she asked Gemma.

"Tell them Andre is a friend from the States. No need to give more details." She studied Andre. "You don't have a criminal record, do you?"

He shook his head. "Not a record."

"So Mr. Andre," Tish said, "do Yanks travel with suits, or do I need to make arrangements?"

"Some do. And some even travel with clean underwear."

A large crowd had already gathered outside the restaurant. They had found her. Gemma's security had also been contacted. As soon as they stepped out of the building, her security enveloped their group and moved them quickly to her car. Andre scanned the faces of the people. He paused, staring at one guy in particular who held a cell phone outstretched. Andre recognized the face. He was sure of it now. He had seen him at both the airport and again in the hotel lobby.

"In the car, sir," the security said.

From inside the car, Andre tried to find the man, but the stalker was no longer there. If his suspicions were right, then he'd have to alert both M&T and local authorities.

They drove off, and as soon as Glen lost the tail, he immediately took Andre to his hotel. Andre and Gemma stared at each other for a few moments, but it was clear Tish didn't know everything. They hugged when he left. Nothing more.

Later, from his hotel room, Andre called an old friend.

"This is Frank Maloff."

"Mr. Maloff, it's Andre Reyes."

"Dr. Andre? What a great surprise. How the hell have you been, kid? When will we have you back at the NSA?"

A good question. Something he would consider in the coming months. The National Security Agency was responsible for collecting and analyzing communications from foreign entities. They secured the U.S. government's communications and related systems. Frank was the deputy director of the agency, and Andre had worked with Frank for years.

"You know my situation. I'm married to M&T with a solid prenup."

"I know. But I want you to know mine is a standing offer. We could use you here."

"Thank you. I'll call you on that someday. For now I need to ask you for a favor."

"We don't do favors. We repay debts. What do you need?"

"I need the source code of the utility we wrote for monitoring the sleeper cells in Madrid."

"Whoa! Are you tracking terrorists?"

"Close."

Thirty minutes later, Andre had the source code and was developing a new tool.

CHAPTER TWENTY-FOUR

*"Success is a journey, not a destination. The doing is often
more important than the outcome."*

~Arthur Ashe

Gemma's car arrived at Andre's hotel at 7:30 p.m. She had
hoped they would have spent more time together the night
before. But when the paparazzi found her, the only choice
was to first lose them and then covertly drop off Andre.
Today was a new day, with new possibilities.

All night yesterday, she had hoped they'd be able to pick up where
they had left off in L.A., but with Tish there, her hopes had been
thwarted. She had not been transparent with Tish when she had asked
her to arrange Andre's flight. She had not admitted she had already fallen
for Andre. She had only said she wanted a chance to know him better as
friends. A lot better, to be accurate.

She was attracted to him, no doubt. And she thought he felt the
same. Not wanting to leave things to chance, she had taken some
matters into her own hands. For one, her new dress was perfect. A
silky black number that hugged her body with a hint of subdued
seduction, while it still tipped on the side of classy. Also, this dress
brought enough shape to her chest, feminizing her boyish figure.
Additionally, now that her thigh was stronger, she wore two-inch
heels, making her as tall as Andre. But she also knew heels made her

calves pop. She didn't see anything wrong with showing a little bit of the goods.

She watched Andre step through the hotel doors, her security flanking him on either side. They were focused and alert, while he floated with ease. Thankfully, no paparazzi were in sight. As always, Glen had done a superb job of losing his tails.

Andre wore a three-button tuxedo and a white scarf. She struggled with how a twenty-something carried himself like a thirty-something. He walked with long strides, while the tips of his shoes kicked out slightly. He seemed comfortable with everything he did.

Andre stepped into the limousine then froze in place, mouth partially open.

"What's wrong?" she asked.

"You look…" He paused, appraising her. "I don't have the right words—only clichés come to mind."

Gemma blushed. Her dress had worked, and his face said it all. "You're being silly."

"No. It's true. You'll slap me any second now—I can't peel my eyes off you."

"I won't slap. Maybe an upper cut."

He studied her. "Any fallout from yesterday?"

"Not that I'm aware of."

"You want to talk about it?"

She grinned. "Not that I'm aware of."

"Whenever you're ready. In the meanwhile, can I see your cell phone?"

"Sure, why?" She handed him her mobile.

"A little experiment."

"What are you up to?"

"A harmless virus that your contacts will receive from you."

"A what? Don't do that." She reached for her phone.

He tapped her hand away. "Trust me. Nothing will get damaged, and they'll never know. What we get in return is information."

"Is this legal?"

"Technically? No. But your peace of mind is more important than silly legal considerations."

"Are you planning on telling me what you're trying to find out?"

"Sure. As soon as you tell me about Georg and why you wanted to dismember him."

Gemma didn't know what to expect of the evening, but had decided she would make the most of it. They arrived at the Prime Minister's residence on time. Ten Downing Street boasted over one hundred rooms, and had been the home of Prime Ministers for nearly three hundred years. Security was tight, but she and Andre passed through the prominent blast-proof steel door without trouble. They stepped into the entrance hall onto the famous black and white marble tiles.

"Gemma," a voice boomed from another room. Prime Minister Beckford strode toward them, arms widespread, his wife next to him.

"Good evening, sir," Gemma said.

He held her shoulders and kissed her on both cheeks. "Welcome."

"Thank you. May I introduce you to—"

"Dr. Andre Reyes," the PM said.

She spun from the PM to Andre, who was smiling too.

"Good to see you again, sir—I mean, Jeffrey."

The PM eyed Andre. "It took Gemma for you to finally visit?" He shook Andre's hand vigorously. "How are you, son?" He cupped Andre's neck—an act of endearment, like an older brother or a loving uncle. She wasn't sure what to make of this odd scene.

"I am fantastic," Andre said. "It's nice to see you both. It's been too long."

"How many times have we asked you to visit?" the PM's wife asked.

"Excuse me, but you know each other?" Gemma asked, confused.

"Yes, my dear. You keep great company. We've known Andre for years. Also, this young man has done more for the United Kingdom than I can possibly say. In fact, I can't say—it's classified." He winked.

"Let's go to the drawing room, shall we," his wife said, taking Andre's arm. "The guests are eager to see you, Gemma."

The Pillard Drawing Room, though sparsely furnished, held a majestic aura. A portrait of Queen Elizabeth I hung over the fireplace and a luxurious Persian carpet covered the majority of the hardwood floor.

As Gemma stepped in, the eight other guests applauded and cheered.

She was certain her tanned skin reddened. In a moment of inspiration, she curtsied, to everyone's delight.

Over the next hour, she introduced Andre to the guests. She observed how he melded easily with the aristocracy of London. Yet he remained constant. He was the same person, no matter whom he met or where he was.

She was asked about the American by some, to which she replied, "He's an old friend, who has also worked with the Prime Minister in the past." She was grateful no one pressed, but also hoped she wouldn't see articles about him anytime soon.

Inside the State Dining Room, Andre and Gemma sat together. She wondered if anyone would run to the press about her and Andre. She hoped not.

Andre leaned in and whispered, "You're somewhere else. Be in the moment. Enjoy it."

She put her hand on his and mouthed, "Thank you." When she turned, she saw the Prime Minister observing her, grinning. She withdrew her hand.

The ringing of silver on crystal chimed through the room.

"A moment, please," the Prime Minister said. Conversations came to a close, and the faces turned to him. "I'd like to say a couple of words. By now you are well aware that I'm not shy about saying a few words."

Polite laughter rolled through the room.

He raised his glass and studied Gemma. "The United Kingdom is proud of you. Your heroic battle last week brought an unparalleled feeling of hope to the people. You are an inspiration to all."

Applause filled the room.

"Most of you may also know I'm fairly competitive and a sports fanatic. Therefore, I'd like to make a request of you, Gemma."

The PM raised his glass higher.

"Next week, you embark on Wimbledon. This is our country, our sport, and you are ours. Win the championship for your country."

The guests applauded and cheered, but Gemma heard nothing. She felt as if she had been shoved in a bathtub filled with ice water, drowning and numb. She could only pass one command to her brain—*smile*—as the weight of England itself settled on her shoulders.

"If I may," she heard Andre say as he pushed his chair back and stood. She studied him as he lifted his glass. "My uncle used to say, '*Do what you love and magic is possible.*'" Andre and the PM exchanged smiles.

"I have known Gemma for some time now," he said then glanced at her, their eyes locked, "and I can comfortably say that whatever happens, on or off the grass, she is a warrior unlike any other. Gemma, we all want to see you fully recovered so you can bring us all years of magic. First, get better. When you do step on the grass, bring the love, the passion you have for the game to your opponents. With love, magic is possible. And while you're at it," he scanned around conspiratorially, "be sure to kick some 'Merican arse," he said in a flawless Scottish accent.

The room erupted in laughter, applause, and side conversations.

"We may have just witnessed the making of a new American politician," the PM said.

"No sir, not me. I solve problems—not cause them." The laughter thundered through the dining room. He glanced at her. She winked at him, thankful for coming to her rescue. Again.

After dinner, the guests went to the terrace. The scent of cognac and Cuban cigars floated over the rose garden. Andre was talking to the Prime Minister when Gemma slid her hand through the crook of his elbow.

"May I steal him for a few moments?" she asked the PM.

"Of course." He turned, but paused, considering something. "Gemma, I just had a brilliant idea. My only daughter, Emily, is getting engaged in a couple of months. Why don't you join Andre as his guest?" He glanced at Andre.

"Oh, thank you," she said, staring at both men, who seemed to be locked in a staring contest. "That's very sweet." They continued staring at each other. "I'll be sure to get details from Andre. Thanks again."

"It's my pleasure," the PM said, grinning, still locked onto Andre. He winked then walked away.

She tugged Andre, moving him deeper into the terrace. "What was that all about?"

"The man's a brilliant politician and strategist. Never mind. How are you, Gem?"

"Tired, elevated, and scared. But who cares about me? I want to know how you know the bloody PM."

"That is classified, Miss Lennon," Andre said in a dignified, thickened voice.

"You've done work for the UK?"

"Without giving away classified information, one of the services I provide is to help track terrorists through their communication—chatter."

Her mouth opened. "You do that type of work too?"

"It's my specialty. In fact, that was my claim to fame when I was fifteen. I helped Homeland Security and the National Security Agency decode a bunch of chatter that led us to arrest a lot of bad guys. I got to meet the President. Can you imagine? A fifteen-year-old kid meeting the President of the United States because he helped get the bad guys."

"Unreal," she said. "You must suffer from superhero complex."

"No, not at all. I don't see it as a complex."

They strolled farther into the shadowy terrace. She squeezed tight into him.

"Do you really believe with love, magic is possible?"

"Absolutely. I think you do too. At the Aegon you tapped into something primal when the rest of us thought you had reached the end of your championship run. If you can tap into the source, then you can accomplish anything."

She managed to smile. "I'd like to tap that source right now," she said as the space between their lips disappeared. His lips were gentle, warm, and loving. The taste of cognac on his mouth, which should have made her sick, was somehow sweet and pleasant now. Her hands dropped to her side, giving in to him. She wanted to worry about the people there—the people who would betray her, but she was powerless to speak or move. Instead, she remembered his words. *"You're somewhere else. Be in the moment."*

A flare of heat rumbled in her chest and expanded.

"I think they're over here," someone said, her voice dangerously close.

Gemma broke her lips away and spun to Andre's side before his eyes had even opened.

"What—" he began, but Gemma stopped him.

"Are you looking for me?" Gemma said as she briskly walked in the direction of the voice.

"No, my dear," the PM's wife said, "I was showing the guests my prize rose bushes."

Gemma's shoulders slumped. *Great.*

The paparazzi waited outside the PM's residence. Andre and Gemma rushed into the car, and Glen took off. Yet again, he was doing all he could to lose the tails.

During the ride back, Gemma wordlessly cuddled in Andre's arms and closed her eyes. Andre lay his chin on her head and tried to moderate his erratic heartbeat. With each conversation, each visit, each day, and passing moment, he wanted more from her. Unlike anyone else, she accepted him as he was. She treated him like she needed him—not something from him, but him, his presence. And that concerned him.

She was a busy and committed professional who led a life that did not accommodate relationships. As for him, he would have to disappear for months. How would that play out with her?

No matter how he looked at it, this was not the right time. Unless... could he cut his ties with M&T sooner without evoking the early termination penalties? Could he have it all?

Over the past couple days he had been considering options and alternatives. He would have never considered it before, but with her in his life, he realized new tactics would need to be considered. Could his idea work?

If he truly believed he had to live in the moment, then how could he justify holding off his feelings for her for another six months? He could barely stay away from her for six hours.

She opened her eyes, sat up, then turned to him. "Sorry, I must have crashed."

"It's okay."

She studied his eyes. "Are you okay? You look lost in thought."

"It's no big deal."

"I'd like to hear what's on your mind."

He took a deep breath. "In about six months, my contract with my firm ends. It's gotten ugly for me lately. All I can think of is the end of my contract."

"You'd quit your career?"

"Yes."

"Just like that? This is your talent, your gift."

"I'm not quitting my talent. Just the way I've exploited myself."

"I see. What would you do if you quit?"

"Sleep for a few days."

"If it's bad, then why even wait? Can't you just leave?"

"I'd love to, but I can't. I've made commitments that if I broke them now, let's just say it would be problematic. And to top it all off, I have a significant project coming up which will bury me for three to four months. I have to see that one through before I leave them."

"A project that'll last three to four months?" She continued to study him. "How will that work? What I mean is, will I be able to see you?"

"I don't know."

"I am not overwhelmed with confidence."

"I'll figure something out."

"I certainly hope so. Otherwise..." She kissed the side of his lips. "I may have to take matters into my own hands." Then she nibbled his lip.

Suddenly the car accelerated and the privacy window lowered. Gemma spun around.

"Ma'am, paparazzi on motorcycle approaching on the right."

She immediately slid a few feet away.

They locked eyes. He pointed to the wide space between them. "What happened?" he asked.

She shook her head. "I don't want pictures of us in tomorrow's tabloids."

"Gemma, are we always going to have to stay apart when there's another living soul around us?"

She broke off eye contact for a few moments. "Maybe. Sometimes."

"When will you and I be able to spend time together? No Tish. No event with other people. Just us."

"Tomorrow," she said. "Definitely maybe tomorrow."

Once again, they separated in less than ideal circumstances. Fortunately Andre's hotel hadn't been discovered by the paparazzi yet, but the threat of their potent lenses kept Gemma nervous throughout the rest of the ride.

Once in the elevator, Andre felt more alone than ever. He wanted to be with her. Yet, they continued to scurry apart like roaches. How long would it have to be this way?

Once in his room, he called his dad.

"Did you call Linda?"

Silence.

"Dad?"

"I will call her when I'm ready. I'm busy working on something. When I'm done doing that, then I'll call her."

"You're kidding, right? It's been almost six years. Six. And you're busy working on something."

"I know how long it's been. You don't think I remember my only brother? You don't think I miss him?"

This was the first time Andre had ever heard his father express any type of sincere emotion for his brother. "Then why do you always talk about him like you hated him?"

"Because I was mad at him."

"Mad?"

"What I would have given to have his brain. He had thousands of ideas. I hoped I'd have something, anything like him. But nothing. I got nothing. When I tried to convince him to take some of his ideas and start a business together, he was not interested. He didn't want to even try. And you know why?"

Andre said nothing.

"Because he was scared. So when you showed the same capabilities, he tried to scare you too. But I wouldn't let him. He was trying to stop you from reaching your potential. I loved him. But hated him too. He had a gift and he threw it away. I'd rather die than to let you do the same."

"He may have disagreed with you and mom, but he always loved you."

"And I loved him too. I will always love him even though I never told him."

"You can tell his daughter. Or his wife."

"One day I will."

"Then what are you waiting for? Linda is your only remaining connection to your brother. A blood connection."

"What I'm waiting for is for all of you to stop bothering me about this. I will do what I have to do first. Then and only then will I talk to them." The phone line went dead.

Why was it so hard to do the right thing? Linda had already given up. She wasn't resentful about it. Just resigned.

Andre tossed his phone on the bed then grabbed his laptop. Within a few minutes, he was logged into NSA's web server. Time to see if his application had penetrated Gemma's circle. Like a virus, once one contact caught it, the others got infected as well—and the friend, and the friend of the friend.

His application crawled into the data exchange layer of the contact in question. All communication was captured and loaded into NSA's proprietary multi-threaded, neural mapped, pattern-matching engine.

Eighteen percent penetration in four hours was a good sign. It meant a lot of activity and chatter. Based on past experience, at sixty percent, the data produced interesting heuristics, although sometimes luck walked in and delivered unexpected results.

He was analyzing the data, when something caught his eye. "Hello." He cocked his head then covered his mouth, analyzing a stream of unexpected communication. "What have we here?"

CHAPTER TWENTY-FIVE

"To hell with circumstances; I create opportunities."

~Bruce Lee

Gemma shouldn't have, but she called off the late afternoon practice and texted Andre instead. He had been right the night before. Isn't that why she had brought him here? To be together. Alone.

Mid-afternoon was a perfect time to go to the Hurlingham Club. Exclusive and practically empty at this hour—except for the octogenarians who never seemed to notice her and her type. The lush grounds were awe-inspiring, the food prepared by world-class chefs, the security tighter than most palaces, and the staff discreet.

They nestled into a booth.

"There's something I've been meaning to ask you—" Gemma started.

"I thought you'd never ask. I like to take long strolls on the beach, my favorite color is black, if I was a vegetable I'd be a—"

She pinched his arm.

"Ouch." He rubbed his arm. "Man, you're violent."

"Now that we have a common understanding, let's start with the things I want to know. Are there others in your family who have shown some of your talents?"

"Yes."

This was perfect. She had often wondered about her athletic gifts and if what she had was genetic.

"My uncle—Linda's dad—was one of those scary-smart math guys. When he was in third grade he was studying calculus."

"That sounds horrible. Like child-abuse."

He eyed her. "By third grade you were beating fifteen-year-old kids at tennis. What do you call that?"

"Don't change the subject. I'm interrogating you." If his talent was inherited, then maybe she also had inherited her athletic gifts. This would support the idea that maybe her real father had indeed been a professional footballer.

"Of course, I didn't know about his gifts until they moved from Argentina to L.A. And I found out because he and my dad got into arguments over me. The sad part was my parents called him a loser, afraid, you name it."

"Oh no."

"Oh yes. They didn't want me to be influenced by him and follow in his footsteps. The way they saw it, he had wasted a one in a million talent when he decided to become a teacher instead of some money-making businessman. And yet, when I was eleven, I met Prime Minister Beckford through my uncle. Not bad for a loser."

"You admire your uncle."

"Admire. Love. I spent practically every summer with them, whether in Argentina or in Spain. Those were the best days of my life. He was the warm version of my dad—the one I actually wanted to live with."

"Things aren't well with you and your parents?"

"Sort of. I guess. Don't get me wrong; I respect them. In their own way, they thought they were doing the right thing. And I can't deny what I have today is because of them. As I talk about it, I'm conflicted. Love and animosity can't co-exist in one space." He raked his hands through his hair.

"Should I stop?" she asked.

"You can ask anything."

"You'll regret giving me that much freedom."

"I don't live life with regret."

She couldn't make the same claim. She had plenty of regrets. "Have things improved now between your parents and uncle?"

He paused for a few moments, until his eyes glistened. "Nearly six years ago, my uncle and his oldest daughter were driving home when a drunk kid smashed into them. They both passed away."

"Oh, Andre, I'm so sorry."

"Life is fragile, Gem. One day I had them, the next I didn't. And I guess in some ways, when I lost him, I also lost my way—he was my moral compass. But when you think of poor Linda, five years after she lost her sister and father, she lost her fiancé."

"I didn't mean to dig up painful memories," she said, placing her hand on his.

He lifted her hand to his lips and breathed a small kiss on her bruised knuckle. "Memories can't hurt people."

He was wrong about that. Dead wrong. Even so, sad story, funny tales, or even in silence, he added depth and warmth to her. His presence brought equilibrium and consistency she desperately needed. With him, she felt safe. She wanted to feel that way all the time.

"By the way, Nikon will be hosting an event tomorrow night. A new ad campaign for Wimbledon. Will you join me?"

"Is it a good idea for me to be there? Press and all?"

"We celebrities have an entourage wherever we go. You're one of my minions."

"That sounds like a promotion."

"Well deserved one at that."

Andre ordered dessert and coffee. He was a bad influence, ordering all the things she wanted, but didn't dare eat. But there it was, pistachio *crème brûlée*, staring at her. She decided to taste a bit. Two spoonfuls later, she wanted to eat the whole thing.

"I shouldn't indulge," she said, as she picked up a piece of hardened sugar crisp.

"You're right," he said, pulling the plate away from her. "You shouldn't. This is mine—I did not agree to share."

"Sharing is caring. Didn't anyone teach you that? Where do you put all the junk you eat anyway?"

"In a very comfortable place." He rubbed his mid-section.

"Seriously. How do you burn it off?"

"Hyperactive metabolism for the most part. Climbing and running keep my heart rate high, sort of like a perpetual burn. But there is one activity in particular that burns calories and works my body like no other," he said then offered nothing else. Instead he placed a spoonful of the custard in his mouth.

"Go on. What is it?" she said, then paused as soon as she asked.

"It's not proper to talk about in public." Andre leaned in and whispered, "Some consider it inappropriate to discuss—taboo. I'd be happy to demonstrate in private if you like."

Her face went slack. She blushed and her ears burnt. "Are you serious?"

"Yup—full contact mixed martial arts," he said, scooping more custard.

"You bastard." She pinched his arm.

"Ouch. What was that for?" He put on a badly rehearsed innocent face. "You didn't think I meant—Gem. Shame on you." He covered his ears. "Get your head out of the gutter. I'm way too civilized for you savage Brits."

"Why you bloody Yank!"

CHAPTER TWENTY-SIX

"Love is composed of a single soul inhabiting two bodies."

~Aristotle

They left the Hurlingham Club shortly after dessert. "Where to, ma'am?" Glen asked once they sat.

"Can I recommend something?" Andre asked.

"By all means—go ahead," she said.

"Glen, take us to Soho. South end of Wardour Street, near Piccadilly Circus."

"Soho?" she asked. "Why there?"

"Trust me."

Thirty minutes later, they arrived.

"Perfect. Right here," Andre told Glen.

"Here?" she asked, incredulous.

"Come on, let's go."

"Outside? With all those people? I can't go out there. The paparazzi will be all over me. And then there's the little issue with the rain."

"Anything else?" he asked. "Air out all your reasons."

"Those should do."

"Good. Look at the people walking. What do you see? Observe them."

She shrugged impatiently. "I don't know. They're walking... holding umbrellas... getting wet."

"What else? Look."

She searched then she got it. "They're looking down."

"Right. The rain makes others invisible. The focus changes from who may be in front of you, to where you're going. No one will notice you."

"Brilliant," Glen said. They both turned to him. "Sorry, ma'am." Glen turned beet red.

"Okay," she said, "so you may be right. But why here?"

"Stop questioning everything. Let's walk and enjoy your anonymity. When was the last time you walked the streets of London?"

She thought for a moment. "Five bloody years ago."

"Isn't it about time?"

She nodded then opened the door.

"Ma'am," Glen called out through the open window, "some of these streets are blocked off, or one way."

"Glen, don't worry," Andre said. "If we need anything, we'll call you."

Glen glanced at Gemma, who nodded. "Very well." He rolled up the window then drove away.

"Wait. We didn't take an umbrella. I'll call him back."

Andre held her shoulders. "Feel it, live it."

Andre's arm across Gemma's back and her head on his shoulder, they strolled through Soho toward Oxford Circus. People sped right by her, not noticing, nor caring. This was a freedom she was not used to.

"Every time I visit London, I make a point to end up here," he said as he guided her through the narrow roads. "I stroll the streets and imagine what it was like thirty or forty or four hundred years ago. There—" he pointed to a building "—the Beatles and the Rolling Stones recorded a few songs up there. Can you imagine the energy generated by the musical genius of the twentieth century? What it must have felt like to be in the same room with them?"

She listened to Andre's stories and absorbed the world around her. It seemed improbable that she was strolling the streets of Central London with so much freedom. Her hair was damp, and the air cold, but with her body pressed into his, her arm wrapped around his waist, she had never experienced warmth like this. Their bodies connected, and their

181

heartbeats thundered through thin layers of clothing. Their synchronized breathing and body heat purred.

They turned onto Kensington Street and strolled westward to Hayden Park. They wandered into the empty park and approached the pond. Hundreds of coins lay inside, most covered in algae.

"I made a wish at this pond years ago," she said.

"And here I am. Your wish come true."

She glanced at him. "It's your humility above all else that makes you lovable."

She studied the pond. Their reflection gave her pause. In all the pictures she had seen of herself with other men, she didn't think she had ever looked as complete as she did in Andre's embrace right now. She appeared free, unencumbered.

"There's something about this part of town, an energy, that makes me wonder if one day I'll make London home," he said.

Her heartbeat picked up. "You've thought of living here?"

He spun her around to face him. She slid her arms through the inside of his coat, around his waist. He brought her body into his, tight. Her breath caught momentarily.

"I was looking for a good reason to live in London."

She blinked.

"I think I have one now." His eyes bore deep into hers. "If I had a place here, maybe we could make time to see each other more often. Or all the time."

Her mouth opened slightly, as the drizzle picked up in intensity. His hair, face, and lips beaded with raindrops.

He drew her closer, and when he spoke, his voice was solid, unwavering. "I want to be near you. I need to be with you. When we're apart, I feel empty. Like something important is missing. I realize we've just started, but I know what I feel. And I know what I want. I want you in my life."

Her eyes stung, and her heart threatened to explode out of her chest. As if the words had been plucked out of her mind and spoken through him. He understood her completely. A tear fell from her eyelash and rolled down her cheek.

With both hands, he cupped her face delicately. In the clasp of his strong hands, she felt precious, yet protected. He drew her face into his. When their lips met, air swooshed out. She was flying, gliding in the ecstasy of the moment. The scent of his cologne, the scraping of his stubble on her chin, she wanted and accepted all of him with greed, wanting to hold onto the moment. Her body merged into his. Coursing through her was release and freedom. A certainty that she would never believe life was meaningless. In this moment, her life overflowed with meaning and joy.

When their lips parted, his dark eyes burned into hers. She was unable to stand properly. Her heart and body raced with heat, the type of warmth she had only ever dreamt of. A burn roiled within.

"Are you okay?" he asked, his voice hoarse.

She uttered a sound, her throat unable to form words. Another tear rolled down her cheek. He wiped the tear track with his thumb then kissed the corner of her eye. Her eyelashes fluttered.

"Don't worry," he whispered as he placed another gentle kiss on her brow. "Just be here—right here, right now."

"But I *am* worried. Look at us. How can we make this work? Your life is… and my life…"

"Don't fight it. Let it roll. Like the surfer in Malibu. He didn't fight the wave. He understood the wave would decide where he'd end up."

He gazed into her eyes.

"I used to be one of those other guys. The ones who chased every wave. I was after more, faster, better. Then, when Rob died, I understood. I got that life is about living—you never know when it'll end. Let the wave we're on guide us. We'll figure out the rest—together."

She eventually whispered, "Okay, together."

They walked silently for a few minutes, holding each other tight. Gemma never expected the day to take this turn. Walking the streets of London, talking, laughing, crying, acting like kids, and of course the blissful moments under the rain in his arms. What did that make them now? A couple? Was he serious about getting a flat in London? She ran her hand over her wet face and dared to smile.

"What's your story, Gem? Do you have a sordid family story like mine?"

"Well, as you know, I'm adopted."

"What?" He stopped. "No, I didn't know."

She studied him. "Everyone knows that. It's part of my aura. You haven't read about that?"

He shook his head. "I haven't read anything about you or researched you. Why would I when I can just ask you?"

She froze. He continued to find ways to surprise her. She slipped her hand around his waist and proceeded walking.

"My birth mum, Ginger, passed away during the delivery. My father, Javier, freaked, didn't know what to do, so he abandoned a newly-born me. Very little is known about him. I know he was from Spain and by some accounts he may have been a professional soccer player training with Liverpool. But that's about it."

"Have you tried to find him?"

"I've tried. I placed adverts, hired PIs, even went on TV, anything I could think of. Eventually, we found a couple who knew my mother. Through them I was able to track her parents. By then, only my grandfather survived. Unfortunately, I have nothing on my father. Only a name and one picture. An old-school selfie with my mum. A portion of his face is cut off. He had longish black hair and wore sunglasses. So all I know of him is his smile. They looked happy. Complete." For a moment she thought of her reflection with Andre in the fountain.

"Have you kept in touch with the couple who knew your parents?"

"Yes. In fact, Xavi and Mari live in my Malibu home."

"The guy who gave me the evil eye?"

"Exactly. We grew very close. They'd tell me stories about my mum. Stories I would not have known otherwise. They told me in the eighth month of her pregnancy, she used to rub her belly and call me her black bird."

"Your tattoo."

She nodded. "The best bit is that Xavi's been like a father to me and also quite the guru. Few people know this, but after the Australian Open, I had decided to quit tennis. For weeks I sulked in L.A., but one day he explained being sad changes nothing. He told me life was about choices and action."

"Choices and action," Andre repeated in a soft whisper.

"He told me to choose the future I wanted and then be in action. So I did."

"Do Xavi and Mari know what happened to your father?"

She sighed. "They barely knew him, but Mari tells me weeks after Ginger's death, Javier returned, trying to find me, but the hospital and adoption agency refused to provide him the information. For all I know, he may still be trying to find me."

"How do you feel about him?"

"I'd do anything to find him. Before I knew his story, I resented both my parents. I assumed the worst. But the situation, the way things unfolded, I could see how a young man would make that decision."

"You must show me the picture. I need to see their faces. The curiosity is killing me."

"Next time we're in L.A. It's in my Malibu home."

Suddenly, the innocent drizzle converted into a torrential storm, and rain drops the size of nickels pelted them. They ran for shelter. Visibility approached zero. Their shoes, coats, and hair were drenched. When she thought it couldn't get any worse, it did.

They slid under a bookseller's canopy.

"That's some rain." Andre shook his hair, spraying water everywhere. "I told you we'd need an umbrella."

"Your attempt at humor is tempting me to hurt you. For your sake, I'll call Glen instead." She dialed, but the connection dropped.

"Look over there. Three blocks west—my hotel. Let's make a run for it. We'll dry up while Glen comes to your rescue."

"Right, good plan." She dialed one more time. "Glen, if you can hear me, we're heading to the Kensington Hilton." She glanced at her phone and disconnected in exasperation.

Andre grabbed her hand, and they ran. The impact of their feet on the overflown streets kicked up more water. They were drenched and getting cold, but she giggled like a schoolgirl.

They crossed the street toward the main lobby. The porter opened the door, concern carved on his face. "Are you okay? Can I get you something?"

They were still laughing. "No, thank you. All's under control," he said.

A handful of guests and hotel staff spun and gaped at the couple. Then directly at Gemma.

CHAPTER TWENTY-SEVEN

"When you have the opportunity, you strike."

~Rod Lever

Gemma and Andre stepped off the lift and found their way to his suite. "Try Glen now," he said as he opened the door and stepped in. Gemma moved slowly, observing his movements. He threw the card key on the table, then removed his wet jacket and marched through the spacious suite.

He was always in action—never a wasted moment.

"I'll get you towels. I bet my sweatpants and shirt could fit you." He found articles of clothing and took them to the large bathroom.

No matter what he was up to he was always the same person—no different personas. He was the same guy on the beach as when he spoke to the British aristocracy.

"We should call for tea and soup." He added towels to the clothing then walked toward her with an oversized towel.

Choices and action.

"Your hair is drenched," he said, as he placed the towel on her head. She said nothing while he towel dried her hair. "We'll need a blow dryer. This won't do." His eyes dropped to hers. "Do you know if Glen got your message? Did you try him again?"

She shook her head, not losing eye contact.

"Are you okay?" He stopped drying her hair.

She stepped into him, placed her hands behind his neck, and lowered his head. As their lips came together, electricity ran through her spine. A humming sensation washed through her legs. When he grabbed her hips, her body arched and pressed into his. Their breathing shortened, and their lips parted in acceptance. Their wet bodies came together, attached, molded to each other's contours.

The rain pelted the windows as she reached for his belt.

Then a repeated sound. *Thud. Thud.*

Her eyes opened. So did his.

Thud. Thud. Thud.

"Ma'am, it's Glen." A voice from outside.

Her eyes widened. They stopped, out of breath. Her body wavered.

"I was in the lobby when you arrived. I received your earlier calls. I wouldn't have disturbed, but it seems people in the lobby saw you."

Gemma blinked. "One moment," she said. She leaned in close to Andre's mouth. "I'm sorry. I have to leave," she whispered.

"No," he said, "stay with me."

"I can't." She pulled away. "That was careless of me. The hotel staff and guests saw me. They'll need to see me leave."

"You're not serious."

She took the towel off the floor, threw it on her head and stepped backward to the door.

"I'm sorry," she said, opened the door, then left.

He took a shower then changed, intent on finding a solution to these games. How long did she plan to keep their relationship a secret? Until a couple of weeks ago, Andre had been focused on achieving financial independence. Now he understood independence without the right person to share life with would be incomplete, a sham. Did she feel the same?

This cycle had to stop. Maybe the cell phone virus would help. He powered up his laptop then monitored the status of the web service. Forty-five percent penetration by his virus and patterns were already emerging.

The headache knocked on his skull. He closed his laptop and decided to go downstairs for a late dinner before the kitchen closed.

As he stepped out of his room, he saw his stalker from a few days earlier. The stalker came to an abrupt halt, eyes wide. Andre strolled toward the man, pretending he didn't recognize the man. But the stalker spun and sprinted down the hall.

"Stop!" Andre yelled, then broke into a sprint also.

The stalker had thirty yards on him and was a few feet from the elevator. Andre's adrenaline catapulted him forward. The elevator door opened. The stalker slid in. Only fifteen yards to go and the door began to close. Andre saw the stalker's face in perfect detail. He jumped toward the closing door, but was too late. He slammed a fist against the closed doors.

He spun, searching for the stairwell. For fourteen flights he ran, leaping from landing to landing. Sweat dripped from his face.

When he reached the first floor, he slammed the door open and stumbled into the lobby. He spun around, looking. Nothing. He sprinted to the porter. "Did you just see a twenty-five-year-old male, five-foot-seven, black curly hair, red rain jacket?"

"He just ran out. Nearly shattered the door. Turned west onto Kensington."

Andre ran into the unforgiving rain. With no visibility, all colors faded. He could not make out anyone in red. He turned back.

"Have you seen him before?" he asked the porter.

"I'm not sure, sir."

"Do you have security cameras on the fourteenth floor?"

"Yes, we do."

"Please make sure all security footage is saved. I'm calling Detective Chief Inspector Whitby. We will need those tapes."

After one hour with the DCI, Andre returned to his room. They had enough to launch an investigation. But why was he being tailed? Was the stalker related to past work, as he had suspected, or was this about Project Sunrise? Had his involvement been compromised? *My contract.*

The DCI was concerned for Andre's safety. Andre didn't share the concern, confident that Whitby would find something. He was one of the best.

Andre studied his cell phone—a message from Gemma. He listened to the voicemail. "*Sorry. I hope you're not mad. Please call me.*"

He wasn't mad. He was confused. Did she really have to leave? Would the hotel staff say something to the press? And so what if it leaked? He was new to this domain. So he would have to follow her lead—for now.

He grabbed a beer from the minibar and collapsed on the couch. He needed to settle before returning her call. He turned on the TV and flipped the channels. The volume was low, but the picture stopped him cold. He sat up and increased the volume.

The talking head announced, "*Gemma Lennon has been seen with someone new. Who is this mystery man? Is it really over with Johnny?*"

They had pictures of them. Pictures from the day at Maurice's and others showing Andre in a tux, entering her limousine. None of the pictures proved they were together. But if they were followed tonight, there would be pictures of them holding, embracing, kissing.

Was the stalker involved?

If so, then the media blitz was about to go on a feeding frenzy. But that didn't make sense. The first time Andre had seen the stalker was at the airport. Gemma had not been there. This was about him, not her.

He downed the beer while watching the program, amazed at the amount of drivel that could be generated from nothing. Looking back, it was fortunate she had left when she did. She was right—the hotel staff would have probably sold the story—if they hadn't already. But how did the press know about them? He was beginning to see patterns and possible answers from his virus, but nothing conclusive.

His phone rang. It was Gemma.

"Are you upset?" she asked.

"They have our pictures, Gem."

"What are you talking about?"

"TV. They're talking about us."

"They what? How the hell? Channel, please."

They listened to the talking heads in silence. He elected to not mention his stalker. No sense in worrying her further. This was his problem. She already had plenty on her mind.

"Do you think we were followed tonight?" she asked.

"I don't know," he said then thought about the stalker. "Maybe."

"If they got pictures of us… in the rain… this could be disastrous."

"Disastrous? Aren't you being a bit dramatic?"

"When you've lived twenty-four hours in my shoes, then feel free to lecture me. Otherwise trust me. This shit gets ugly fast. And I don't want any part of this. I better ring Wesley. He'll know what to do."

"Gem," he said, but the line was already dead.

CHAPTER TWENTY-EIGHT

"It is dangerous to let the public behind the scenes.
They are easily disillusioned and then they are angry with you,
for it was the illusion they loved."

~W. Somerset Maugham

Andre awoke to a blistering headache. The breakfast and double espresso at the hotel restaurant were starting to help when he caught a segment on the overhead television. He crept toward it.

"Can you increase the volume?" he asked the waitress.

Two toothy hosts smiled.

"Is Gemma prancing around with an American? Sources tell us there is a special person in her life, and he's here in London."

They cut to some of the same pictures he had seen the night before. Back to the co-host.

"She doesn't waste time, does she?"

Laughter.

"No, she doesn't. Odd timing, wouldn't you say? Wimbledon begins this weekend and with her injury, you'd think she'd want to be focused on her game."

"I'd say few tennis diehards will be surprised. She's always been more interested in the celebrity side of her life than on the competition."

"A shame. She had a brilliant Aegon tournament, then this. It's a questionable time to be playing Romeo and Juliet days before Wimbledon."

"Typical for her, I'm afraid."

"I'd venture to say the tennis gods don't mind having a celebrity in their midst. She has drawn more new eyeballs to tennis than any other athlete. She may never win a Grand Slam, but she'll have her rabid fans."

Andre spun to the waitress. "Another double espresso, please."

Why were they browbeating her? Was this typical? Also, how did they know he was an American? Who was their source? Multiple variables, but not impossible to solve. The emerging patterns from his virus were providing an interesting angle. If the data was right, Gemma would have to watch those around her carefully.

After his meal, he took a stroll through Notting Hill. He breathed in the scents from the restaurants and bakeries. He thought of the invisible forces, the controlling puppet masters that hid in the shadows. She was the puppet, and everyone else was riding her to the bank.

At the newsstand, he picked up the gossip paper. She was splashed on the cover.

"Who is her mystery American lover?" A sub-heading wrote. *"She's ready to quit tennis for him."*

He read another newspaper's headline. *"'She cheated on me, again!' Johnny confesses to a friend."*

Andre laughed then clenched his fists. He bought all the papers at the newsstand then hurled them into a trashcan. "My contribution to eliminating pollution," he told a gawking passer-by.

Gemma stepped into physical therapy and was confronted by an anxious Wesley.

"Why are you here?" Gemma asked.

"Anything else you want to share with me?"

"I'm here for therapy, and you're not therapeutic."

"Haven't you seen the damn headlines?"

She frowned. "We talked about this last night—"

"The new headlines. Gemma and her *American* lover. Those headlines."

Her jaw dropped. She had not read today's newspaper yet. How did they know he was an American? She composed herself. "What's your point?"

"Five years ago you told me you wanted to be bigger than anyone else.

I did that for you. What I expect is the truth. You owe me that much."

He was right. He'd been there for her when she'd thought her career was over before it'd even started. But she'd been a child then. So much had changed since. "He's a friend, that's all." She wouldn't—couldn't—tell Wesley the truth. She didn't need his lectures, nor did she completely trust him after the Johnny Flauto mess.

"So how did this get out?"

"Rubbish is fabricated every day. You should know, you've created plenty in your time. Let them say what they want. My personal life will not be addressed. Who I choose to befriend is my business."

"The word in the press and TV is you are not focused on Wimbledon—"

"That's nothing new. That's their favorite tune."

"And you have confided to someone you will quit tennis for him. The sponsors are calling me, demanding an official position. Tell me that's not true."

Her entire career they'd said the same thing about her. Time and again, her dedication to tennis had been questioned. They spoke about her dismissively, conceding she had the talent, but her actions were those of one who was more interested in landing an acting role rather than competing on the big stage. And she had gone and done just that with *Triton Warriors*. She wouldn't give them one more reason to discredit her. She needed to show the world she was the real deal.

"Where do they come up with this trash?" she asked.

He held her shoulders. "Did you consider maybe it's your new friend who spread that rumor? Trying to make some money off your friendship?"

She laughed. "Bollocks! Solid crap!" She shrugged his hands off her shoulders.

"Gemma, celebrities need to stay with celebrities. The average person can't be trusted. They don't get this world. It's not their fault. They just don't have the slightest clue of how this world works."

"So celebrities can be trusted? Say, like Johnny? Wesley, instead of second-guessing my ability to choose friends, why don't you find out who's spreading this shit. In fact, find out why the paparazzi always seem to know my whereabouts. Work on that and don't worry about my priorities."

"Gemma—" he said

"Wesley, please leave. I need to prepare for Wimbledon."

"Call me. We need to discuss this. We made a commitment to each other. We need to work through this together."

When he left, she dropped to the bench. *Why now?*

Hours later, Tish joined Gemma in her kitchen, huddled over a countertop littered with the day's newspapers and online articles about Gemma's new romance.

"You've shaken the hornet's nest," Tish said.

"How the hell did I manage to do that?"

"By bringing him here. The press have gotten wind and now the word is out."

Gemma felt drained. Her therapy had been solid and her training even better. She would be ready for Wimbledon, and furthermore, for once, she was happy. Andre was hers. But when she had stepped out after therapy, the larger than ever crowds, and the dozens of voice messages about the 'American' proved this time the media wanted answers.

Now they knew his name. This thing was spinning out of control. From TV to Twitter to Facebook, the rumors were flying. They had taken some truths and combined them with lies, giving credibility to the story. She wanted this to go away.

"And you invited him to tonight's Nikon party. Might as well call it your official coming-out party. I bet the paparazzi will be clamoring for his picture now. G, you say you two are friends. This is a lot to put a friend through. If there's more to you two, you need to tell Wesley so he can protect both of you."

"He's a friend. That's all."

"Just friends? Nothing more?"

"Tennis is what matters. Tennis wins over everything and everyone."

She wanted to collapse. Already she was lying about him, to her best friend now. With each lie and deception, the walls closed in further. Could she trust anyone? Even with Tish, she had to be elusive.

"I'll call Andre. He'll understand," Gemma said.

"You brought him here, and now you're asking him to hide? Even if he only comes to the matches, he will be in your reserved seats, there for everyone to speculate."

Gemma's shoulders sagged. She had not thought this through properly.

"Furthermore," Tish continued, "if we don't do something to manage the stories, they'll get worse. More lies will be added, and before you know it, the whole thing will implode around you. Look, I'll admit Wesley sometimes is all over the place, but I honestly think we need his advice. He'll come up with something."

Gemma begrudgingly agreed. When Wesley was called, he, as always, was eager to show he was a strategist. A smug one, but a competent one as well.

"We need them to reconsider the credibility of the source," Wesley said.

"How?" Gemma asked.

"They expect to see you with him, and you are planning to take him to the Nikon event. That's perfect. At the event we will confirm that such a person is real, but he's not your lover. Big misunderstanding. Yet again, the press misread the clues."

"And how do we pull that off?" Tish asked.

"He'll show up with someone else. He's in Gemma's circle, but not with Gemma. Natural confusion."

Silence. "But the damn event is tonight. Who can we trust? Conspiracies don't last long," Tish said.

"How about you?" Wesley asked.

"Me? Are you drunk?"

"That would make for the most reasonable explanation. He knows Gemma through you. We don't have to say he's your lover. Just that he's your friend."

Gemma rubbed her temples—a vise would have been preferable. "Won't it be easier if we avoid the whole thing?"

"Maybe for today," Wesley said, "but it doesn't give me the opportunity to redirect the chatter and kill it off, allowing you to focus on the tournament. I don't want to be a broken record, but the other question is, can we trust this Andre guy?"

"Wesley, you are a broken record, and the tune you play gives me a bloody headache."

"Hear me out," he said.

"No, I've seen what your idea of a good pairing earns me."

Silence.

Her heart was not in it, but over the years, Gemma had learned to follow Wesley's instincts. She didn't know if the plan would work, or how Andre would take it. He was a level-headed chap who solved complications, not created them.

And what if she actually told the truth?

No, this was not the right time. The press would zero in on her lack of focus. For once, she wanted the press to respect her. Once she won her first Grand Slam, then she could be free with everything else. She wouldn't need to balance anything.

"Tish, what do you think? What if we pretend he's your guest?" Gemma asked.

"What am I supposed to do, hold his bloody hand like we're an item or something?" Tish asked.

"Why not? Who's it going to hurt?" he asked.

Who indeed. Silence stretched for a few moments.

"Bloody shit, Gemma. Fine. I'll do it. But I'll remember this one when it's time for my raise. The things I do for you."

CHAPTER TWENTY-NINE

"There are a terrible lot of lies going about the world, and the
worst of it is that half of them are true."

~Winston Churchill

A ndre's face froze and his smile faltered. "I must have slept for a few days and missed something. I'm supposed to pretend what? And why?"

They were in Gemma's limo heading to the Nikon event. He scanned from Gemma to Tish and then back to Gemma again, searching for some clarity, but their faces gave him none. Tish's phone rang. She answered it.

"Wesley believes this is the most sensible approach," Gemma said, her voice now low. "This way we get them off my back until Wimbledon is over."

"I see. I'm a great supporter of sensible ideas. I'm just struggling to find the sensible part of this plan."

Gemma leaned closer. "No one needs to know about us," Gemma whispered. "Not Tish, not Wesley. That's our business. Let Wimbledon pass."

"And what happens after Wimbledon?" He held her gaze. Why would they go through so much to hide something so natural?

Gemma finally blinked. "Just bear with me for now. I don't need the distraction."

He slid closer. "I understand your request and will honor it. But by

197

playing these games, are you crushing the distractions or bringing more attention to it? This is a risky move. Whoever is the source of the rumors may already know more. And if new pictures show up? Or more details slip out? What then?"

They gazed at each other for a few moments.

"Okay, that was Wesley," Tish said as she hung up. "He's already throwing hints through his sources."

"That's good to hear," Andre said, trying to hide his sarcasm.

Andre's phone rang. It was Roger.

He was on vacation. Why was that so difficult to understand? He tapped the *Ignore* button.

The limousine pulled up to the red carpet. The flashing bulbs throttled like an uninterrupted cascade of blinding thunderstorms.

"All right, Tish," Andre said, "give me your hand. We need to make a good showing of this."

"Shite. I need a drink."

Gemma's door opened. As she stepped out, a roar of cheers, questions, and lights engulfed her. She was a silhouette against the blinding beam of fame. She was a portrait of calm and composure.

He and Tish stepped out holding hands. Dozens of cameras swiveled, and questions were hurled at them. He scanned the crowd and absorbed the situation. Too many people, too many voices, faces, movements, and flashes.

Andre and Tish remained silent and stood near Gemma, who was asked to pose over and over again. She was asked about him, but she smiled and offered nothing. As if the question wasn't even asked.

More pictures, more lights, more questions, and fake smiles—everyone wanted something from her. The needy begging for handouts.

The press were not expecting him to be holding Tish's hand. He hated the games, the lies, the stupidity of it all. Why would she—

Andre's headache burst from his right ear. Every single word came in Technicolor. With effort, he raised his hand to his ear, wanting to push the headache around—spread the sharp pain. He tried to shut out the chaos surrounding him. He wanted it to end. But it was no use.

"Are you okay?" Tish asked.

He forced a smile. "Headache."

"Migraine?" Tish whispered.

He blinked and held his posture, hoping to wait out the torture.

"Let's go in. Gemma can handle them."

She tried to walk quickly, but his balance was suspect. Tish supported him as they stepped into the venue. He stumbled into the restroom, ran cold water and drenched his face, meditating away the enemy within.

After a few minutes, color returned to his skin. He studied his eyes and regulated his breathing before he stepped out. Tish and Gemma were waiting for him.

"Are you okay? You scared me," Gemma said, her eyes bloodshot, cheeks red.

"Just a headache."

Gemma placed a hand on his chest. "Do you want us to leave?"

"I'm fine—" Andre started, but a frantic looking woman cut in.

"Miss Lennon, we need you backstage now. The video starts in twenty seconds."

Gemma glanced at her and nodded. "I'm ready."

The woman rushed Gemma around the back as Tish and Andre moved into the main reception area. A large silver screen showed a countdown.

Three, two, one.

To the music of AC/DC's "Back in Black", the new Nikon commercial rolled.

In black and white, the shot started from Gemma's shoes, up her lean powerful legs, all the way up to her face. The lighting and gray tones gave her body the appearance of a statue. First sign of color: Gemma's ice-blue eyes. The camera paused on her face. "I'm back," Gemma said.

With that, cleverly edited footage of Gemma hitting one winner after another thundered by. Spliced in-between the shots was a spinning, gunmetal black Nikon camera. Finally, a tight shot of Gemma's black bird tattoo. The camera then zoomed out and spun around Gemma for a head-to-toe shot of her glistening, powerful body. "Yes, I'm back," she said, and the commercial ended.

The invitees and press broke into a roar of applause and cheers. At that moment, through a cloud of smoke, Gemma walked onto the stage to a raucous crowd.

Andre had to hand it to her: she knew how to work her sexuality and her story. She was definitely back.

The rest of the evening dragged. Tish held his hand a little tighter now, remaining close, like a personal cane. They mingled, always a cluster away from Gemma. She was the sun, and all flocked to her.

From the body language of those in the 'respectable' media, they obviously had expected him to be with Gemma. And the way Tish held him—tight to her—added to their confusion. Most intriguing was Gemma. She never made eye contact with him. Not once. Yet another version of Gemma.

The evening wore on for another two hours. He waited for her to speak to him or something, but nothing came. Speeches, platitudes, announcements, small talk, cocktails, and more stares.

"You seem to be doing better," Tish said.

"I am. Didn't mean to worry you."

"Well you did, you dumb ox."

Andre observed Gemma. "Why isn't Gemma talking to us? Did I miss something?"

"It's all part of the act."

"What act?"

"This is the celebrity Gemma."

"Hmm. Interesting. How many Gemma's are there?"

"That's an odd question. I don't know. A few. What does it matter?"

"I'd like to know which ones I can speak to, so I don't inadvertently bring down this house of cards you guys have built. There must be rules to this game."

"The rules are simple: don't screw up."

"Great. Thanks. I'll keep that in mind."

Eventually it was time to leave.

When Gemma stepped out, staff photographers and paparazzi jumped and rushed the velvet rope. More bulbs, more cameras, more questions, and more rain. The air was cold now. Steam rose from the press corps.

Andre studied the press then tapped Tish's shoulder. "Looks like this plan of Wesley's worked for today," he whispered. "They're definitely confused. Just hope it's sustainable."

"Hope you're right. She doesn't need the distraction. Maybe we should make sure they don't second-guess what they've seen."

"And what do you—" he started, but did not finish. Her kiss came without advance notice or warning. It was his turn to keep his eyes open. It was a quick kiss, but it left him stunned. "Well," he said, "that's one way."

She laughed. "You 'Mericans are funny."

He glanced toward Gemma. She was locked onto Andre, unblinking. The same pose from her commercial.

CHAPTER THIRTY

"And if you gaze for long into an abyss, the abyss gazes also into you."

~Friedrich Nietzsche

The rain rattled against the car's roof. The windows were streaked with droplets that in turn picked up the city lights. Tish was on the phone with Wesley, while Andre focused on the world outside.

Gemma didn't know what had happened between Tish and Andre. Whatever the reason, it was making her nauseous. She would remain calm for now. She'd get to the bottom of this once she could ask privately. But the itch to understand was too much to bear.

She pulled out her mobile and sent him a text.

"What was that? With Tish," she wrote.

He studied his mobile then typed, *"Her idea of leaving the press with no doubt."*

"I see," she wrote.

"No, you don't. Why are you hiding us? When they win, we lose," he wrote, then dropped his mobile in his coat pocket.

She read his note a few more times, then glanced at him. She wanted to go to him, but how could she? If she had told Tish the truth, that kiss would never have happened. And what if the truth came out? What was the worst that could happen?

"I'm sorry," she mouthed.

He didn't acknowledge her. Instead he turned his gaze back to the streets.

Her heart sank. This was why. This was why she didn't want a relationship. She hadn't asked for this. She hadn't wanted to fall in love, but it had happened.

Love?

Heat spread across her cheeks. She continued watching him, the seconds ticking away.

"Wesley's all over it," Tish said as she hung up. "He's calling his contacts to give them the scoop that there is no scoop after all." She studied both of them. "Did I miss something?"

"No, just exhausted," Gemma said.

A few moments later, Andre sat up. "There's the hotel now. I'm going to stay away for the next few days. Let's not give the media more raw meat."

Not a question. A statement. She wanted to argue, disagree. But she couldn't. That was his plan, wasn't it? He was forcing her hand. He knew she would not say anything in front of Tish. He was testing her. She had lied about them, even to her best friend. She was left without options.

"But you will come to the matches, won't you?"

"Of course."

"Andre, look," Tish said, pointing to the hotel entrance. "Paparazzi are camped out in front of your hotel."

"Okay," he said, and without a second thought, stepped out and closed the door.

Gemma watched him walk away. No kiss. No hug. Not the slightest touch.

Once home, Gemma tried Andre's cell, but it went directly to voicemail. Gemma's head sagged. Why wasn't he answering his phone? She had marginalized their relationship, but knew she could clean it up. They would talk and all would be okay again. Because that's what they had—they could fix anything.

She tried again, with the same result. Had he shut off his mobile?

He had not been given a choice. He was told to play along in the games she had been a part to for nearly five years now.

I am an idiot.

At midnight, Andre went to the hotel gym, hoping a good run on the treadmill would release the tension in his neck. It took forty-five minutes for the headache to finally exit his skull. Sweat dripped off his body, his shirt was drenched, and his veins pumped with blood.

What was he to Gemma, he wondered? What was more important to her? Their relationship or some obscure concept of privacy? He could have been a flowerpot there. Why even invite him, if that's what she was going to do?

He ran faster. The machine whined under his thundering clip.

How could he have been so wrong? He had been willing to do anything to make it work. Now he wondered how he could have been so off base. She wasn't ready. He wondered if she ever would be.

Almost finished, he assured his legs. His thighs and calves were numb. His lungs were unable to take in deep breaths—only shallow, small gasps of oxygen through gritted teeth. Pure adrenaline and momentum pushed him on.

The treadmill's display showed thirty seconds remaining.

The music that blared through his headphones was now overpowered by his thudding heartbeat in his throat.

60 MINUTES flashed on the display. He slammed the "Stop" button and tumbled off.

Andre collapsed, one knee on the floor, head bowed. Sweat ran down his face. Eventually, he summoned the energy to stand and walk back to his room for a much-needed shower.

Under the steaming water he wondered where their relationship would go from here. Maybe a few days apart would clarify what she wanted. He had a full day ahead with the DCI. He'd spend Saturday and Sunday investigating. Monday was Gemma's first match. Maybe by then she would know what she wanted.

He stepped out of the shower, haphazardly dried himself, and wrapped a towel around his waist.

The next move is hers, was his last thought as he stepped out of the bathroom.

CHAPTER THIRTY-ONE

"Dream as if you'll live forever. Live as if you'll die today."

~James Dean

The bathroom door opened. Gemma straightened, and reminded herself to breathe.

Andre stepped out of the bathroom with a large towel wrapped around his waist, his hair still wet, and droplets of water rolling off his chest, arms, and back. Her heartbeat quickened.

He stopped dead in his tracks and glanced up, registering her presence for the first time. "How'd you get in?"

She rose, adjusted her skirt, then found the strength to move toward him. "I have a card key. The room is under my name."

"What are you doing here?"

She stopped in front of him and peered into his eyes. "Today was not a good day. I wanted to—"

"What?" he asked. "What did you want?" His eyes hardened. "Are you allowed to talk to me now? Are we safe enough?"

"I wanted to apologize," she said, then placed her hands on his chest. Momentarily her breath caught when she touched his wet, hard body.

"Gem, apologize only if you don't plan on repeating the same mistake. I don't know what game we're playing and somehow I doubt you do either. What are we doing? Where do we go from here?"

"I don't know," she said. "Can I be allowed to not know?" She stepped into him. "I want to be with you. When we're together, alone, everything is perfect." Her body met his and warm jolts ran down from her navel to her knees. "You asked me to live in the moment. I'm trying."

His eyes softened

They gazed deep into each other's eyes. Their bodies pinned, breathing in harmony, their chests rising in unison. Warm water dripped from his body onto hers.

He ran his wet hand through her hair. "This will not end well."

"No, you're wrong. Tonight ends well. We'll figure out tomorrow when tomorrow comes." She kissed him, tasting his lips again.

She wanted—needed—everything of his. His lips, his chin, his neck, his touch. She slid her hands over his chest then along his back. Her nails raked his skin, causing a slight groan to escape his mouth.

He tugged off her top, exposing a white tank top. Her heart hammered against her ribs. She kissed and nibbled his chest while her fingers teased the skin just above the towel. They stumbled against the wall. His lips burnt into hers. He grabbed the back of her thigh, lifting it, bringing her tight into him. While the other hand slid under her shirt, over her breast.

She gasped for air, writhing and whimpering. Her chest was on fire. She couldn't focus anymore. Her vision blurred as the room spun, and the lines disappeared. Only primal hunger raged with clarity. Unlike anything ever in her life, she needed him.

His warm mouth devoured her neck then found her ear. Her hands slid down, below the small of his back, squeezing in until the towel snapped loose and dropped. Her nails dug into his flesh. His body tightened.

He reached behind, grabbing her hands, then pushed them up and above her head, holding her there momentarily when he swiftly peeled off her shirt. He worked her lips, bit her chin, kissed her throat, down her chest, and hovered over her navel.

Kneeling in front of her, he glanced up into her eyes. Her knees bounced when he unclasped the skirt and the garment slid down slightly. She ran her fingers through his hair. His hands on her skirt, he kissed the flesh just above her waistline then slowly tugged the garment and underwear down. She trembled. With each inch, he kissed the newly exposed skin, down her hips, over her thighs until she was completely bare.

He rose and slammed his lips onto hers. She threw her arms

around his neck then wrapped her legs around his hips. The world spun as he carried her into the bedroom. He lay her down but then stepped away. When she heard the tearing of foil, her heartbeat quickened. Moments later he slid next to her. The sheets were soft, his body hard, damp, on fire. As they kissed, he rolled on top of her—his weight, presence, and warmth enclosing her. He bore into her eyes, communicating without words.

She answered him.

Their bodies melted into one.

In that instant, lightning illuminated the skies, thunder rolled, and hail covered the streets of London.

The tap-dancing of the rain against the window was therapeutic. The room's lighting cast a glow on Gemma's skin. She was sleeping, at peace. Andre lay on his side, memorizing her smooth skin, the dimple below the small of her back, and her curves. He wanted to remember everything about her.

Without touching, he traced the tattoo of the graceful black bird on her shoulder blade. As if by the suggestion of his touch, she stirred. He moved in and held her tight—her soft flesh against his. He nuzzled her hair, the faint smell of jasmine still detectable. She faced him. Only a whisper of air separated their lips.

"What time is it?" she asked.

"Don't know—don't care," he said, and kissed her.

"I better call Glen," she said, her voice barely audible. She covered herself with the bed sheets then sat up. She glanced over her shoulder as she stepped toward the pile of clothes sprawled across the suite. She found her phone then entered the restroom.

He lay back and watched the ceiling, daring to imagine a life of happiness, when distant thunder growled.

He could hear her soft voice. A few moments later she came back, the pile of white sheets still engulfing her like clouds embracing a rainbow. She crawled into bed.

She was a young girl now. Joy, innocence, and uncertainty transformed the face of the fierce competitor and shrewd athlete. She was a different person, and he had to protect that innocence from the people in her world who tried so hard to break her.

She scooted tight next to him, inches away from his face. He held her gaze. They remained silent, the sounds of breathing, accompanied by the percussive rhythms of the rain infiltrated the room.

"I don't want this to end," she said, her voice strained. "But I'm afraid it will. Like all good things in my life, this will end too. Don't let it end."

He pulled her to him and held her face. "Why do you talk that way?"

"I inadvertently made a pact with the devil. I think. Professional success at the cost of happiness. I'm cursed and destined to be alone forever. So this—this dream we're sharing now—will be over and I will be alone. Again."

"You do know you're full of shit, right?"

"Well, that's very sweet," she said, chuckling.

"This dream ends when both you and I say it's over. No witches, doctors, or managers will tell me what I can and can't do. This thing we have is completely in our hands. No one else. I have no plans on withdrawing from this game. You?"

She was silent, looking at him. Then she moved up and kissed his lips. "Thank you," she whispered. Her fingers caressed his healing chest burn then traced his abdomen, down below his navel. A wave of heat traveled along his skin.

"You're welcome," he mumbled in return.

And as she kissed him, she rolled on top, still kissing him. "I told you," she said in a warm, sultry voice as she straddled him. "Tonight ends well."

A flash and the rumble of thunder woke Gemma. She sat up in the strange bed, confused at her surroundings.

"You okay?" a man asked.

No! She snatched the bed sheets and haphazardly tried to cover her exposed body, while at the same time she tried to scurry away from the voice.

"What's wrong?" the same man asked.

She whirled to the voice and focused on his face. It was Andre. She was fine. It was Andre. She tried to control her reaction, even tried to smile, but it was no use. She was trembling now.

"What's wrong, Gem?" He sat up. "Why were you scared?"

She didn't speak.

He scooted next to her and gently placed his hand on her head, looking into her eyes. Her tears welled up.

"Christ, Gem. Who hurt you?"

One simple question and the floodgates opened. Her head collapsed on his bare chest as tears flowed freely. He cradled her in his arms and held tight. His fingers slid through her hair, a gesture she had come to adore.

Why was she still hurting over the past? She had put that episode behind her. She was a strong woman now. Back then she had been a child. She hadn't known how to handle life and its challenges.

"You're safe with me," he whispered. "I won't hurt you. I can't. I love you."

Her eyes opened wide, but she didn't move a muscle.

He lifted her chin and peered into her eyes. "I love you."

Her expression didn't change, but inside she burnt. *He loves me.*

"Together, remember?"

The best she could do was nod and burrow into his chest. *Andre loves me.*

Some moments passed before she was able to meet his gaze.

"I was sixteen," she said. "A newly minted pro who had just stunned the tennis world by reaching the semis in my first Wimbledon Grand Slam. My agency organized a celebration in my honor." A smile flitted at the distant memory. "I was finally a pro. I would earn a living doing what I loved. I would repay my parents for their sacrifices, and pay my way through my professional career. It was a surreal feeling.

"The party was a madhouse. Loud music, alcohol, heat. I was given one cocktail after another until the night became a blur. At sixteen, it didn't take much to intoxicate me. There was another tennis pro there. He was nineteen and had just broken into the top twenty. He was talented, handsome, and I had been crushing on him for months, but he never paid me much attention. That night, he asked me to dance.

"We danced, more drinks, and then… he told me I was pretty. After that, like a daft child, I stuck to him like fur on cat. I had been hoping for him to notice me for months. And here he was, interested in me. We found a secluded place and kissed. It was fantastic. I was already imagining a future with him. Until he lifted my skirt."

A burning tear slid down her cheek.

"I felt his hands, his body, his breathing. It hit me then. I realized what was happening. But I was too drunk. I could barely stand, much less fight. I told him to stop. He didn't or couldn't hear me. I asked, then said, then yelled. The stench of mixed drinks was on his breath. I was helpless, without strength. I tried to stop him. Instead, I lost my footing and landed on the floor. Like a fuckin' animal he was on top of me. I remember tears. Maybe from the pain, but mostly from the humiliation."

A few moments ticked away.

"I was on the floor, tears were smeared on my face, and he asked if I had enjoyed it. I did the best I could—I spat at him. He laughed and said he had taken pity on me. That I looked like a little boy with my flat chest and muscular shoulders. Next thing I knew, someone was peeling my fingernails from the bastard's face. It was Wesley who found and rushed me out of there. I will never forget how he came to my aid."

"Was Georg arrested?" Andre asked.

She straightened. His voice had an edge that exhilarated her. But how had he figured it out? "No."

"You didn't press charges?"

"Wesley advised me not to. He told me Georg would most likely claim I was a willing participant. Everyone saw us dancing and drinking. And many knew I had been after him for months. It would have been my word against his. Also, my tennis career would have been forever marred. Wesley, like always, was thinking about the long-term impact." She paused, tried to force a smile, but she didn't have it in her to pretend.

A solid hand raised her chin. "I'm not Georg. You have nothing to be ashamed of. Nothing. You are sharp, beautiful, gifted, and powerful—you are perfect. You were taken advantage of by an asshole. Simple as that. That was five years ago—a lifetime ago. You're not that sixteen-year-old girl anymore. You are amazing. You have so much to offer this world. Don't look at the world through the eyes of that sixteen-year-old."

Gemma said nothing. Instead she absorbed his words. His eyes held no judgment. She had been right about Andre. He did understand, and he didn't blame her either. Years of apprehension and distrust lifted. The air seemed cooler, fresher.

His eyes said it all. He kissed her lips gently.

"Are you okay?" he asked.

"I'm perfect," she said then kissed him.

She held him as tightly as she could. She had found the one. The only one. They leaned back as he kissed her head—little pecks that soothed her heavy heart. With her cheek on his chest, she listened to his deep and rapid heart rate. With that rhythm, she drifted off to sleep.

PART IV

DOUBLE FAULT

The server has two opportunities to place the ball in the designated service box. The first missed shot is a fault. A second consecutive mis-hit is a double-fault. Although the aggressive serve can generate winning points (Ace), a double-fault is usually a sign of mental and physical fatigue—both conditions which will contribute to eventual defeat.

~Tennis Basics

CHAPTER THIRTY-TWO

"It is our choices that show what we truly are, far more than our abilities."

~J. K. Rowling

Gemma woke to the shrill sound of her mobile phone. She stumbled from bed and glanced out the window. The sun was not supposed to be there. What time was it? She grabbed her phone, forcing her eyes to focus. First she noticed the name—*Bedric*. Then she noticed the time—*9:00 a.m.*

"Holy shit!" she yelled. She was an hour late.

Andre sat up with a jolt. "What? What happened?"

She answered the phone. "Sorry, I lost track of time."

"Are you well?" Bedric asked.

"I'm fine. I'm sorry. I just—you know—lost track of time."

"Gemma, you must learn to choose. You said you wanted to win. You called it a new chapter. What are your priorities?"

She glanced at Andre, who stumbled past her to the bathroom. "There is no confusion. Give me an hour." She hung up.

"Crap! Bugger! Shit! I am so late!"

Andre popped his head out, studying her.

"What?" she asked.

"There's my drunken sailor."

Gemma was waiting for her team to arrive and escort her from the private exit of the hotel.

"What are your plans for today?" she asked Andre.

She noticed his hesitation. "I'm taking care of some urgent business."

"Will you be free tonight?"

"I'm expecting a call by noon. I'll know the exact plans then, but should be free at night. Why do you ask?" He slid his hand through her hair.

"As fun as it was to have the hotel's general manager sneak me in, my place is infinitely safer. Come over tonight. We'll have dinner."

"Is it wise? The tournament starts tomorrow and your first match is on Monday. You should focus."

She grinned. "It's settled then. I'll have Glen pick you up at 8:00 p.m." She gave him a peck on his lips.

He pulled back slightly. "Gem, is this wise?" he asked again. "I don't want to be a source of distraction."

"You don't distract me. You center me. At the Aegon championship, it was your voice in my head that carried me through. You're good for me."

He beamed. "Okay, then. 8:00 p.m. it is." He brought her face to his.

Just as they kissed, his mobile rang. She glanced at the number. "That's Tish."

He answered it. "Good morning, Tish... yes, I'm free in the morning... sure, sounds fun... I'll meet you there in an hour." He hung up.

"She wants to give me a tour of Wimbledon." He smirked. "Are you jealous?"

"Nice try. I asked her to call you."

"So you weren't jealous? Not even a bit?"

"Maybe a bit." She draped her arms around his neck and gave him a long, loving kiss. And in the privacy of her mind, she thought, *I love you.*

Andre recalled her face, her words, her smile, her scent. He was utterly happy, which concerned him. He had never enjoyed the luxury known as happiness.

He'd have to manage the situation with M&T. How could he stay away from her for three, four, maybe five months? If he worked around the clock, maybe he could wrap it up in two or three. But that was wishful thinking. Once Sunrise started, he would be buried, flying from one military base to another. How much harder could he work?

He wanted to be a source of support, not distraction. She had to focus on Wimbledon. If he brought it up now, it would probably cause more problems. But he couldn't wait until after Wimbledon either, because that's when he had to start his project. The upside of an early loss was that he could tell her sooner.

He didn't even want to think about that scenario. She had to win, for her own sake. Although her fans loved her, the press wanted to see her fail—gloriously if possible. They would write one segment after another. A celebrity who hit rock bottom was infinitely more entertaining than one who stood above the fray.

He'd have to tell her soon. He just had to wait for the right opportunity.

Tish greeted Andre with a hug and a kiss on the cheek. "Let's go into the inner sanctum of tennis's greatest destination." She held his hand and led him into the park.

They spent the next two hours talking to officials, touring the grounds, watching the crews tend to the grass, and talking to the broadcast crews. They eventually settled and ate the famed strawberries and cream.

"So what do you think of her world, her lifestyle?"

"It's a crazy world, where little makes sense."

"Maybe to you. But it's the way the world of the gifted and celebrity works."

A headache cut through his left eye. "Really? Running from one group of salivating paparazzi, to another? That's the world of the gifted?"

"We may not like it, but when you're as big a celebrity as she is, you need to be willing to play the game."

"Until it breaks her."

"She's much stronger than you give her credit for."

Like a saw, the headache ate away at his brain. "We're all more fragile than we want to believe."

"We're made stronger by those who surround us. She needs people

215

she can trust. People who have her well-being at the forefront of every decision."

"And how well do you think she's doing there?"

She hesitated.

"That's what I thought," he said.

"It's not that. Look, everyone is doing the best they can."

"Do you really believe that?"

He studied her eyes, saw her sincerity. "I do. This stuff is so confusing sometimes. Everyone is running one way, then the other, then we're told to do more of one thing, then less of another. It's with the best of intentions. But sometimes things go wrong. No one wants that to happen, but it does."

"Chaos will always produce unexpected results. That's the goal of chaos. You guys have to eliminate the things that create the spirals. Not feed into them."

Gemma glanced at the clock every few minutes, her nerves on full alert. It was 8:22 in the evening. She was estimating how long it would take Glen to pick up Andre and drive back. Fifteen minutes? Maybe twenty? She kept checking her hair and lightly applied makeup. She studied her reflection, happy with what she wore. A strapless one-piece dress, a handful of inches above the knees, with heels to accentuate her legs. Her smile froze. *You're behaving like a little schoolgirl waiting for her prom date.* Not that she had ever been to a prom.

Her mobile rang. It was Glen.

"Ma'am, Mr. Reyes is not back at the hotel yet. I've checked with the front desk, and it appears he has not returned since morning."

Her heart sank. "I'll call him on his mobile."

Three rings and he picked up.

"Gem, I am so sorry. I should've called."

"Where are you?"

Noise in the background. "I'm still stuck on the business I told you about. I'm sorry, but I won't be able to make it after all."

"I see." Her jaw clenched. "That's it then. I guess we'll speak tomorrow."

"I'm sorry. I promise to make it up to you—"

"No need," she said. "Cheers." She hung up and was tempted to throw the phone against the wall. Instead, she leaned against her mirror and closed her eyes.

Andre wanted to bash his head against his cell phone. He had known two hours earlier he would not be able to pull away. He should have called her then and there. But he got distracted, and now he felt like the prize idiot.

He glanced at Detective Chief Inspector Whitby, who was studying him.

"All's well, Doctor?"

"No, I'm an idiot."

"Aren't we all?"

The video surveillance images from the hotel had been close to useless. The stalker had successfully blocked enough of his face when passing the cameras that the image matching applications couldn't find a hit. It would have to be up to Andre.

He had already gone through the images of suspected and known perpetrators who belonged to various terrorist organizations and their sympathizers. One by one, he had scrolled through the images, relying on his photographic memory to find the right person. But the exercise had been a bust. No hits.

A new approach would be needed.

"What if we expand the search to include anyone who fits the stalker's physical description?" Andre asked.

"Not just terrorists or friends of?"

"Let's not limit the search. Let's see everyone."

DCI Whitby rubbed his face. "I can't even hazard a guess as to how many faces you'll need to analyze."

"Let's not guess. Just bring up the files."

Half an hour later, after they had filtered the faces for known physical attributes, Andre leaned close to the monitor and scrolled through the images, faster and faster, looking for key markers that differentiated each person.

"How do you do that?" DCI Whitby asked. "I'm getting dizzy just watching you."

Andre didn't respond. He blocked sounds, scents, and self-doubt. For a long stretch he studied the images, slowing down when he needed to blink. He would push through this until—

He stopped scrolling. His heart rate spiked momentarily.

"Did you see something?" Whitby asked.

Andre scrolled back slowly until he landed on the face that had given him pause.

"Is that him?"

"That's my stalker."

Whitby took over, pulling the man's information.

Andre leaned back, rubbing his temple and eyes.

"This is unexpected," Whitby said.

Andre studied the rap sheet. "Abe Munem. Who is he?"

"Not a terrorist, that's for sure. He's a hired gun, an investigator of sorts."

"A private detective?"

"Not exactly that classy. Also, he's talented at hiding."

They spoke for a while. Andre considered the implications of their findings. Although some details were still speculation, the news was significant. Who had hired him? And why? Andre would have to deal with this development the best way he could—head on. More importantly, he had to protect Gemma. She could not get stuck in the crosshairs of his mess.

Chapter Thirty-Three

"People are where they are because that is exactly where they really want to be—whether they will admit that or not."

~Earl Nightingale

Gemma was familiar with this feeling—emotional hangover. She was furious and depressed. She understood that eventually this would be a way of life. With his career and hers, physical proximity would be the exception, not the norm. Their relationship had grown with velocity, and with each passing day they had gotten closer. All her vulnerabilities and concerns had been exposed to him and he in return had been her anchor.

For the first time she understood the meaning of bliss. But when she was not with him, the emptiness was there in abundance. She missed him, and the thought that she would not have him whenever she needed him bothered her.

He had once told her nature abhors a vacuum. Emptiness would eventually get replaced with something else. For Gemma, sadness filled her lonely heart.

She crawled out of bed, dragged her feet across the house, and sat for breakfast, newspaper at her side—her father's tradition she had now adopted as her own. She unfolded the Sunday paper, pulled out the sports section, and raised the teacup to her lips. She froze, her cup tilted slightly and her mouth open. She blinked, and read the headline again.

"Gemma's Secret Lover Exposed."

She read quickly, picking up the key pieces of information.

"Gemma and Dr. Andre Reyes met in Paris during the French Open… Their romance blossomed just as she dropped her semifinal match against Sonia Wilkins… They left the country together for a brief romantic getaway in Malibu, California… After her injury, during the Aegon games, she sent for him, and he came to her side… She is ready to quit."

She stopped reading.

Her mobile rang. Wesley. "Not now." She pressed *Ignore*. Her home phone rang. "Don't answer it," she told her staff.

Newspaper in hand, she ran upstairs to her bedroom, slammed the door shut, and dialed Andre.

"Hi, Gem," he said, clearing his throat. He sounded like he had just woken up.

"How did this shit get out?"

"What are you talking about?"

"The bloody newspapers. They know everything about us. What the hell is going on here?"

"I don't have the slightest clue."

"This is great, Andre. Just fantastic. The tournament begins today, and my first match is tomorrow. Do you know what this'll mean?"

"No, I don't. I haven't read the article, but assuming they haven't created vicious lies, the most it means is they know we're together."

"It's not that simple."

"Yes. It is simple. Calm down. There's no reason to get excited over this. Don't get thrown off track."

She would have to talk to Wesley and plan a response. She would need to address the fears of her sponsors. Why did it have to happen now? Couldn't this have been buried for a few more weeks?

"I need to go," she said, and hung up.

Although Andre had advised Gemma to relax, he was furious. He would have to call the DCI and see if this article was related to his stalker. He hoped not, but maybe the DCI could pressure the newspaper to release the name of the source.

He got out of bed and checked his laptop. Gemma's virus was completely attached now. He ran the analyzer tools and watched the results. His eyes froze, and his mouth opened slightly.

At that same instant, his cell phone chimed. He had a text message from his assistant. The message was simple and to the point: *"911 - Rome."*

He stared at his phone, considering the implications. It was midnight in L.A. This was bad. He was dialing his assistant when his cell rang. It was Roger.

"Hi Roger, I just got the notice about Rome."

"That's not why I'm calling."

"Oh?"

"We've gotten word about you in the newspapers."

"Okay."

"And you need to distance yourself from the media and press ASAP. If the press and paparazzi begin to follow you, the Pentagon will cancel the project. They can't have you in the spotlight. Your actions are compromising Project Sunrise."

Gemma spent all day training, canceling interviews, and planning with Wesley. To her relief, Wesley was rolling with the developments; the smug bastard was finding ways to spin the news. Unfortunately, two days ago they had concocted the appearance that Andre was with Tish. And now the backlash was five-fold. It gave credibility to some of the more damaging lies. The questions surfaced again: was she about to quit tennis? Also, some of the raunchier papers questioned the type of friendship she really had with Tish. Bad taste had no limits.

Her phone chimed with a new text message from Tish. *"Just friends?"*

Gemma rubbed her temples. Now her best friend was calling her out on being less than honest about Andre.

It was late afternoon when she got around to returning Andre's voicemail and text messages.

"Glad you called. I thought we wouldn't connect before I left."

"Left? What do you mean?"

"I have an urgent matter in Rome. One of my clients is on the verge of losing their license with the Italian government. They need me there for a Monday morning meeting."

"Monday? You'll miss my first match."

"I know, I'm sorry. I tried to find an alternate solution, but no one else can represent their technical strategy."

She didn't know what to say.

"Gem, I'm sorry. But I have to do this."

"I wanted you at my match," she whispered.

"It won't be like this forever."

She heard the sincerity in his voice. She'd have to at least try to understand.

The next morning, Gemma emerged from her world of dreams—drenched in sweat. The first day of each tournament was always the worst. Her nerves dominated her dreams.

She shuffled into her kitchen, feeling profoundly sad and lonely. She picked up her phone and called Andre, but his mobile went to voicemail.

"You forgot to wish me luck," she said.

She waited patiently for his call, but when she didn't hear from him, the sadness evolved into passive aggression.

A few hours later, when she was in the locker room preparing for her match, her mobile rang. She leapt at her bag and snatched the phone.

"Hello," she said.

"Good luck, Gem. I'll have the match streaming on my cell. I'm there with you—thirty-second delay, but still there."

"Thanks for calling," she whispered.

"Go. Win. I love you."

She grinned like a kid. "I'll see what I can do about that."

She won her first match.

But she was rusty, committing too many unforced errors in the first set. She even dropped one of her serves, allowing the first set to go to tiebreaker. She eventually won the set, and when the second set started she didn't look back, winning 6-0, not conceding even a single game to her unseeded opponent.

She walked off, waved at her boisterous fans, and smiled for the camera, but once in the locker room she was ready to spit venom. She removed the strap around her thigh and slung it across the room. Maybe she played poorly because of her strained hamstring. She doubted it. The cause was Andre.

He should have been here at the match, not in Rome.

An hour later, after she finished her last interview, her mobile rang. It was Andre. She ran into an empty room.

"You were awesome!"

"Thank you," she said, not fully agreeing with his assessment.

"I sat at the head of the table with the phone on my lap, stealing glances. But I couldn't take it anymore. Near the end of the first set, when it went to tiebreaker, I excused myself and went to the restroom to watch the match in the stall. Each time I wanted to cheer, I'd flush the toilet."

She laughed. This time she would cut him a little slack. She leaned against the wall and closed her eyes. She missed him. She loved him.

On Tuesday, after practice and interviews, she went home and changed. Andre had invited her to his suite for dinner. He had promised something special.

She wondered what he had planned. Whatever it was, she looked forward to spending a few hours with him. She couldn't spend the night there; she had a match the next afternoon. But she could afford a few hours of down time.

With the help of the hotel's general manager, she once again entered from the private access. Andre walked her to the sofa and planted her in front of the coffee table. She studied the variety of knickknacks, trying to understand.

"Fresh baguettes from a bakery in Notting Hill," he said as he exposed the basket of fresh loafs. "The Serrano ham and wine are from my grandfather's estate in Spain. The cheese I brought from Rome last night. And the movie on the laptop is one of my all-time favorites: 'The Big Picture,' with Kevin Bacon."

She breathed in the scents. Her tired shoulders relaxed. She kicked off her shoes and pulled her legs up beneath her. Bread, cheese, wine, and a movie in the company of a loved one was the epitome of romance.

She cuddled next to him. "What's the movie about?"

"It's about a young director who allows conceit to nearly ruin everything that matters. He thinks that in order to make it, he needs to be someone else. He puts at risk his passion, his friends, and his love—not to mention his identity. What do you think?"

"Stop talking, get me half a glass of wine, and press play."

Some time later, the bottle was empty, the food was gone, the movie credits rolled and her head was on his chest. She listened to his breathing and heartbeat.

"I'm sorry about the last few days," he said.

She sat up and pulled him by his arms.

"I'd like to try something new with you," she said as she unbuttoned his shirt.

He hesitated. "And what's that?" he asked, his voice a bit hoarse.

She undid the last button and exposed his chest. She leaned into his neck and whispered, "It's called make-up sex," then nibbled on his ear.

He cleared his throat. "I've never—" he took a breath "—heard of this game."

"In order to be forgiven," she said as she laid soft pecks on his chest, "you need to bend to all my demands." She stopped kissing then studied his eyes. "What do you think?"

His eyes were foggy. "I love this game."

Gemma's second round match on Wednesday was a blood bath.

She was brilliant. One ace after another, one broken serve after another. Her opponent won only two games. The match ended 6-1, 6-1. Gemma didn't break a sweat.

At the end of the match when she waved at her fans, she turned to her reserved seats and waved at Andre, who was standing and whistling.

My lucky charm, she thought, as she marched off the court, convinced that with him, she was unstoppable.

On Thursday morning, Gemma was ready to cry.

Tucked inside her newspaper was an unmarked envelope. Hidden inside was a picture of Andre and her, kissing in Hayden Park. Not a perfect picture. But the picture was irrelevant.

IF YOU LIKE IT, I HAVE MORE. I KNOW YOUR LITTLE SECRET TOO. £1 MILLION TO KEEP IT SAFE. SO HARD TO TRUST PEOPLE, BUT YOU CAN TRUST ME, GEM.

What little secret? Georg? Her fingers trembled as she dialed Wesley. Afterwards, she called Andre.

Within twenty minutes, Andre and Detective Chief Inspector Whitby were in Gemma's home. As were Wesley and Bedric. Gemma's staff and security team explained the newspaper was dropped off as always. They had not noticed anything out of the ordinary. The surveillance tapes did not show any tampering after the paper had been delivered by the service.

The DCI interviewed Gemma, Bedric, and Wesley. Tish was a no-show. Whitby was a heavyset man, barrel chested, with a perpetually wet upper lip. His dark eyes didn't miss a thing, reminding her of the black, soulless eyes of a great white shark.

No, there had been no previous actions of this sort. Yes, she received crazy fan mail regularly. No, although she had been sued frivolously in the past, never had she been blackmailed. No, she had no idea who would be behind this.

"Ma'am, the extortionist refers to a 'little secret.' Anything you're able to share?" the DCI asked.

"No," both Gemma and Wesley said at the same time. She glared at Wesley then faced the DCI, barely able to keep her emotions in check. "I want to pay this bastard off and be done with it."

The DCI shifted in his seat. "Ma'am, if I may. You're world famous. Any real secret from your life would be worth considerably more than £1 million. My guess is the pictures alone would bring in a small fortune."

She held her breath, considering the implications. "So what are you saying?"

"There's more to this than a simple blackmail. It's either the first of many, or there's a larger agenda at play."

"Hold on a minute Mr. DCI," Wesley said as he shifted forward. "What are you driving at? This seems fairly straightforward. Someone with access to private information is ready to make some quick cash. You need to look into who could have access to sensitive information."

The DCI grinned. Decades of nicotine had marred his teeth. "The Met always appreciates expert advice. My ears are wide open."

They stared at each other.

"What if—" Wesley started.

"Wesley, please," she interrupted.

Wesley grunted. Bedric crossed his legs, not a trace of emotion on his face.

"I'm willing to take your advice and follow your lead. But I can't have my life and career ruined. I need this handled."

"I will place the best on this case," he said, then exchanged glances with Andre. When Andre and Whitby arrived together, she had been confused. But now it was clear they knew each other.

When the interview was over and the evidence collected, she asked Andre to join her in the kitchen to speak privately.

"I am very worried about this," she said. "What little secret? Could it be about Georg?"

"I don't know."

"No one in my family knows. Not my mum, not my grandfather, Xavi, or Mari. This would devastate them. I can't let this happen to them."

"I won't let that happen. I'll help Whitby and his team crack this one."

She studied him. "Who would do this to me? Why?"

"I don't know yet. But I will—"

"And then the note refers to me as 'Gem.' You're the only one who calls me Gem."

He cocked his head.

"No, I don't think you're behind this. But I don't know what to think either, Andre. The blackmailer is making a direct connection to you. And when I called you, you showed up with the DCI. What are you not telling me?"

He took a deep breath then nodded. "Someone has been following me since I arrived in London. This extortion letter may be from the same person. We're not sure yet, but the DCI and I think it the most probable scenario."

Heat bloomed. "But… why did you keep this from me?" Her voice trembled.

"I didn't want to concern you. I didn't believe my tail was in any way related to you."

"That doesn't make sense. Why would anyone follow you?" Her words came out in a harsh whisper.

"Calm down."

"Maybe you need to be less calm," she snapped. "Explain why someone would follow you?"

"Gem, this has happened to me in the past. I have provided services for governments and kingdoms. Those entities have enemies."

"Enemies? Like terrorists and the like?"

"Yes, which is why I got Scotland Yard involved."

She wanted to snap at him, even blame him, but what he had done was reasonable. As frustrated as she was, he had gotten all the right people involved. "But why wouldn't you tell me this? If I had known, or even suspected, I would have stayed away from your hotel. You could have come here instead."

"This has been my life for nearly seven years. From one classified project to another. I've already told you that immediately after Wimbledon I will be on another classified project. I can't just expose you to that side of the world. And until I'm done with my contract, this is what I have to deal with."

"And in the meanwhile, these bastards get to humiliate me and break the hearts of those closest to me?"

"Gem—"

"Please, don't call me that. Not now. Not after that goddamn note."

He studied her.

"You asked me to trust you," she said. "Yet it's our relationship that has brought this mess into my life. You should have warned me."

"I thought I was shielding you from this stuff. I wanted you to focus on Wimbledon. I didn't want to distract you."

She slumped on the kitchen stool.

"I've been working with DCI Whitby since last Saturday. We're close."

She wasn't angry with him. She was angry at herself for being so careless. She should've known better. This was exactly what she should have expected. Always the same story.

"Also..." He hesitated. "I'll be gone for a few days."

She turned to him. "Why?"

"Depending on our findings, I may have to return to the States."

"Fantastic. I feel like seagulls are flying overhead and one after another is pelting me with their turd." She placed her hands on her face, forcing back tears. "When will you be back?"

"Early next week."

"Please," she said then bore into his eyes, "whatever you have to do, do it. I need to shield my family from this story. All this happened because of us. Solve it."

Gemma caught up to Bedric before he stepped out of the house. "Talk to me, Bedric."

"There is nothing to say."

"I won't let it happen again. You have my word."

"It already has happened again. The performance on the court is the symptom, not the problem." He walked out of the house.

Wesley remained with Gemma long after the investigators left. "We need to be careful, G," he said.

She stared at him.

"How well do you really know Andre?"

"Wesley, don't go there." Even though she already had.

CHAPTER THIRTY-FOUR

"One important key to success is self-confidence. An important key to self-confidence is preparation."

~Arthur Ashe

In the locker room, Gemma waited to be called to the court. A full day had passed after receiving the extortion note. Thankfully, nothing had been leaked to the press yet.

She had received a text message from Andre twenty minutes earlier wishing her luck. She had not responded. There was nothing to say because the truth was, if not for Andre, her family would not be in the crosshairs right now. She needed to focus on her match.

Gemma's third round match promised to be a challenging one. She was to play Veronika Rezníkováč, and she didn't like the scouting report on her. Veronika was five-foot-three-inches tall, which gave Gemma a distinct advantage. But what Veronika lacked in size, she made up in strength, talent, and spunk. Gemma could not afford to underestimate her. She had shocked everyone during last year's Australian Open by reaching the Grand Slam final. She was a dangerous opponent through and through.

From the first serve, Veronika proved to be lethal. The first set went to tiebreaker. To Gemma's bewilderment, *her* crowd started to cheer for Veronika each time she saved herself from set point.

Make them make mistakes.

She wiped his voice from her head.

Gemma changed things up, trying different tactics. She served and volleyed. She tried drop shots. And in one horrifying instant, she dropped the first set to Veronika. The stadium fell silent.

Gemma opened the second set serving. And in less then two minutes, she dropped the first game love-40.

The murmurs in the stadium spread like fire. She took the bench during the switch over and massaged her tightening hamstring. She'd have to break Veronika's serve, otherwise fighting back from a deep hole would be near impossible. But if Veronika played with this same level of energy, then Gemma's dreams would die in an early exit.

She rubbed her hamstring again. Gemma was about to call for the match medic when she saw his run briskly to Veronika's side instead. Gemma watched intently. She had been so deep in thought, she had not realized Veronika had called for assistance. The minutes passed by as she watched the therapist try different movements and extensions on Veronika's lower back. Fifteen minutes later, Veronika withdrew. Gemma embraced her sparring partner, who was frustrated but composed. The tennis gods had dealt Veronika a bad hand.

In the locker room, Gemma thought about the bullet she had dodged. It was highly likely she would have lost the match, or maybe withdraw because of her hamstring. Now she had the entire weekend to rehabilitate. She couldn't help but feel the root cause was not a strong adversary or a tightening hamstring. More likely, all the events of the past week and the on-going roller coaster with Andre were the real reasons for her poor play.

She leaned against the wall then lowered herself to the floor. Her arms perched on her knees, she glanced at the ceiling, hoping to find answers. She should have known better. Her throat dried.

It had started again. Each time she had fallen in love, her world had crashed around her. He was different; he was supposed to be the one. Yet the same circus had come to town.

Andre spent all of Friday with the interrogators at the Met. Finally, after eight hours, they had the smoking gun. Abe had given them a name. Now they needed to tie the fingerprints of that name to the gun.

On Saturday morning Andre took the first flight to Washington D.C. His colleagues at the FBI were ready to assist. He remained focused on the task at hand and tried not to think too much about Gemma's lack of responses to his texts and messages.

Saturday stretched on in agonizing reminders that Gemma was completely in the dark. Yes, it was self-inflicted. She could have answered his calls. But she was upset, angry, and every other emotion that lay scattered throughout the spectrum of love and hate.

She submerged herself in her work—exercise, rehabilitation, interviews, more conditioning, more of anything she could think of just to keep her mind off of him. But now the press produced new stories, fabricating explanations about his disappearance.

Some games had no winners.

"We have a hit," the FBI agent told Andre.

"The voice patterns match?"

The agent pointed to the monitor where sound waves from two different sources had been compared by the analyst. "Ninety-eight percent probability. It doesn't get much better."

He had suspected it, but now he had confirmation. He would not dwell on it, just act. The NSA had confirmed the source of the e-mails Abe had received, and the FBI had matched the voicemail Abe had turned over. What remained was tying-off a loose thread. He wanted to know why.

At the airport, Andre sent DCI Whitby the latest, then boarded his flight—the red eye to Los Angeles. He had to take care of some things at home.

Exhausted, he attempted to sleep during the flight, but sleep eluded him. Also, the headache that had been with him since Saturday afternoon accompanied the six-hour trip. All the medication in the world didn't seem to help.

He had sent Gemma various text messages over the last few days, and not one had gotten a response. He couldn't understand her behavior.

After all, he was on her side. He thought she knew that.

Gemma and Tish hit the football field at the Cobham Training Centre, the training ground of the Chelsea Football Club. They had not spoken much since the publication of the article that exposed the true details behind her relationship with Andre.

Gemma had waited long enough. It was time to break the ice.

They ran a few laps at a fast clip. She always preferred running on grass. Maybe it was because grass was more forgiving on knees and ankles. Quite possibly it was because the morning dew left a nearly imperceptible coat of cool water on her legs as she sped around the field. Either way, running and playing on grass had always been her preferred venue.

Although she always though of herself as a fit runner, Tish was on a different plane. It seemed she had limitless stamina. Tish didn't have the explosive speed needed for a tennis match, but she could go on for hours.

"Bloody hell, Tish. You're not even winded."

Tish glanced at Gemma then refocused on the path ahead. "I suppose."

It was time to clean this mess up. "I'm sorry, okay?"

Tish didn't bat an eye. "For what?"

"You know." Running and talking was not easy. "Andre. And not telling you."

"Oh, that." They rounded the corner. Tish picked up speed. "I forgot all about that."

"That's good to hear, because—"

"After all, just because you gave me this whole speech after the Aegon tournament, doesn't mean that we all have to meet that standard."

"Stop," Gemma said as she tugged Tish's shoulder. "I can't even talk when you run like that."

Tish placed her hands on her hips and peered at Gemma.

Gemma caught her breath and opened her mouth. "I—"

"Don't," Tish said. "You don't owe me an explanation. I get it."

Gemma studied her friend's eyes. She saw sincerity. "I should have told you the truth."

"Maybe. But it's done now. And..." she paused, then broke eye contact. "God knows I've been less than perfect."

They started walking the path. "Can we turn the page then?" Gemma asked.

"Of course. That's not even a question."

Gemma made a move to embrace her friend.

"Oh, no. You're a sweating mess. You can hug me after you've cleaned up."

"You should accept me as I am."

Tish took a few steps backwards, creating space between her. "No, thank you."

Gemma moved toward her. "Best friends for ever."

"BFF, not BO. Stay away, you." She spun and sprinted away.

"Bloody coward!"

That had been easy. Maybe too easy.

Before Gemma went to sleep on Sunday, she called his mobile. It went directly to voicemail. She should have tried earlier. Then again, maybe this was for the best.

After the previous hellish week, she needed a bit of calm in her life. She had her Round of Sixteen match in the morning, and she did not like what the pundits had said about her last match against Veronika. She needed to win convincingly. She needed to drive home the point. As always, the need to prove others wrong was what drove her to fight and win. Also, she wanted to remind herself she could win, with or without him.

Even though she loved him, she could go on without him if she had to.

Win she did.

Gemma had a brilliant match, defeating her opponent quickly and swiftly. She wondered what the experts would say now. Not that it mattered. She needed to prepare for her next match with no time to rest. Because of rain delays, the quarterfinal match was scheduled for the next day.

She would not stew over her life. Yes, she had yet again miscalculated. But she couldn't dwell on that. For now she would revel in her preparation and focus only on the next round.

But when she grabbed her mobile, the message from Andre derailed her plans momentarily: "*You were epic.*"

She studied his name on the mobile's screen and thought of the last time she had seen him. He was in her kitchen, trying to reassure her. She missed him. She loved him. He was supposed to be the one. But she couldn't stand the uncertainty and lack of stability she was now feeling because of him.

On Monday, Andre quit.

"You can't quit!" Roger yelled.

"Here is my letter of resignation."

"I won't accept it," Roger said.

"You can't keep me employed against my will."

"No? Are you ready to forfeit your bonus and pay back all your commission for the last three years? Are you ready to give up millions in bonus? You're not that stupid." Glee radiated in the man's eyes. But the redness that blossomed across his cheeks told a different story.

"Do you want more money? Is that it?" He walked over to his bar, spilled whiskey in his glass, then drank it with gluttony. One drop ran down his chin. "Name your price."

"I want out, and you will pay my bonus. We will call it a done deal and go our separate ways."

Roger's hoarse, phlegmy laugh caused him to cough. "Have you gone stupid on me? Are you on drugs? Bullshit! We will go after every penny. With interest."

"No, you won't," Andre said, and pulled out a document. "Here's a contract I wrote up. It says you will not exercise any of the punitive damage clauses of our contract. My exit is the end of our relationship."

"There is no way I'm signing that piece of shit." Roger downed the rest of the whiskey. "What happened to you? You were doing so well. Now you want to throw it all away? You've gotten yourself mixed up with the wrong crowd. Running around with celebrities, drinking, and who knows what else."

"I want out."

"We built our five-year strategy around you. If we lose money, you'll lose money."

Andre would not bite. The chess game was on. "A few months here or there will make no material difference to your revenues. And when you sign this agreement, I will sign this one." He threw another document on the desk.

"And what's that?" Roger asked.

"For a period of one year, I will not work for any consulting firm that competes or provides similar services to any client that would be deemed a prospective client of M&T. I'm getting off the grid for twelve months. No one gets me." He reached into Roger's coat pocket, removed his gold pen, and placed it on the papers.

Andre had considered all possible permutations of this game.

Roger scanned the document and turned pale. "Legal needs to read it. I won't agree to anything until they sign off."

"I'll give you ten minutes. Like I said, I'm willing to get off the grid if you sign. But if you don't, in about one hour I will have a meeting with Vektor Consulting—your favorite competitor. Then another one with Homeland Security. Tomorrow I meet with the NSA. I'll ask for and receive a signing bonus that will cover litigation or payoff. In return I'll commit to a five-year deal with them starting immediately. Vektor will destroy your hold on the Global-100. They'll also get an exclusive agreement with Homeland and NSA when I join. Either we all win, or you lose. Your choice." He glanced at his watch. "Seven minutes."

The game was coming along just as he had anticipated.

"Bullshit. No one will give you that kind of deal."

Andre took out an envelope from his coat pocket, opened it, and placed the letter on the table.

"Now what?" Roger asked.

"A written offer from Prime Minister Beckford. The United Kingdom has already made me an offer. The signing bonus is there as well. I'd rather not move to London, but I will."

Roger rubbed his face, turning crimson, then slammed the table. "No. No deal," Roger said, and raised his chin. "You need me. I'm the one who can prevent some leech from destroying the good reputation of your girlfriend."

Check.

"I'm listening."

"I received video, pictures, and audiotapes. Video of the two of you having an intimate moment in the rain. Then running into your hotel room. And audiotapes of a conversation between you two—of a certain 'rape' from some years back. The blackmailer discovered you were with us and sent a copy." Roger's forehead was littered with beads of sweat. "I agreed to his demands to save your reputation and your woman's name—but more importantly, because I didn't want our company name to be associated with scandals of this sort. You know well our clientele is sensitive."

Roger wiped his forehead with his handkerchief.

"So you have a copy of the video and audio material from the extortionist?"

"That's right. High quality stuff."

Checkmate.

"That certainly changes things." Andre strode around the office. "Now, this wouldn't happen to be the tape Abe Munem took?" Roger suddenly lost all color from his cheeks. "Two nights ago, Scotland Yard—the Met—arrested him."

Roger's eyes widened.

"You're thinking of the e-mail you got from him this morning, right? Nah, not him. What's interesting is his story is different than the one you just spun." Andre walked around, running his fingers on the furniture. "He said you hired him. Can you believe the audacity? He even provided phone records as proof. I spoke to Josh Kinsey—you remember Josh, don't you? FBI special team on extortion and blackmail. Sure you do. Anyway, I visited him yesterday, and he confirmed the authenticity of the phone communication between you and Abe."

Andre walked up to Roger's bar, opened a forty-year-old bottle of Macallan, and poured an overly-stiff shot in a crystal glass. He studied the color, took in the aroma, then sipped. "Oh man, this is good."

Andre sipped more whiskey. He had to time this well. Allow the facts to sink in for Roger.

"Yes, sir. Scotland Yard has Abe. The question is, what will I do with you? I do recommend you sign my original offer. Maybe I can convince the feds that jail is not the best option for you. And just to be clear, no, I will not stay with M&T. The good reputation of this firm depends on the choice you make in the next..." he studied his watch, "... sixty seconds."

Andre studied Roger. "Why'd you do it?"

Roger set his chin. "For you. I did it for you. Don't you see? She will ruin your career—she already has. You could've made partner here. I took you under my wing because I wanted to see you succeed. I—"

"You wanted me to make you money. As much money as humanly possible before I collapsed. So don't try to justify your actions by—"

"I don't have to justify anything. Don't forget who you're talking to. You think you're so smart with your little dramatics here. I've seen this play before. The same story repeating itself. Brilliant kids, straight out of top universities, wanting to make it. And they do by working hard. Their money gets them noticed by the ladies who are on the look for their kind. Then they think they've fallen in love. Suddenly they can't go on those extended trips. They want someone else to fill their spot. They need vacation time. The woman in his life wanted him for his money, and now is demanding the money and the person. So the stupid kid does it. Follows the woman. Does what she wants. Ruins his career. All for what? A divorce that will invariably come, because that's how it always ends. And that will be your story too. The difference this time? She'll dump you. Because her sun is brighter than yours. You are nothing next to her, and you will be left with nothing after her."

"Roger," Andre said, "Cooperate with the FBI. Hand over everything. I don't want you to go to jail."

Andre had one more loose end to handle. He drove into his parent's driveway. Time he had it out with his dad. No more recommending or requesting. On one hand he had Gemma, who would give up anything to find a connection to her family. And here his dad, who still had a niece, was acting like a petulant kid.

He opened the door and stormed into the kitchen. He found his dad tasting his homemade marinara sauce.

Gabriel looked up. "I thought you were in England. I saw you on TV."

"I'm going back later tonight."

His mom showed up from the den, a glass of red wine in her hand. "What are you doing here?" she asked.

"Mom, I am tired of waiting."

"What are you talking about?" his mom asked.

Gabriel chuckled. "We've been drinking, and he's the only drunk in the house." Both his parents laughed.

"I'm here to talk about Linda," he said. At that same instant, the sliding door to the yard opened.

"What about me?"

Andre stared in disbelief. Linda had three ripe tomatoes in her hands.

"What are you doing here?" he asked her.

"We asked you first," his mom said.

"I came to…" he didn't know what to say.

Linda showed the tomatoes to Gabriel. "Will these do, *Tio*?" she asked.

"Yes. Perfect. Wash them then peel the skin. I'll find the grater. Also prepare two garlic cloves. Then I'll show you my father's secret ingredient for *Pan con Tomate*."

Linda nodded then went to the sink. She glanced at Andre. "Will you join us for dinner? My mom should arrive any minute now."

"I don't understand," he said. "I came here to…"

She grinned. "Your dad came over last week. We went to the beach and talked for a long while. *Tio* Gabriel just needed time."

Andre pulled his dad to the side. "What made you finally go to her? Was it our talk?"

He shook his head. "I told you, I was busy doing something."

Andre stared at him, trying to understand.

"Your *tio* had hundreds of ideas. He would sketch them on any random paper in the house, then forget about them. I kept all of them—four boxes of ideas. I put together all his thoughts and notes into an album. It wasn't easy. Not because it was a lot of work—though it was. The real hard part was remembering him and how he'd get excited over a new idea, talk about it, get me excited, and then lose all interest a week later. Each one I read brought fresh tears. It was draining, but also exciting—some of his ideas are still amazing. I finished the album last week and gave it to Linda. Maybe one day you and Linda can turn some of his ideas into reality."

Andre's mouth had gone dry. "That's amazing, *Papa*."

"You don't have to solve all the problems, *Andres*," his father said. "Sometimes the problems will solve themselves if you give it time."

Andre tried to nod—wanted to hug his father, whom he had never hugged before.

Someone pulled his elbow.

"Come, Andre," his mom said, tugging him toward the den. "Let's drink wine while they prepare dinner. I want to know more about the British girl. Does she do yoga, because those legs and that ass. It's just not fair."

On Tuesday, after having eliminated her opponent in the quarterfinal match, Gemma thought about her strong run in the last two matches. Maybe she had been right after all. Andre was a distraction. Without him, she had dismantled her opponents. But according to his earlier text, his plane was due to land soon.

She had to be careful. She didn't want to lose momentum. She had one day's rest before her semifinal match on Thursday against Sonia—her third chance this year.

Her mobile rang—*Andre*.

"Welcome," Gemma said.

"It's great to hear your voice again," Andre said. "Are you busy tonight?"

"Sorry, yes I am." As she spoke the words, something collapsed in her heart.

"How about tomorrow?"

"Andre, it's best I remain focused on my upcoming match."

A beat. "Sure, no worries. Well, I wanted to tell you in person, but good news should be shared. The Met arrested the extortionist."

"Are you serious?" Lead lifted off her shoulders.

"Yes. DCI Whitby has his hands on the evidence. Original footage and more. I will be visiting the team in the morning to help scan the systems for uploads, transfers, or copies. We'll know if any other pieces of the material exist, and put this story to bed."

For a moment she considered calling him over, but stopped herself. Though on mute, the footage on the telly was clear: a news segment showing the arrival of Andre at Heathrow and the paparazzi surrounding him. Must have been video from minutes earlier. Bedric had been right. It had already happened. She refused to allow a replay of Australia. Not with Andre, not with anyone.

Andre hung up and closed his eyes. He had not told her that he had quit his job, nor that the stalker had been hired by his employer. She didn't want to deal with any of this until after the tournament. He could and would respect that.

He was finally free, but had no good way to celebrate. The cab was driving him to Gemma's home. No point now. He picked up his cell and dialed.

"I'm back in town. Are you free?" he asked.

After a brief conversation, he hung up and tapped on the driver's glass partition.

"Change of plans. Please take me to Ten Downing Street."

"The PM's residence?" the driver asked.

"That's the one."

"Did it work?" the Prime Minister asked.

"Like magic. I can't thank you enough." Andre didn't want to share more than he had to.

"Glad to hear it," the PM said, sinking deep into the sofa seat. "Clearly I'm happy you broke the chains. I'm also happy I don't have to actually pay that kind of money."

They drank a toast.

"As I said that night at your home, I needed something to bluff with." At the time, Andre had not expected M&T to bury themselves with the extortion letter. In their attempt to hold on to him, they had made it easier for Andre to leave.

"Andre, I would have gone directly to the Queen and asked her to personally fund it if it meant we would have your services for the next five years. And I would be a great boss."

Andre laughed.

"I'll take this as your R.S.V.P. for Emily's engagement. I knew you'd come up with a clever plan. What will you do now? Professionally, I mean. I'm sure you have expenses—"

"I'll be fine. I have no financial worries. You and my uncle can rest comfortably."

"Well. Fantastic. Now on to a more important matter. What's the story with you and Gemma?"

Andre leaned forward. "Have you ever watched the sunset on a tropical island?"

The PM gave a curious look. "Sure—Tahiti a few years back."

"Can you describe it?"

"Beautiful, immense, reminded me of how small we are and our relative insignificance. Also, I felt sad, I admit. It lasted but for the briefest of moments."

"Mortals can't hold on to the sunset. It will set when it wants to. Gemma's life, the circumstances, and the circus that has grown over the past two weeks have thrown her off. She's closed herself off again. Her survival instinct has kicked in."

"So what's the plan? How will you address this?"

He shrugged. "I don't think this is a problem I'll be able to solve." What was he going to do? Prepare a Power Point presentation? Build a spreadsheet that showed why they were perfect for each other? This one was up to her. And as much as the implications scared him, he knew that was the only way.

"I'm sorry, Andre," the PM said.

Andre forced a smile. "At least we're in the semifinals now," he said, as he raised his glass in a mock toast.

"It's only a game, son. Just a stupid game."

CHAPTER THIRTY-FIVE

"Ability may get you to the top, but it takes character to keep you there."

~John Wooden

G ame day tradition remained the same as always. She leaned forward, elbows on knees, looking at a point in space. A light sheen of perspiration dusted her arms and legs, and her breathing was moderate. Everything appeared to be in place, except her mind wasn't actually focused on the game. Instead she was pretending, going through the motions.

Her thoughts were not the typical mantra of 'one point at a time.' Instead, her brain activity was erratic and confused by thoughts of a future with Andre that were now in question.

A couple of weeks ago, she would not have dreamt that sitting here, waiting for her seminal match at Wimbledon, it would be thoughts of Andre distracting her.

She had planned and expected to win many Grand Slams—a current-day Steffi Graf. She wanted the record. But after five years of trying and disappointing the experts and herself, she would be happy with one. And if she were to win one, she hoped it would be Wimbledon. For her. For her dad.

What would be her legacy? She thought of the 'beautiful' ones who had played the game but never won a Grand Slam. Was she destined to go down as one of them? She wanted to matter.

Gemma entered center court. The explosion of cheers and applause upon her arrival was heartening. The overwhelming majority of the crowd stood and gave her an ovation. Fans waved UK flags of various sizes. The national pride unmistakable.

She wore an all-white outfit. She recalled what Andre had said about her outfit: *"White against your tanned skin makes you look like a black pearl nestled in Caribbean sand."*

When she sat on the bench, she glanced toward her seats. He was there with Tish. For an instant a smile threatened to break through, but she stopped it. There was no reason to smile.

The clouds overhead promised rain.

The umpire spoke. "Quiet please. Thank you." With that, the match began.

The first set was over in thirty minutes. Gemma was being humiliated.

She was slow, unable to reach the returns. Her motion during the serve was tight, producing weak, pitiful hits. After each point, she grimaced and squeezed her hamstring.

Why like this? Why couldn't she lose like she had in the French Open—with dignity? Instead she was playing like a rank amateur.

Down 1-3 in the second set, rain drenched them and the umpire called a break. The ground staff sprinted on the court and covered the grass. But just as quickly, the rain stopped.

While the officials debated closing the roof, Gemma was downright panicking. She was down one set already, and the second was quickly slipping away. She was being outclassed. She couldn't exit like this. The press would ruin her. She would be the joke of professional sports for years to come. Maybe the rain stoppage had been a lucky break? Could she bear down and focus now?

She glanced in Andre's direction. Why had he shown up? To watch her be embarrassed? To see first-hand what his handiwork had caused? It didn't matter. She would take care of him in due time.

With the score 1-3 in the second set, Sonia needed to win three more games and Gemma's Wimbledon dreams would end in yet another semifinal trouncing. That would mark the end, not only of this tournament, but possibly of her career. She was imploding, choking in a fantastic way—a repeat of the Australian fiasco. It was one thing to lose, quite another to get manhandled. A crushing defeat in her own country, in front of her people, in front of the Prime Minister, and Prince William and Catherine.

The soap opera of her life was repeating itself. No matter who she chose, the same dark cloud followed her.

She readjusted the strap on her thigh while the ground staff uncovered the grass again. The players were asked to warm up. Gemma didn't rise from her chair.

She focused on a point in space. She would go through the mental preparation now. Unlike most sports, in tennis, even if the athlete had only one point left, she could fight her way back and win the entire match.

"You can do it, Gemma!" someone yelled, and the audience roared.

She remembered her first loss. She remembered her first win. She remembered her first tournament championship, the rape, the articles about her, the anger, and the promise she made to prove them all wrong.

Gemma! Gemma! Gemma!

She remembered putting her trust and love in one man. She remembered it all.

We love you, Gemma!

She removed the strap off her thigh and tossed it into the crowd. Widespread cheers and applause bounced throughout the stadium.

She didn't need to warm up. It was game time.

It was Gemma's serve, and she had to hold serve. If she dropped this one, then it was all but over—*fait accompli*. She would fight for it, one point at a time. *The only point that matters is the next one.* She would not think of the final result, but this moment only—this point only.

Done.

She walked to the base line and asked for three balls. The light drizzle brushed against her. She inspected one ball and popped it away. She placed the extra ball underneath her skirt and stepped up to the line. All her motions and timing were calculated. *Frustrate your opponent. Create anxiety. Produce drama.*

She took a deep breath, glanced over at Andre, then at her opponent. Sonia was relaxed, hovering near the extreme edge of the court, bouncing slightly on her toes. Her body language exhibited full and complete confidence.

Gemma stared her down until Sonia noticed her eyes. Sonia's back straightened slightly and her heels touched the grass. Gemma immediately shifted her weight and tossed the ball high. It swirled in slow motion. She timed her leap, maximizing the crushing force of her racquet—her weapon of choice. Her racquet cut through the air, while at the same time she growled and torpedoed the ball down the middle. Sonia didn't even attempt a return. She was left planted on the court.

Ace.

The crowd erupted with a standing ovation.

Gemma's first ace of the match. Gemma walked to her line, then scanned the crowd and found Andre, leaning forward against the rail, fingers intertwined.

One point at a time. One love at a time—the time is for tennis. She knew what that meant—what it would have to mean. She would not throw away sixteen years. Not like this. She had worked too hard.

Everything else—everyone else—is a distraction.

Sonia moved a bit closer to the center to prevent another dead-center ace. Gemma tossed the ball, and when she struck it, she sliced the ball at a deep angle, willing it to go to the extreme end of the court, away from Sonia—the lefty's weapon. Sonia's eyes widened and she leapt for the far side of the court. Her racquet made contact with the grass, not the ball. Gemma's second ace in a row.

She now saw it all in slow motion.

Gemma tore another serve, clocked at 118 miles-per-hour down the middle. Sonia made contact, but the ball flew into the crowds. The umpire could no longer control the cheers.

Gemma took her time in picking the right ball, frustrating Sonia further. She walked up to the line, then watched her adversary, one of the best who had ever played the game, who now appeared confused by the turn of events. Flustered, Sonia murmured, seemingly talking to her racquet. Gemma took her position, tossed the ball in the air, and when she made contact with the ball, she knew she would not lose this set.

Gemma won five straight games, coming back from down 1-3 to win it 6-3. They were now tied at one set apiece. The tiebreaker set was next, but lightning shattered the skies and heavy rain drenched the court and players.

The officials scrambled to first cover the grass, then close the roof, but in the end elected to postpone the tiebreaker set to the next day, citing the late hour as the reason for postponement. It was nearly ten in the evening. By rule, they could play until eleven, but she understood the real message. They could get a lot more advertising revenue by playing up the storybook drama for one more day.

Gemma's dressing room door opened, and Tish rushed in and gave Gemma a hug. Andre followed.

"G! I can't believe it. You were down for the bloody count. An amazing comeback. Utterly brilliant."

"Thank you," Gemma said. "Not over yet." Her eyes traveled to Andre's.

"You were phenomenal," he said, his eyes trained on hers. "Amazing transformation."

"Transformation?" Tish asked, still smiling. "What do you mean?"

Andre did not break eye contact with Gemma. "She released a burden. Like Atlas, she was carrying the weight of the world on her shoulders. Once released, she was back and ready to dominate the game."

"Tish, can you give us a moment?" Gemma asked. She had to be strong and decisive. She could not back down now.

Tish glanced at her, then Andre. "Sure," she said, then walked out.

Andre stepped up and stood in front of her. Two feet separated them. The same distance as the first time she met him in Paris.

Staring into his eyes, she almost lost her resolve. *One love at a time*, she reminded herself.

"We can't go on like this."

He said nothing.

"You've—our relationship has become a source of great distraction for me. I can't have this in my life. Not again."

He remained silent, boring into her eyes.

"All the madness that comes with us, it's just not healthy. I can't throw away sixteen years of tennis like this. It needs to stop. We need to stop and go our separate ways."

Still nothing.

"Will you say something?"

"Gemma, you can blame me for everything. The choice is yours. But it won't change anything. Not really. Was I to blame for the Australian Open? How about the French? Or the years before this one?"

A slap would have been better.

"You have to take a serious look and understand why you sabotage your own success—in all areas of your life. What are you afraid of? What will happen if you win it all? What could've happened if you'd fallen in love with me?"

She needed to sit, or grab on to something stable.

"There's one constant in this picture: you. Look at the chaos around you. It was there before me, and it'll be there after. I didn't ask you to lie to the world about us. I saw this coming, but you chose to continue the madness. I've remained the same person throughout. I've never pretended to be someone or something I'm not. Can you claim the same?

"The celebrity game you play assures you'll always have something go wrong. I'm sorry bad things happened to us. Those are curves on the road—they are not the road. If we can't handle these, how can we handle the big rocks—the tragedies? You're right: if we're not on the same page, if we're not willing to stand side by side, then we shouldn't be together."

Andre caressed her face. She trembled inside, but fought hard to maintain her composure. He held her face delicately. A tear threatened the bridge of her nose. She swallowed and held her breath.

"I love you, and I'm willing to fight through anything for us. Anything and anyone. At the core we are the same. When you're ready to have a partner who'll stand next to you, let me know. When you're ready to be the Gemma who lives and loves freely, then find me. Right now, the Gemma in front of me is the character she's created with Wesley. It's the one you devised to keep you safe. Life is not safe. Life is lived at risk. The domain of survival feels safe, but survival is another way of admitting death is catching up with you. I refuse to live that life."

He dropped his hand and planted a warm, long kiss on her mouth. "If that's the last kiss I give you, then I hope you'll remember it as the kiss from the guy who loves you and will always love you because he saw the possibility of a life of happiness with you."

He turned and walked out.

Gemma remained frozen, still trying to find the words she wanted to say to him.

Andre stepped out of Gemma's room then leaned against the door, his eyes sealed tight.

"What's wrong?" someone asked.

His eyes popped open. It was Tish. "I have to leave."

"Wait a bit and we'll all go together."

He shook his head. "No, I'm leaving. Going home."

"What? Why? What happened?" She searched his eyes.

"Before I leave, I have to ask you for a favor."

"Sure. What?"

He held her shoulders and peered into her eyes for a few moments. She flinched.

"Don't tell Wesley what Gemma does all the time. Where she's going, who she's with. Don't listen to him when he tells you to kiss me. Your instinct was right when you said no to him initially. I want to believe you thought you were just doing your job. But your job is to protect her. Don't let anyone get to her."

Her large eyes turned glassy

"I won't be around to help her. She'll only have you. You! Don't misuse her trust."

She blinked.

"Do you understand?"

Tish nodded, tears streaking her cheeks.

The weather opened up on Friday, and the semifinal match between Gemma and Sonia was set to continue. Gemma searched for Andre, scanning her reserved seats, then glanced over at the PM's. But he was nowhere to be found. Had he given up on her? Why wouldn't he? She had given up on their relationship after all.

She'd broken up with him to end the madness. But how was she to deal with the overwhelming sadness she was now feeling? She had been impulsive. But how could she clean it up now? Her life was still a mess.

Cleaning up the chaos in her life had to start somewhere. It would start on the tennis court. Gemma redirected her focus to the third and tiebreaker set.

She'd have to generate the same electric energy as the day before. Sonia was shaken. Gemma could see that. But Sonia had the opening serve. Gemma understood the psychology of the game—the brutal truth. All athletes at this level were talented, technically equivalent. But the champions understood the mind games. Once doubt penetrated the mind, nothing could save someone from sinking. She had to remind Sonia of the momentum shift of the day before. Gemma had to break Sonia's first serve.

Sonia launched the first serve. Gemma's return was decisive, forcing Sonia to sprint to the other side of the court. In that instant, Gemma risked it and rushed the net. When Sonia returned the ball, Gemma was there to spike it away.

Love-15.

Gemma set the tone. She'd be aggressive and take chances. On the second serve, Sonia compensated and lobbed the return, forcing Gemma to sprint away from the net toward the baseline. With her back against the net, Gemma realized the ball was above and behind her. Like a basketball player performing a fade away jump shot, Gemma leapt and spun in mid-air, her racquet behind her head. She dropped the hammer and cut through the ball's trajectory. The ball tore across the court, just barely missing the net.

Love-30.

On the next serve, Gemma crept up on the baseline, daring Sonia to attack her body. Sonia bit, and when the serve came, Gemma adjusted her grip and returned the ball straight down the line.

Love-40.

Gemma never looked back, breaking Sonia's serves twice, and never faltering on her own.

Match to Gemma: 6-3.

The standing ovation and cheers would not end. She saluted the crowd, the Prime Minister, and the Prince. When Gemma extended her hand to Sonia, the graceful champion embraced her opponent instead.

"I always knew it was just a matter of time," Sonia said. "Good luck. This one's yours."

After another hug, Gemma marched off the court, waving to her fans. Mixed with the perspiration, tears dripped from her face. Tears of joy, tears of loss.

She sat in the locker room and remembered Andre's words. *What are you afraid of?* She closed her eyes and recalled his honest eyes and lovely smile. Then she remembered something else. *With love, magic is possible.*

Gemma was in her living room nursing a glass of red wine, while Tish sat silently.

"What happened with Andre?" Tish asked, breaking Gemma from her thoughts.

She turned slowly to Tish. "I fucked up. Badly."

"Yes, it appears that way. And now what?"

Gemma shrugged. "I need him. But I can't have both a career in tennis and a relationship. You saw what happened; they can't coexist. Paparazzi following us, taking videos of us, private details showing up in the papers. I can't live that way. My life can't be a soap opera. But... I don't know. Without him, I'm lost." A tear rolled down her cheek. "I need to find a way—"

Tish leaned forward then rose. She tugged on her braids, not making eye contact with Gemma.

"What's wrong?" Gemma asked.

Tish dropped back into the seat, took a deep breath, and spoke. "I should have known. It's so obvious now, but I didn't see it. I thought all of it was being done for good reason, never bothering to ask why the bloody hell we did what we did."

"What are you talking about? You're not making any sense."

Tish covered her face for a few moments then peered at Gemma. "I think you can have it all."

Gemma gazed at her friend. "Is that so?" She wiped her cheek.

"This may be the worst time to say this, but you need to know the truth. Or at least what I believe is the truth."

"What are you talking about?"

"What happened to the two of you was not his fault or yours. Someone else orchestrated the drama."

Gemma set her glass down. "Explain. Very. Slowly."

"Okay," Tish said, "but first, I have to resign as your assistant. And ask that I speak to you as a friend who loves you and wants to see you happy."

"Gemma, what brings you—?"

The hard, fast slap threw Wesley's glasses off his face.

"What the hell, Gemma? Have you lost your mind?" His eyes were wide, his mouth askew.

"After all these years how could you betray me?"

He leaned down, searching for his glasses. "What are you talking about?"

"It was you all along. You've been doing this. You were the one who was meant to protect me. Instead you try to ruin my life."

He laughed as he rose, glasses in hand. "Is that what you think? You think I was trying to ruin your life?"

"It's not what I think. It's what I know."

"You don't know shit, Gemma. Nothing. You act all innocent and confused now. That's rich. Look at your homes, your bank accounts. You think those came for free? Years ago I promised you'd be bigger and more powerful than anyone. I asked you to let me do my job and you do yours. I made you famous. I made you filthy rich. Now you're shocked you had to give up something in the process? Another five, maybe six years, you'll be gone from tennis. No one will remember you. But I made sure you can live the remainder of your life in comfort, at the level only a handful of people have ever had the privilege of experiencing."

"Did you bother asking what I wanted?"

"You wanted to be famous. You wanted to be rich. You wanted everyone to love and respect you. You wanted to matter. From your birth parents, to Georg, to any of the countless people in your life who had doubted you or hurt you. You got what you wanted. I put everything on the line to get you there. I did it out of love for you."

251

She dropped her eyes.

"When I saw you that day with Georg, I swore I'd do everything I could to rebuild your confidence. Look at you now. You've become the most loved person on the planet. You are a presence, a force. You're practically royalty, and royalty needs someone extraordinary next to her. You need a prince, not Andre. He's a nice enough guy, I'm sure. But we need to keep you in the limelight. Single, available, always with celebrities, the equally rich and powerful. Years from now you can think about settling down. Now's not the time. You need to ride this train." He slid his glasses back. "I understand what you're feeling. You're in shock. Not able to think clearly. But take an objective look at where you are today. You're one match away from having what you wanted professionally. And financially you are better off than most professional athletes combined. You already have it all. I don't expect this to be obvious to you now, but you will thank me later. You will understand."

Something dawned on her. A reality she would have never considered before. "Wesley, five years ago, you were Georg's agent, weren't you? That's why he was at my party."

His face froze for an instant then recovered. "But I dumped him immediately after what he did."

"But you asked me to not press charges. Why? What would I have learned if I had?"

He just stared into her eyes, not moving, not reacting.

"An ideal pairing that went terribly wrong... Christ, Wesley."

"Listen, you're—"

"Wesley," she interrupted, stepping into his face. "Don't ever come near me or speak to me again. We are done."

"You're being irrational. You're not thinking clearly. Don't forget who you're talking to. You have everything you ever wanted because of me."

"Wrong. I lost the only person I needed because of you."

CHAPTER THIRTY-SIX

"My greatest point is my persistence. I never give up in a match. However down I am, I fight until the last ball."

~Bjorn Borg

On game day, when Gemma awoke, she stumbled into her bathroom and stared at her reflection in the mirror. The sun's rays flooded the room and specks of dust floated in air. Specks—nothing more.

She thought of her future. She was a standout tennis player—for now. But so were many others. So many had come and gone. So many more waited in the wings. She didn't want to be one of those: one more athlete who made noise, won, and then disappeared. She was a speck amongst millions of others.

"You have so much to offer this world," Andre had said.

It was still hard to believe. She was about to play in her first championship match at Wimbledon. This had been her dream. This was what she had worked toward since she was five years old. This was for her father.

She had destroyed her happiness to get the title match, and she would not let that sacrifice go in vain.

Gemma stepped onto center court, waving and walking briskly. The thundering cheers draped the entire stadium. It seemed all of England had come out to support their favorite daughter. She marched with a sense of clam and ease, her chest light, her breathing smooth. She glanced at her adversary. With Sonia out, the smart money was on Mina Pavlova, who had already won Wimbledon once before. She had defeated Gemma each time they had met. Winning against Mina would be a phenomenal end to her championship run.

Gemma was certain she would win. Not because she believed she was necessarily better than Mina. No, she would win because that's what she needed to do. It had to happen that way. She refused to sacrifice so much just to be the runner-up.

Gemma scanned through the crowd. Was he here, watching her, supporting her? She looked at Tish, who shook her head. She had asked Tish not to let him out of her sight if she saw him.

A pang shot through her. *Please, be here with me.*

Gemma didn't like to romanticize anything. But as the match progressed, she thought of herself and Mina as two warriors clashing on a battlefield of grass. The same grass where thousands before had lost their lives. Two souls put on this field to motivate and enchant the next generation of tennis players.

They fought against each other, against the field, and against exhaustion.

They battled for each point. They yelled, screamed, grunted, and growled. Gemma's arsenal of different serves frustrated Mina, while Mina's thundering returns kept Gemma honest. But Gemma was driven by knowledge, a certainty that she was destined to win. She could not lose.

The first set went to tiebreaker, but when Gemma tore a laser beam backhand down the line, Mina lost her footing. With that, Gemma won the first set.

Destiny was on her side.

The second set was a horse race as well. Each one holding serve. With the set tied at 6-6, they entered the tiebreaker phase. Back and forth the gladiators fought. The player who earned the two-point advantage would win the set. For Mina it would mean a tie game and an opportunity to play a third set. For Gemma it meant the culmination of a dream: a championship.

The cheers were uncontrollable. The British crowd would not relent. They understood two more points meant their player would win Wimbledon. Try as she might, the umpire could not get the crowd to be silent. Everyone—the crowd, Gemma, and maybe even Mina—could feel the game was at an auspicious point.

They'd been going back and forth until Gemma broke Mina's serve and tied it up at 13-13. Gemma would receive two possessions. If she just held her serves, she'd win.

Gemma had racked up twenty-two aces in the match. One right now would deflate Mina. *The utmost amount of presence, with the least amount of effort.*

She closed her eyes, took a deep breath, and tossed the ball in the air. Catapulting upward, she ripped her racquet with all her remaining strength. The yellow bullet went down the middle, catching the outside line. A perfect ace.

The crowd erupted. 14-13.

Mina, like Sonia in the previous match, was left planted on the grass, unable to challenge the invisible ball. Her head dropped.

Gemma noticed the crowd, who pointed at the tachometer, their mouths open in shock. She was clocked at 132 miles-per-hour. Was that a new record? It didn't matter.

She didn't smile. The match was not over. One more point. That was all she needed.

Gemma served again. This time Mina returned the ball cross-court, forcing Gemma to sprint for it. Gemma reached the ball and sliced it back, taking pace off the ball. But Mina had attacked the net, ready for a quick put-away. She forehand-volleyed the ball to the other side of the court. A perfect angle, completely on the other side of Gemma.

One point was all Gemma needed. Every point sacred. *There is no tomorrow!*

Gemma sprinted, but she knew she would be short. She stretched, and in the last instant leapt, flying toward the ball to get the two additional inches she needed.

Contact.

The ball lobbed high up, with just enough on it to make it past the net.

Just one point.

Gemma hit the ground and her racquet popped out of her hand, skidding on the grass. She glanced at Mina, who was shuffling to the net, tracking the looping ball as it started its descent. Gemma got on one knee, grabbed the racquet, and pushed off. She attacked the net. Mina was at mid-court, racquet raised, prepared to spike the ball.

Just one.

Left, right, or center? Gemma had to make a split-second guess. Mina's foot shifted slightly. *Left!* She leapt again, stretching for the ball, racquet held tight.

One!

Mina's spiked ball hit Gemma's racquet dead center. The ball flew past Mina's ear. The stadium held its collective breath. The ball hit the grass and rolled innocently.

For one second the thunder of the crowd deafened her. She watched the ball roll to a stop. Gemma jumped to her feet, whirled to the line judge who had his hands down, then spun to the umpire, then to Mina, who dropped her head and racquet.

In!

The ball was in!

Gemma lost control of her knees. She fell to the grass, then collapsed and covered her head. The crowd sounded like waves. Like the waves she heard when she climbed Point Dume, when she sat on the sand with Andre, watching the surfers, and when they gazed at the sparkling stars over Leo Carillo. But this time he was not with her. She was alone, and she cried like she'd never cried before.

Eventually Gemma stood and waved to the cheering crowd. The roars were persistent and relentless. She ran to her box and hugged her mum, who was crying like a newborn. Next to her were a tear-drenched Xavi and Mari. Tish cried on Bedric's shoulder, while he nodded in approval.

With love, magic was possible.

Once Andre was clear of the crowds, he leaned against the wall, threw his head back, and yelled as loud as he could. He removed his sunglasses and wiped tears. She had done it. She had defeated her own demons. She was a champion.

His newly acquired throwaway phone chimed: a text message reminding him his flight was in three hours. He dropped the phone in his pocket and left. It was time to get off the grid and see how the chess match would play out.

Gemma eventually regained her composure, but when she raised the golden plate, tears came again. The interviewer tried to ask her questions, but she was barely able to put words together. Finally, when she caught her breath, she spoke.

"Thank you for your undying support," she said to the fans. The crowd erupted in applause and cheers. "Winning this tournament against the best in the world, in my country, is a storybook scenario."

Mina, the proud warrior, smiled graciously.

Gemma noticed the Prime Minister. He was wiping his tears.

"To my fans who believed in me and supported me, thank you. My love for my family, fans, country, and this game is what has carried me to this point." She pointed to the sky. "I did it, Dad!" The crowd erupted, chanting her name.

"This has been one crazy and stressful run to the championship for you," the interviewer said.

"You think?"

The crowd roared.

"Yet you pulled through in dramatic fashion."

"I pulled through because of one person, and I need to thank him. Andre, I won this for you—because of you. Thank you for your unwavering love."

"*Gemma's in LOVE!*"

The news agencies ran with those words. "*Where is Andre?*" was the follow-up question the news programs wanted answered. It was a calculated move. Gemma had hoped by throwing it out there, he would hear about it. More importantly, she was making a statement—she no longer feared the truth.

Sunday evening was soon upon her. As a junior player and throughout her climb up the ladder, she had dreamt of the day she'd be the guest of honor at the famed Wimbledon champion's party. Being there now, she was incomplete. She wanted to celebrate with Andre. Find him and make things right again.

She found a quiet corner, said a prayer, and dialed his number.

An odd ring, then an unexpected message: *"The number you are trying to reach is no longer in service. Please check the number you have dialed and try again."*

CHAPTER THIRTY-SEVEN

*"Take things as they are. Punch when you have to punch.
Kick when you have to kick."*

~Bruce Lee

Gemma woke the next morning determined to track Andre down. She wouldn't give up. But as soon as she started, she realized she didn't even know where to start. Was he still in London? She called a couple of hotels, but quickly hit dead ends.

How would she find him? She glanced at her watch. It was early in Los Angeles, but she was desperate.

"Sorry for calling at this hour, Linda. It's Gemma," she said

"Gemma?" Linda cleared her throat. "Congratulations! You were awesome. Extraordinary! We were all at Dan and Dina's watching the match. What a nice surprise. How are you?"

"Fine. Horrible. I'm trying to find Andre, but his phone is disconnected. Would you know where I can find him, or maybe you have another number for him?"

"I called him immediately after we heard your speech. I got the same message. I'm sure he'll resurface soon."

"Do you know if he's back in the States? I'm against the clock. He was going to start a project right after Wimbledon. I need to speak to him before he leaves."

"Project? Gemma, when he was here last week, he quit his job. There is no project."

Gemma decided if nothing new turned up by end of day, she would take the next flight to Los Angeles. Andre had told Tish he was going home. That's what she would do too. Go to his home.

Gemma's phone rang.

"Ms. Lennon, I have the Prime Minister for you," the voice said.

"Hello, Gemma," the PM said.

"Hello, sir. What a pleasant surprise."

"Gemma, I've been carefully observing the situation."

"Situation, sir?"

"The situation with you and Andre."

Her heart skipped a beat.

"Would you like to come over for tea?" he asked.

They sat on the terrace, her memories drifting to the other night, when the world was full of possibilities and all they had to do was hold each other tight.

"Has Andre told you how we know each other?" he asked.

"Yes, sir. He told me you and his uncle were friends."

"That's right. But there's more to it. When Andre was eighteen, his uncle passed away. As I sat in church hearing the speeches about this man whom I had come to regard as my friend, I made a promise I would look out for his nephew. Andre never had a fair chance to achieve a life of happiness. He was taught to chase the money. To go after success at all cost. His uncle was a stabilizing force in his life, so when he passed away, I tried my best to be the voice of reason. I feel personally responsible for him. Can you understand?"

She nodded.

"The first time I saw you together, I knew he was happy. And in turn that made me happy." He studied her. "You do realize today is the infamous Fourth of July in the States. It's a meaningless holiday for us, but today is the day the Americans won their independence from England. I do hope you won't let Andre declare his independence from you. He does not want to be independent—he needs you."

"Sir, I can't find him," she said.

He drank his tea. "How unfortunate. How very unfortunate indeed."

"Do you have any suggestions?"

"I certainly couldn't betray secrets." He produced a sly smile. "Did you know his grandfather was from Barcelona?"

"Yes, he told me."

"Have you been to Barcelona?"

"Not recently, sir." She rose.

"When you go there, say today or tomorrow, be sure to find this little beach paradise south of Barcelona in Tarragona. I think you will fall in love with Vilfortuny. I hear it's beautiful this time of year."

She hugged him. "I think I'm about due for a holiday."

"You do seem a bit pale."

Gemma called Tish from her car. "Do you want a chance at redemption?"

"Anything."

"Search for properties in Barcelona under Andre Reyes. Specifically in Vilafortuny, just south of Barcelona. Do a ten mile radius search."

"Okay, I'm on it."

"One more thing," Gemma said. "Arrange a flight for Barcelona. I want to be there today."

"Should I get you a hotel room?"

"Only for tonight. I have confidence you'll find Andre's home."

Gemma landed in Barcelona that evening. In her hotel suite, she pored over a map of Vilafortuny, drawing out a plan of action while she waited on Tish to come through. Vilafortuny was a small community with beach houses. He was a beach man, and she knew he'd want to be on the coast. That's where she'd start.

Her mobile rang. It was Tish. "We have a hit."

"Go on."

"As I said earlier, nothing under Andre Reyes. But after I searched every property, I hit gold. The Estate of Andres Van."

"Van? That sounds Dutch. Why do you think it's him?" Gemma asked.

"I don't think it's him, I *know* it's him. I just got off the phone with his cousin, and she confirmed a little detail he mentioned over dinner at

Maurice's. His paternal grandmother was of Armenian descent, born in Van. Back then it was in Armenia, now it's in modern day Turkey. He wanted to honor her by including it in his estate declaration. Also, it's *Andres* with an *s*. The Spanish version of his name. His grandfather's name."

Gemma grinned. "Absolutely brilliant."

"I'm texting you his address."

Gemma's eyes stung. "Wish me luck. Tomorrow I go hunting."

CHAPTER THIRTY-EIGHT

"Create your future from your future, not your past."

~Werner Erhard

Gemma arrived in Vilafortuny at 9:00 in the morning. The address Tish had provided proved to be challenging to find. She'd have to walk the small streets that cut off and continued in irregular patterns. She parked the hired car, slid on her sunglasses, and walked through the streets of the carefully manicured beach villas.

She found the street name and took the pebble path until she saw the beach break through. This was definitely the type of street that would call to Andre.

Just before she reached the sand, she scanned around. To her left was the yard of a charming glass-enclosed house. This had to be his. She could see him falling in love at first sight. She didn't bother checking the address number.

She opened the gate and stepped into the backyard. The smell of fresh jasmine stopped her cold. A heavy punching bag hung, abused, and sliding doors stood open. Her ankles wobbled.

"Andre?" she called out. No reply.

She knocked, yelled out. Nothing. She stepped in and took in the decor. Simple, comfortable furniture, designed with the beach dweller in mind. The house boasted an open architecture. The kitchen, den, and living room were all one large space. Overhead, sizeable skylights brought more natural light into the spacious living area.

She glanced through the books on the coffee table—mystery and suspense novels. She sat on the love seat and imagined him lounging for extended hours. She pictured herself lying there next to him. She spotted a gallery of guitars hanging on the wall. Eight in total. Five electric, two acoustic, and one missing.

"Andre?" she called out again. Still nothing.

She returned to the yard and peered toward the ocean. It was a little windy, but pleasant. The friendly breeze would keep the beach dwellers glued to the ocean. Not a lot of people yet. She absorbed the scents of sun tan lotion, sand, and ocean water.

Gemma stepped on the sand and glanced to the left and then right. She noticed a beach cafe in the distance, red Cinzano umbrellas adorning a few tables. She strolled in their direction. The cafe had seating both on the sand and in a covered area. In the center was the cafe, with both a bar and a kitchen for *tapas* and sandwiches. The path led her to the covered area.

She heard faint music. At first she thought it was a radio, but when it stopped abruptly and continued again, she whirled toward the sound. As her eyes adjusted from bright light to shade, she saw clearly.

Her breath caught.

With his back to her, Andre sat at a table, clutching his guitar, focused on the ocean. He wore red trunks. No shoes, no shirt. White earbuds delivered music from his mobile, and an empty cup of coffee kept him company.

The cafe was mostly empty. She went to the bartender, got a glass of juice, then sat a few tables away.

To the rhythm of the Mediterranean Ocean's waves, he played a piece that sounded familiar, but she couldn't place it. Had Dan played it at Zuma Beach?

Andre set his guitar down, then leaned back and closed his eyes.

She observed him, convinced she could stare at him forever. But that's not why she'd come. She rose from her table and walked to him. His eyes were still closed when she quietly pulled out a chair and sat next to him. He was still unaware of her presence.

She slid off her sunglasses then touched his shoulder. He spun. Shock transformed to surprise. Surprise transformed to a small smile. He removed his ear buds.

"Do you take requests?" she asked.

His gray eyes turned nearly silver. His face softened, and she thought she saw redness invade the white of his eyes.

"Hi, Gem."

Two simple words—two words that meant the world to her. She collapsed into his arms, digging her face into his neck. She wept and shook while he held her tight.

Moments passed.

She finally raised her face and gazed at him. He studied her with gentle eyes, his fingers caressing her forehead and cheeks, stroking back her hair.

"You found me," he said.

"You didn't make it easy." Her voice was hoarse. "I tried to call you, but you disconnected your mobile."

"I wanted you to find me, not call me. Did you cheat?" he asked.

"Yes."

"Which one? Linda or Jeffrey?"

"He recommended I take a small vacation. He said I'd fall in love with Vilafortuny."

"Well, what do you think?"

"He was wrong. I was already in love—I just found my love in Vilafortuny."

"Love?"

"Yes, love. Mad love. When you saved me from the paparazzi in Paris, I fell for you. When little Haley was in your arms, I was jealous. When you lost at Wii tennis, I wanted to kiss you. When you made Georg kneel in front of me, I wanted to make love to you. Each time you make me laugh, I want to hold on to you forever. How can you expect me to walk away from the one person, the only person I have loved?"

"For how long?" he asked. "When will you give up on us? Which article? Which picture? Which loss? When will you ask me to step away, or decide it's time to leave?"

"Can we take a walk?" she asked.

He handed his guitar to the bartender.

"*Gracias, Gustavo*," he said to the bartender.

Gustavo? Was he the same Gustavo whom Andre had spoken to on the plane?

Gemma slid her hand through the crook of his elbow then leaned her head on his shoulder. They moved slowly.

"I took your groundbreaking advice," she said. "I won a Grand Slam."

He chuckled. "I know. I was there."

She spun to him. "You were? So you heard what I said? And you still don't believe me?"

"Gem, I want to believe you. But do you believe you?"

They sat on the sand, facing the ocean.

"When I won, a tidal wave of emotion rushed through me. Everything I had hoped for was finally in my hands. I had proven to everyone, and myself, that I was a champion. But when the wave had passed, I was alone. I could not share it with the only person I loved. I realized the game, the championship, all of it was part of the journey, not the end."

Small waves broke, and white wash tickled her feet.

"Also, the emotion of winning dissipates quickly. Much faster than the emotion of loss and regret. All the stuff I have—the accolades, championships, commercials, homes—are the result of my work. But I have nothing I can truly say I value and treasure."

She grabbed his hand. "Only you, Andre. You were the only one who made me feel right, centered, and normal. Like I mattered as a person. I'm still that five-year-old girl who was told she was born with a gift. And you're still that eleven-year-old boy who was told he could change the world. In some ways we are still those two kids. And it seems to me we have a chance to live the life we bypassed as kids. The one we took for granted. And I figure, if I have the opportunity to live a life I love, it should be with the person I love."

She held his hand tight, never wanting to let him go.

"I've been thinking," she said, "since you don't have a say over any of this, we need to figure out the best place for us to live. We can live here if you prefer. Or move to London, or L.A. I'm flexible. I've got nothing planned, other than being with you."

"What about tennis?"

"It won't be easy, I won't lie. But I'm going to try to slow things down now. I achieved my goal. I won Wimbledon, the one I wanted. I'll try to enjoy the game now and play only in a handful of tournaments. My sponsors will be upset, I will get fined, and my ranking will suffer, but who cares about some arbitrary number next to my name? I won't get the preferred seeding, which means I may play against the best in the first or second round. But isn't that why I play the game? To play against the best."

"And how will your manager take this news?"

"I no longer have a manager."

"What happened?"

"Tish told me some things. It was your phone virus, wasn't it?"

He shrugged.

They leaned back on the sand. She lay on his chest and noticed the burn marks were all but gone. Her face inches away from his. The colors of the beach cast rainbow hues in his gray eyes.

"I hear you're unemployed now."

"I am gainfully unemployed and loving every second of it. You may need to support my habits."

"Which habits?"

"An unstoppable need to stalk my favorite tennis player."

She gave him a playful wink. "We can work something out, I'm sure."

He held her tighter.

"I didn't come prepared," she said, "but I have a question for you."

"Shoot."

"Will you marry me?"

"What?" he tried to sit up, but she wouldn't let him. "Gem, we have a lot of time—"

"Stop," she said. "I love you. Why wait when I know? Why waste time? Life is fragile—things can change without notice or warning. The only moment that counts is now. We're better together than apart. So answer my damn question and don't disappoint me. Will you ride this wave with me?"

In seconds, Andre would kiss her. For now, he stared, with a passing realization that his mouth might be open. He was not in control. He was once again lost in her azure eyes.

EPILOGUE

One month after Gemma found Andre, they returned to Malibu. Gemma had the newly-delivered flowers moved to the entrance, and then back to the great room. Two minutes later they were in the entrance again. The curtains were closed, opened, and then left partially open. She didn't know what to do with herself. She didn't want any complications—not tonight. Within a few hours, Tish and Bedric would arrive, followed by Andre's friends, parents, and aunt. Her mum was already there, taking a nap, and if all went well, Prime Minister Beckford's family would join them by 6:00 p.m.

They were all coming to celebrate Gemma's championship—the lifting of her albatross. What the guests didn't know was once they were all there, Gemma and Andre would announce their engagement. Her tense shoulders loosened at the thought.

Once the engagement was behind them, and they figured out how to deal with "life," they would plan their wedding. Andre and Gemma had spoken about the wedding at great length. Her celebrity status set an expectation that she'd have a grandiose wedding with all the glamour fitting of someone like her. But she was not interested in any of that. She was simplifying her life. All she cared about was the future and the blissful surprises it held.

Andre sat at the kitchen island drinking a cup of coffee Xavi had prepared. "This is heavenly," he told the man.

"For me, espresso is an art-form."

Gemma entered with frame in hand. "Here you go. This is the picture Mari gave me of my mum and dad."

He studied the photo. "My God, your eyes and hers—it's scary." He glanced at Xavi and Mari, who were also smiling.

"Do you want to take a walk on the beach?" she asked Andre.

"Give me a few minutes. Xavi and I are discussing religion."

She studied the two men with espressos in hand and shook her head. "I'll be by the pool. Come out when you're ready."

She kissed him, ruffled his hair, and walked out.

"We are very happy for both of you," Mari said.

"Thank you. You have a lot to be proud of."

Mari whispered a little prayer as she crossed herself.

"You don't know this yet," he said, glancing from one to the other. "She will tell you in about an hour or so. Please be surprised when she does. The plan is once all our guests arrive, we will announce our engagement."

A sound escaped Mari's mouth. Xavi's eyes turned glassy.

"And I thought it appropriate I ask her father for her hand." Andre stared at Xavi directly in his eyes.

The air left the room.

"She doesn't know," Andre continued in a soft tone, "and I will not be the one to tell her. This is something that will remain between the three of us if that's what you want. But I think she could use her father today."

Mari wept.

Andre had suspected—from Xavi's protective stance, his height, physical build, and large, powerful calves—all telltale signs of an athlete. But Xavi's smile sealed it. The partial face in the picture had enough elements for Andre to make the match with the man who stood in front of him. The jaw line, the lips, the teeth. Gemma had the same smile. But it seemed to Andre that Xavi—or Javier—had not smiled in a long time. How could he when he had abandoned his own child all those years ago? Guilt. Embarrassment. All of the above. The choice Xavi had in front of him would not be an easy one to make.

"She's outside, waiting to take a long walk on the beach. And I'm a bit tired," he said then eyed Xavi. "Maybe you'd like to keep her company?"

A beat. "Choices and action," Andre said.

Xavi turned to Mari, her eyes expectant. Xavi drank his espresso in one shot then marched off. He stopped, came back, and hugged Andre. "Thank you, *hijo.*"

Mari sat next to Andre and held his hand.

"You came to Javier's rescue after Ginger passed away?" he asked.

She nodded and wiped a tear. "What do you think will happen?"

Andre studied her hand then gazed into her hazel eyes. "I don't know. I really don't. But I am convinced love has magical powers."

AUTHOR'S NOTES

Morning of May 26, 2010, Paris: I stumbled into the hotel elevator. I had not slept well, which was typical for me on international business trips. I was in mid-yawn when the doors slid open and walked in the talented Dominika Cibulková. Not my coolest moment, I admit, but I recovered fast enough to wish her luck. Thanks to me, she won that afternoon's match. ☺

The French Open was in full swing and many of the athletes were staying at the same hotel. So over breakfast I thought about a tennis star's lifestyle. Can a celebrity athlete have a "normal" life? Can they trust anyone? Then I remembered a "What if…" situation I had jotted in my journal months earlier. It all came together and in that moment, the random idea found its soul. On my return flight, I wrote the "breakfast scene." The seed which was found on a business trip, transformed into this novel.

Some may wonder about Andre's gifts. Do people like him exist? To just say yes, would probably not satisfy the doubter. To say that Andre is a composite of three different individuals that I have met over my years in the technology industry would be better. In the story, Andre recounts how at the age of fourteen he attended *USC* in Los Angeles (my alma mater). Amongst other programs, Andre was probably admitted into *USC's Sidney Harman Academy for Polymathic.*

A quick search on polymath will lead to people like Leonardo Davinci who were gifted in diverse fields. Polymath focuses on how you think, not what. And unlike disciplines that focus on pure technical skills, polymath focuses on the intersection of technology, art, philosophy, and communication (yes, super intelligent people who can communicate like politicians—a scary concept which we may have to address in another novel). So yes, they are real and live among us. I also hope the truly gifted are like Andre in that they appreciate hard work, a good cup of coffee, and a healthy dose of Nutella.

ACKNOWLEDGEMENTS

This writer became an author thanks to a tribe of professionals and friends.

My superstar agent, Stacey Donaghy, fell in love with the story and opened the doors to my dreams. And when things could have gone terribly wrong, she was my rock—a true partner.

Lisa Gus, Eugene Teplitsky, Andrew Buckley, Nikki Tetreault, Vicki Keire, Clare Dugmore, and the entire Curiosity Quills Press team—you guys are a dream to work with. My editor, Mollie Welsenfeld—you are a rockstar. Eugene, you took on the one thing hat kept we awake at nights—my book's cover—and converted it into something I am in love with. I am eternally grateful.

Freelance editor, mentor, and friend, Jean Jenkins—it's an honor to work, brainstorm, and strategize with you. Michael Levin and Laura Taylor, you always believed in me and reminded me that it was just a matter of time. The incomparable, James Scott Bell whose books, workshops, and personal encouragement helped me evolve.

My critique partners on Game of Love, Andreh Andreson, Aline Ohanesian, Demetra Brodsky, and Norm Thoeming who went through every word, every plot point, and every cliché until we were all proud. Robin Reul and Kendall Roderick, I didn't know you during the creation of this novel, but you are now part of my elite team. Kendall, thank you for giving my "brand" a professional look. And heartfelt gratitude to the rest of the three musketeers (Trey Dowell, Chase Moore, Kate McIntyre).

My Debut New Adult support group: Sophia Henry, Kate Lynn, Marie Meyer, Sribindu Pisupati, Meredith Tate Servello, Laura Steven, Amanda Stogsdill, and Jessica Ruddick. You guys (ladies) are the best.

My family of writers at the Southern California Writers' Conference and the Santa Barbara Writers Conference who are driven by a passion for helping writers: the visionaries (Michael Steven Gregory, Wes Albers, Monte Schulz, Nicole Starczak), the staff, the workshop leaders (Matthew Pallamary, Marla Miller, Janis Thomas, Gar Anthony Haywood, Melodie Johnson Howe, Lorelei Armstrong), and all the conferees. You have been invaluable.

My brother, Armen Grigorian, for honoring me by lending the lyrics to his song, Empty Space. My dear friend, Armen Melik-Abramians, and his partner in photography Alan Falcioni, from FlashCube Photography for the headshots and extensive hours on Photoshop to make me look half-human.

The thousands on Facebook, Twitter, and blog who encourage and motivate—thank you!

And finally, my family and friends—thank you for being in my life. Make no mistake, I chose you. And would choose you every time.

Fight the good fight. Mine has just begun.

PERMISSIONS

The following chapters used quotes which are used by permission from Quotations Book (quotationsbook.com) whose collective work are under the Creative Commons (UK License):

Chapter 1: quotationsbook.com/quote/8880
Chapter 2: quotationsbook.com/quote/19171 (abridged)
Chapter 3: quotationsbook.com/quote/5692
Chapter 4: quotationsbook.com/quote/24232
Chapter 5: quotationsbook.com/quote/16179
Chapter 6: quotationsbook.com/quote/24309
Chapter 7: quotationsbook.com/quote/14168
Chapter 8: quotationsbook.com/quote/6457 (abridged)
Chapter 9: quotationsbook.com/quote/24336
Chapter 10: quotationsbook.com/quote/21537
Chapter 12: quotationsbook.com/quote/15679
Chapter 13: quotationsbook.com/quote/39710
Chapter 14: quotationsbook.com/quote/37299
Chapter 15: quotationsbook.com/quote/40569
Chapter 16: quotationsbook.com/quote/7764
Chapter 17: quotationsbook.com/quote/21647
Chapter 18: quotationsbook.com/quote/12495
Chapter 20: quotationsbook.com/quote/38640 (abridged)
Chapter 21: quotationsbook.com/quote/7541
Chapter 22: quotationsbook.com/quote/9386

Chapter 23: quotationsbook.com/quote/213

Chapter 24: quotationsbook.com/quote/37558 (abridged)

Chapter 25: quotationsbook.com/quote/28721

Chapter 26: quotationsbook.com/quote/24344

Chapter 27: quotationsbook.com/quote/28720

Chapter 28: quotationsbook.com/quote/14160

Chapter 29: quotationsbook.com/quote/23350

Chapter 30: quotationsbook.com/quote/15062

Chapter 31: quotationsbook.com/quote/11431

Chapter 32: quotationsbook.com/quote/49528

Chapter 33: quotationsbook.com/quote/6530

Chapter 34: quotationsbook.com/quote/35435

Chapter 35: quotationsbook.com/quote/69

Chapter 36: quotationsbook.com/quote/29929 (abridged)

Chapter 37: quotationsbook.com/quote/33562

Chapter 38: quotationsbook.com/quote/16496

ABOUT THE AUTHOR

Armenian by heritage, born in Iran, lived in Barcelona, and escaped New York until he found his home in Los Angeles, Ara's first eleven years were both busy and confusing. The fruit salad of languages would slow down his genetically encoded need to tell stories. Until then, an alter ego would be required...

He received an engineering degree from California State University Northridge and earned his MBA from the University of Southern California. Today, he is a technology executive in the entertainment industry. True to the Hollywood life, Ara wrote for a children's television pilot that could have made him rich (but didn't) and nearly sold a video game to a major publisher (who closed shop days later).

But something was amiss until his wife read him the riot act. "Will you stop talking about wanting to be a writer and just do it?" So with her support (and mandate), and their two boys serving as his muse, he wrote stories.

Fascinated by the human species, Ara writes about choices, relationships, and second chances. Always a sucker for a hopeful ending, he writes contemporary romance stories. He is an alumnus of both the Santa Barbara Writers Conference andSouthern California Writers' Conference (where he also serves as a workshop leader). Ara is an active member of the Romance Writers of America and its Los Angeles chapter.

Ara is represented by Stacey Donaghy.

Thank You
for Reading

Please visit http://curiosityquills.com/reader-survey to
share your reading experience with the author of this book!

Peace Cottage, by Lisa Kent

Peace Cottage is an inspirational story about new beginnings in trying circumstances. It's a quiet story about powerful feelings. With the sea as its background, this book asks for a comfortable chair and a hot cup of tea. Lose yourself as you follow Lucy Cook in her journey to home and love.

Adultery, by Rod Kierkegaard, Jr.

Professor Orlando Plummer, philanderer and drunk, first meets the Fliedermans—billionaire Roger and the exotic, neurotic Arabia—at an intimate orgy arranged by his own bored and wealthy wife Valeria. After that disastrous night, Orlando blunders his way through a dizzying sequence of academic back-stabbings and sexual musical chairs until he meets his personal Armageddon: his teaching assistant, Jun Mei, announces she is having his child—and his shaky polyamorous house of cards comes crashing down. Wicked, mordantly funny, and wise, Adultery teaches us a great many things about love, a literary life misspent, and the consequences of too much money.

CPSIA information can be obtained at www.ICGtesting.com
Printed in the USA
LVOW10s1626080515

437779LV00005B/538/P